The Awful Age

Tisha Khosla did her schooling at The Lawrence School, Sanawar. She obtained her master's in English Literature from University of Westminster, London. She has also studied film-making and scriptwriting from New York Film Academy, Los Angeles.

She wrote her first novel, *Pink or Black*, based on her experiences at boarding school, when she was 16 years old. Her second book is a sequel titled *Pink or Black 2, High Drama at High School*. Both books have been bestsellers as they struck a chord with youngsters and sold over 100,000 copies each. She has also worked as an assistant director for Bollywood films *Bodyguard* (2011) and *O Teri* (2014) to gain experience in films.

Tisha conducts fashion and styling seminars for Femina Miss India contestants every year and mentors fashion design students throughout India.

You can get in touch with her through her Instagram @tishakhosla

Author's note: *The Awful Age* is the third and final part of the *Pink or Black* series; however, there's been a long break between the books. Events from the first two books have been recapped efficiently where necessary and *The Awful Age* can be read as a standalone book.

The Awful Age

Tisha Khosla

Published by
Rupa Publications India Pvt. Ltd 2021
7/16, Ansari Road, Daryaganj
New Delhi 110002

Sales centres:
Allahabad Bengaluru Chennai
Hyderabad Jaipur Kathmandu
Kolkata Mumbai

Copyright © Tisha Khosla 2021

All rights reserved.
No part of this publication may be reproduced, transmitted,
or stored in a retrieval system, in any form or by any means,
electronic, mechanical, photocopying, recording or otherwise,
without the prior permission of the publisher.

This is a work of fiction. Names, characters, places and incidents are either the
product of the author's imagination or are used fictitiously and any resemblance
to any actual person, living or dead, events or locales is entirely coincidental.

ISBN: 978-93-5520-009-9

First impression 2021

10 9 8 7 6 5 4 3 2 1

The moral right of the author has been asserted.

Printed at HT Media Ltd, Greater Noida

This book is sold subject to the condition that it shall not, by way of trade or
otherwise, be lent, resold, hired out, or otherwise circulated,
without the publisher's prior consent, in any form of binding
or cover other than that in which it is published.

Prologue

'Show me your friends and I'll show you your future.'

—Anonymous

Betrayed by her friends, used as a scapegoat and suspended by the school authorities, Tiana's future, for a while, had seemed very uncertain. Now she was back where it had started. A rush of hushed whispers and prying eyes were following her everywhere. She was aware of what it meant. She was the topic of their secret discussions.

The last time a girl had been suspended from Hill View High School was 30 years ago. The boys department of the school was famous in this regard; at least two boys got expelled each year and many were suspended. It was natural to gossip about the only girl who had gotten herself suspended after years of impeccable behaviour. She had not tainted her reputation alone, she had taken the entire girls department, including its staff, down with her.

House mistresses had always encouraged the girls to consider their actions as being superior to those of the boys, because the girls were judged by higher standards than the boys. Unwittingly, the girls had developed a strange superiority complex which was always present under the surface of their interactions with boys, even with the boys they liked. The girls believed themselves to be the better social counterparts. Teachers and by extension, senior girls, were often heard saying things such as, 'It's a common thing for boys to get suspended and even expelled from school,' or that 'Boys have a greater affinity to get into trouble, after all.'

However, notorious behaviour became much more sensationalized if it was a girl who had initiated it. When boys used swear words or yelled and screamed in the corridors of the school, everyone would simply brush it off, saying, 'Boys will be boys, no one can control them.' But that didn't apply to the girls because they were meant to be perfect and obedient, behaving as 'young ladies' should. They were supposed to know the difference between wrong and right. The argument was that the girls *should* know better and behave better. However unfair it may seem, it was the girls' burden to bear and they took it *very* seriously.

So, when a girl who is held to those values, fails and falls, she is bound to be the subject of every conversation. She has earned the right to *be* the gossip and she will remain so until everyone decided otherwise. And people were far from bored. Her predicament was going to be stretched and her story fabricated beyond recognition, so much so that what most people heard would differ tremendously from what had really happened.

It was weighing on her, but she was determined to not show weakness of mind or character, no matter how much they were expecting it from her. She would not show any weakness and with iron-strong will, she made her way through the crowd without revealing any emotion.

'It is your reaction to adversity, not the adversity itself, which determines how your life's story will develop.' She had recently read this quote in a book and had taken a liking to it. Now she had to decide what her reaction to this adversity was going to be. They would expect her to spiral. The teachers would have their judgemental, beady eyes on her, and the students would label her a screw-up. In their eyes, she had screwed up.

Three months ago, she had had no clue what she was in for until it was too late. She hadn't had any proof of innocence then, nor did she have it now. Only a few teachers knew the partial truth, and only those students who were in the wrong themselves knew the rest. These students were never going to do anything to clear her name because they would be implicating themselves by doing so.

No, her friends were not going to stand up for her. She was in this alone. Her reaction, she knew, had to surprise everyone. No matter what she was feeling inside, she did not want to give anyone the satisfaction of seeing her rattled. She felt bare in front of every pair of eyes pretending to not look at her. Her ego was going to be her shield and she clung to it tightly. As she walked down the corridor, she smiled at people amicably, receiving only a few in return. But she kept going while hoping that her shield wouldn't crack and betray her true emotions of anger and irritation. The summer holidays were over and it was the second term of the eleventh grade for Tiana's batch. And she had returned to the same gendered approach and politics of a typical high school, but this time she had decided not to become a victim of it.

One

2 Months Ago

'*The people are to be taken in very small doses.*'

—Ralph Waldo Emerson

It was the day the summer holidays had begun. Tiana looked around her drawing room, at the sham 'party' that her brother Sid had thrown at their house. The party had been an excuse for Tiana's friends to apologize to her. Sid was dating Tiana's best friend Leila and he had helped Leila plan the 'apology party'. The evening was thrown at her so suddenly that she didn't know how to react. Tiana had been suspended from her boarding school a month before the summer holidays began and was allowed to rejoin in the new term. She had been home for a month now, returning to school only to sit for her exams, which she did in isolation, in the senior mistress's office. Her friends had not seen her all this time and apparently wanted to apologize to her for their actions.

The party had continued after Tiana snubbed Ronit and kissed Karam, agreeing to date him again. After this, she had hugged her friends and tried to believe she had forgiven them. Her friends Leila, Savera, Bella and her minions, Lilly and Celia, had gotten her suspended when, in fact, she was innocent and they were not. She wished she was over this deep betrayal and tried for the sake of Sid, who was dating Leila and her own boyfriend Karam, who was Leila's brother. They were desperate to end the feud between their respective sisters and girlfriends, and Tiana had played along when they told her the true purpose of the party. She didn't want to seem stubborn, so she had gone and hugged her friends, especially Bella and Leila. It was just a fake show of forgiveness. In truth, it was going to take more than a sorry and a hug. She didn't want to seem stubborn, but she was still hurt.

She had then gone to her new friends, Sara, Sara's cousin Aditya, Jasmine and Diya. From the corner of her eye, she could see Sid talking to Ronit. Sid, Tiana and Ronit were childhood friends. Sid had moved to Bombay right after school. He was attending college there and was also pursuing his dream of becoming a singer. He had already been quite successful, first with his own album and soon he was going to start singing playback for films too. He kept talking about 'networking', whatever *that* meant.

Ronit too had been living in Bombay and ever since Sid moved there, the two had become close again. Tiana could see that, Sid was laughing, while Ronit looked grumpy. That could only mean that Ronit was telling Sid about what had occurred between Tiana and him half an hour ago, when Tiana had told him that she didn't want anything to do with him. Sid seemed too amused by his sister's messy love life. When he looked around and saw her looking at him and the irritation apparent on her face, he beckoned her to come over to Ronit and him.

Tiana made a face to imply she'd rather throw up but Sid kept waving her to come over. As she was taking the party in the stride of not seeming stubborn, she begrudgingly got up from her spot. From there, she had a clear view of the entire room and the people in it. Just as she had been noticing Sid and Ronit, she had also noticed her old friends Leila and Savera whispering and glancing towards her. It seemed as if they could not understand why Tiana had chosen to sit with her 'new' friends. As if it was going to be that easy to win back her friendship and trust! She walked towards her brother while preparing retorts for any comments that Ronit might throw her way, but it wasn't necessary because Ronit avoided eye contact. After their recent fight, he seemed even less enthusiastic to talk than she was earlier.

'What's going on with you two? Can't you get over it already?' laughed Sid, noticing their uneasy expressions.

'Stop laughing,' said Tiana and Ronit together. Then they looked at each other with surprise, after which Ronit averted his eyes.

'Nothing is going on, Sid,' said Tiana. None of her planned retorts came to mind because suddenly she was feeling a little guilty about the things she had said to Ronit during their fight. She had spoken to him rudely and was now feeling an unexpected embarrassment. She had no real reason to be angry. Ronit had chosen to support Bella instead of helping Tiana on the day of her suspension. He didn't need to explain himself. Logically, she didn't have any right to get angry but she couldn't help herself.

'Just remember, we were all *friends* first. You two have known each other since you were seven years old!' said Sid.

'We are not friends anymore,' grumbled Ronit.

'We aren't right now, but eventually we could be Ronit,' said Tiana slowly, not believing the words coming out of her own mouth.

'Have you forgotten our last conversation?' asked Ronit, frowning at her.

'If only you'll let me,' said Tiana, rolling her eyes.

'I don't want you to forget. You're being ignorant and I want you to remember what I said,' said Ronit angrily.

'Ignorant?' asked Tiana, raising her eyebrows.

'Yes, there was a reason behind your break-up with Karam and you are completely ignoring it.'

'My personal life is not for you to discuss and just so you

know, whatever problems I had with Karam, we've discussed them and got over them,' retorted Tiana angrily.

'What if you have the same problems again?'

'I won't know until I give him a second chance, will I?'

'So you can give *him* a second chance,' said Ronit quietly.

Tiana caught the unasked question in his statement. He was asking why she couldn't give him a second chance as well.

'He never did anything as bad as you,' said Tiana slowly.

'Okay, stop it you two. You go to the same school, study in the same class and even belong to the same house! You have to learn to not break into a fight every time you see each other,' said Sid.

'I'm leaving,' Ronit said as he walked away.

'See what I'm dealing with? One minute he is fawning all over me and the next he is fighting and walking off,' said Tiana to her brother.

'Do you want him to fawn?' said Sid in a mocking way.

'I want you to stop discussing me with every guy you talk to. First Karam, then Ronit. You're annoying me,' Tiana irritatedly said.

'Hey, you made up with Leila for my sake. So I promise not to butt in. Even if it's fun,' laughed Sid.

At that precise moment two loud voices called out Tiana's name: it was her father calling from upstairs and Karam, who was sitting with his sister, asking Tiana to join them. As she was not too keen to be near either Leila or Bella, she decided to ignore her boyfriend by choosing to go to her father first. She was not fast enough to reach the stairs because Karam caught up with her and then demanded to know what was going on. All her efforts during the evening to not seem stubborn were in danger of unravelling because she was no longer in the mood to continue pretending. To say the opposite of what she was feeling was taking a lot out of her. She was filled with anger and had no means to vent it out because everybody, including her brother and boyfriend, wanted her to be over it.

'Can you tell me what's going on please?' asked Karam, looking at her.

Looking at Karam, Tiana couldn't help but think what Ronit had just said about being ignorant when it came to her issues with Karam. Suddenly, she had a nagging feeling that Ronit was right. She hadn't really discussed her issues or sorted them out with Karam. She had lied to Ronit about that. Suddenly, she was reminded of why she had broken up with Karam at the beginning of last term. He was always trying to control her and was constantly telling her what to do. Just as now he was forcing her to be friends with his sister when Tiana had no interest in being friends with a back-stabber like Leila. Sure, Leila had once been her best friend but things were different now. Karam forcing her to forgive and forget was beginning to irritate Tiana. A thought began to bother her, maybe she got back with Karam only because he hadn't been involved in her suspension. He was the only friend who hadn't betrayed her, and maybe the gratitude she felt for him confused her into believing she had feelings for him. It had only been half an hour and she felt she had made a mistake by saying yes to Karam again.

On the other hand, it was exasperating how Ronit had gotten into her head again. It was driving her mad that she had been obsessing over him for so long. Her life kept circling back to the things Ronit did and her reaction to his every move. He made her feel angry, sad and feel freaking butterflies in her stomach, all at the same time. First, he spurned her, then two years later, he wanted her. Then began dating her friend Bella and unknowingly helped get Tiana suspended from school and finally, wanted Tiana so badly that he could only fight with her, if they could not be together.

On her part, when Tiana began dating Karam in the ninth

grade, it was an attempt to make herself believe that she was over Ronit. A few months before Karam had asked her out, Tiana had spent her summer holidays in Bombay with her grandparents, who lived in the same building as Ronit. She had known Ronit since childhood but that summer, they had grown up enough to develop strong feelings for each other. Tiana had been crushing on Ronit pretty hard and so when they finally kissed the day before she was leaving, she had been ecstatic.

However, only moments later she found out that Ronit had been secretly dating her cousin, Tea, all this while. Tiana's very first kiss had been ruined. She had been hurt and was trying to get over this ordeal when she began dating Karam. That relationship too was doomed from the start because Tiana still had strong feelings for Ronit which came to the surface when Ronit joined Hill View High last term. Before things could settle down, Ronit, of course, had to ruin things again by dating one of her closest friends. He could have gone after any other girl from any other class, but instead chose Bella. Even though Tiana and Bella had been going through a rough patch at that point, she still considered Bella to be her friend. Bella knew how Tiana felt about Ronit and she still went ahead with him. Neither of them understood her feelings or how awkward it was for her.

It was no wonder that she had impulsively chosen to get back with Karam on her front porch, right before entering the party. Now she knew it was a rash decision.

'Can you please tell me why you aren't hanging out with your friends?' asked Karam.

'I *am* hanging out with my friends. Sara, Diya and Aditya, all of them are my friends,' said Tiana.

'You know what I mean. I thought we discussed it and you were going to forgive them.'

'What makes you think I haven't?' asked Tiana, trying to sound shocked.

'If you think you're fooling anyone, then you should know it's only yourself,' said Karam.

'Okay fine. Everything is *not* fine. I can't be cool the way you want me to be. I know Leila is your sister and this makes things awkward for you, but I just can't. I went and hugged her, but it was only for you and Sid. Not for myself,' confessed Tiana giving up the pretence.

'T, it's not just for me. It's for you too,' said Karam.

'I can't stand to be around her, Karam. I can only deal with Leila in bite-sized interactions right now. Being around her for too long makes me angry. I can't help it.'

'But–'

'Could you do it? If your closest friends ganged up and dumped the blame of their mistake on you? Got you demoted from the post of head boy and ruined all your hard work in the process? Are you honestly telling me you would get over it in a heartbeat?' asked Tiana.

Karam didn't say anything. He tried to pull her into a hug instead, but Tiana resisted.

That's when Tiana heard her father call out her name again.

'I'll talk to you later, Karam,' said Tiana. She went upstairs to where her parents were sitting.

Two

Bella

'Man is a useless passion.'

—Sartre

Bella had been observing Tiana ever since she had made a show of forgiving all of them, before going to sit with Sara. She was not stupid and she understood that Tiana was only pretending to forgive and forget. The problem was that she genuinely felt guilty about her actions. Throughout the first term, she had been extremely rude to Tiana, who had in turn ignored most of the nonsense that Bella had dished out, thereby emerging more gracious than Bella. Tiana had not called her names or said hurtful things, she had always been nice. It was so annoying because how long could she stay angry at someone who was so freaking nice? Bella also knew she was at fault. Despite knowing Tiana's true feelings for Ronit, she had not stayed away from him. She had secretly known that he had only come close to her to make Tiana jealous. Somewhere in between she made the mistake of believing his feelings for her were real and so it was still a rude awakening when Ronit publicly expressed his feelings for Tiana at this apology party.

Looking back at her actions, Bella could see that her jealousy had got the better of her which led to Tiana's suspension. She had not expected that. She had believed Tiana would get detention like the rest of them. Instead, the school *suspended* her! The worst part was that Tiana actually had been the only innocent one. She wasn't even drinking on the campus that night. She didn't drink *ever*. After Tiana left, the guilt had eaten up Bella, so much so that she hadn't been able to sleep peacefully for days.

On top of the guilt, Ronit had suddenly stopped talking to her. He'd been angry at her for posting Tiana's picture online, the one which showed her holding an alcohol bottle on the school campus. That picture became proof and led to her being suspended. Ronit didn't even want to look at her, let alone forgive her. His lively personality was instantly crushed and he lost interest in everything around him. And it really hurt because she had serious feelings for him by that time. Her guilt coupled with a heartbreak was too overwhelming for her to cope.

Now she just wanted to talk to both of them and clear the air. She had seen Tiana go upstairs and decided to wait for her to return. She kept an eye on Ronit instead but she began to feel foolish about practically stalking him at the party. Finally, she couldn't take it any longer. She gathered the courage to go and talk to him. Ronit saw her making a beeline for him amidst the crowd and he started to look uncomfortable.

'Hey,' said Bella.

Ronit just nodded. Realizing that he was being rude, he added a faint smile with his nod.

'Glad to see you can breathe again,' said Bella.

'What?'

'Now that you've seen Tiana and have spoken to her, it seems like you can finally breathe again. During the past month, you seemed so constipated.'

Ronit sputtered out his drink onto Bella's shoes and she jumped back.

'I was not constipated!' replied Ronit indignantly.

'I meant *emotionally*. You seemed emotionally constipated. Relax,' said Bella, shaking her foot aggressively.

'I don't know what I was before and what I am right now. But sorry about your shoes,' said Ronit.

'Shoes? You are apologizing to me about my shoes?'

'Because I got them wet.'

'No, the problem is that you have a lot of things to apologize for, not just my shoes,' said Bella.

'What else am I supposed to apologize to you for?'

'I know what I did was wrong. But regardless of what has been going on between Tiana and me, or you and her, you forgot that there was something between you and me as well. You were my boyfriend, but as soon as Tiana left, you didn't even want to look at me,' said Bella, finally expressing her feelings.

'Tiana came to me asking for help. She wanted me to talk to you, to convince you to not put the picture online, but I chose to stand up for you at the wrong moment. I told her I can't speak to you about her because it would hurt your feelings. The next thing I know is that she is thrown out of school. I knew you had the picture; I should have stopped you even before she came to me, but I was trying to spare your feelings! So, no, I really don't think I owe any apologies to you, Bell,' replied Ronit angrily.

'So not an apology, but at least an explanation would have been nice. I guess I finally got one,' said Bella.

'I'm leaving.'

'Why?'

'This was supposed to be an apology party for Tiana, but instead it has turned into a "we're back together" party for Karam and Tiana,' said Ronit bitterly.

'Jealous?'

'Good night, Bell.'

Bella watched him leave. He didn't even have to go very far, since he was staying in the guest room of Tiana's house until he left for Bombay. They were family friends and Tiana's parents knew Ronit very well. His room was just across the hall. It was strange to her that out of all the things he said to her, the only thing that she could keep thinking about was how he had still called her Bell—his nickname for her. It made her happy, which made no sense. He was fuming over Tiana with intense jealousy, yet here she was, feeling happy because he had called her Bell. All this despite how much he had hurt her and didn't even have the decency to apologize to her. She felt stupid that he still had such a strong effect on her. But she quickly put it out of her mind and sat down to wait for Tiana.

Three

'Luck is what happens when preparation meets opportunity.'

—Seneca

Tiana's parents were sitting in the upper drawing room, from where they could monitor the party without actually being seen. They smiled when Tiana walked in.

'Everything going well down there? I see you have made up with many people,' said her father.

'I tried,' said Tiana.

'Tiana, we need to discuss a few things with you.'

'Okay, sure.'

'Would you agree if we said that despite everything that has happened, we have been very understanding and do not blame you for anything?' asked Tiana's mother, looking very intently at her daughter.

'Umm, yes, you have,' came the timid reply from Tiana because she could sense that this was going to be a serious conversation.

'Good, now we have left you alone for the last month because you were clearly upset and you had your exams going on but I think we should finally discuss a few things,' said her mother.

Tiana looked at her father. Usually, when her mother got very serious about something, her father would try to diffuse the situation with his dad jokes. This time though, he looked just as serious as her mother.

'What do you want to discuss?' asked Tiana.

'Your life, Tiana, and the destructive path it is on now. You must realize that getting suspended from school has ruined all the good work you have done so far. Your teachers liked you, people admired the fact that two years ago, you had the courage to say no to your friends when they were getting into a car being driven by a drunk boy. You too could have been in that accident, but your wise decision is what saved you. It upsets me that this has happened to you now,' said her mother emotionally.

'It upsets me too! But what can I do now? I was blindsided by my own friends!' exclaimed Tiana.

'That's what we want to discuss. We have never stopped you from doing what you want. We let you be with your friends despite knowing that they get drunk and get into accidents. We didn't bat an eyelid when you told us about dating Karam. We want you to grow up making your own decisions but now I think you need our help,' replied her mother.

'You need direction. You need to take some conscious steps to rectify the damage to your reputation.' It was her father who spoke this time.

'Everybody in our social circle knows that you got suspended from school. You are just 17, but I'm scared that you are going to be labelled a "screw up" by everyone who knows us,' said her mother.

'I thought we are not supposed to care about what other people think,' replied Tiana.

'If you actually were this person that everyone now believes you to be, then maybe I wouldn't have cared so much. I would have said that you messed up and that's okay... That you are learning from your mistakes but the problem is that...'

'That you are *not* this person,' interrupted her father. 'Forget drinking alcohol inside your school premises, you don't even drink outside. So your suspension for it makes us feel like we have failed as parents, despite doing everything right. Despite you yourself doing everything right.'

It felt like a ton of bricks had just fallen on her head. This was a hard reality check.

'I'm sorry,' replied Tiana, getting a little teary. She could think of nothing else to say.

'We know you are, T. But we have to figure out how to go ahead from here,' said her mother.

'Okay.'

'First of all, we know that you are dating Karam again. He is a good boy, but right now he is a distraction for you,' said her father.

'I know,' said Tiana.

'What?' asked her mother, a little confused, not expecting her daughter to agree so readily.

'I already feel it was a mistake to say yes to him again. It feels all wrong,' said Tiana.

'Just remain friends with him. He will leave for college next year. You both know that this is a temporary phase. We want you to gain some perspective about yourself first. Right now, you have become infamous for drinking and dating and being a brat,' said her mother.

'Who is saying all this about me?' asked Tiana. She had no idea that people had been gossiping about her. Before this conversation, she had believed that the worst was over. Apparently not. The backlash was just beginning.

'Mostly your teachers. Your senior mistress called us for a meeting and told us all this. Also, some of the parents have been concerned about your return after the summer. They think that you are a bad influence and the school wants us to consider other options,' said her father seriously.

'What do you mean by options?'

'They are wondering if we might consider putting you in a new school,' said her mother.

'What! They want to *expel* me now?'

'No, no, nothing like that. They think you will benefit from a fresh beginning at a new school where nobody knows what happened.'

'Oh, how nice of them,' said Tiana angrily. 'I don't understand this. The senior mistress knows I was not drinking. She knows that other people were at fault. She even told me to my face that I had to be the scapegoat because of that photo Bella had posted online. The only proof they had was of me. That's why I was the only one who got suspended,' said Tiana.

'She was mostly talking about you dating and always being around boys. I don't know. I don't agree with her on this but because of your suspension, we have to be careful,' said her father.

'Everyone is anyway talking about your "drinking problem", let's not give them any more reasons to think poorly of you. All the teachers are judging you and spreading that prejudice among other parents and students. Even if they don't know what happened, you are being discussed as an example of everything that is wrong with your generation,' said her mother.

Tiana suddenly felt angry that she had even attempted to forgive her friends for what they had done. Now that the actual damage done to her was becoming clearer, she was experiencing a strange kind of rage. The kind that wells up like a ball of fire in your throat and makes you want to say a lot of things but instead, it begins to choke you.

'I don't want to leave my school. I don't want to run away. That would be even more humiliating than actually going back and dealing with all of it,' said Tiana with tears running down her cheeks.

'Good, we don't want you to run away either. That's not how we raised you. We know you will come out stronger at the other end of this crisis,' said her mother pulling her into a hug.

'Next, let's discuss your summer plans,' said her father patting her on the back and wiping her tears away.

'What summer plans?' sniffled Tiana.

'Exactly, so far you have none. I know that some of your friends are going for the exchange programme from your school. Now to come back stronger than ever, you too need to do something worthwhile this summer,' said her father.

'Like what?' asked Tiana.

'We have to decide that together. It should be an experience that will give you some much-needed mental stimulation. I mean, your school is great but it is conventional. Academics and sports, that's it. You keep saying that you wish you could learn something new.'

'We have found a few creative summer workshops in Bombay. I really think it will be good for you,' said her mother.

'This is better than an exchange programme because you will actually be learning a new, worthwhile skill. We were thinking that you might be interested in a public speaking and creative writing course,' her father explained.

'Does that sound good to you?' asked her mother.

'I mean, I don't know. What kind of creative writing course is it?' asked Tiana nervously.

'Don't worry, T. It's like a beginner's class. You may or may not be great at it but you won't know until you try. Plus, you'll get to interact with new people and explore different ideas. That's really important at your age,' said her father gently.

'Will there be people my age?' asked Tiana.

'I'm sure but I think mostly it will be grown-ups. I called their counsellor and spoke to her today. She said that very few teens join their workshops, but that they encourage all age groups to sign up.'

'I'm going to be the youngest?' asked Tiana.

'Is that worrying you, darling? It shouldn't. Your age and the fact that you are starting early is going to work in your favour.

You will be doing at 17 what others do in their 20s and 30s. Your age is a gift. Use it to your advantage and get as much experience as you can. Starting early will set you apart,' smiled her mother.

Tiana nodded her head but she still felt intimidated at the thought of being in a classroom filled with grown-ups.

'Also think about how good this will look on your college applications. Your friends are going for the exchange programme and you told me that people who go for the exchange programme become head girls or prefects in their final year. You need something for your resume too. Extra-curricular experiences like this help,' added her mother.

'I get what you are saying. I do need this. But that doesn't mean it's not a little scary,' said Tiana.

'Don't be scared, love. It will be fun. I promise, once you get used to how things work, you will enjoy yourself. Plus, you will be living with your grandparents, so they will take care of you when you feel low. You can always call me or Dad if something goes wrong. We just want you to have a good experience,' said her mother.

'So, what do you think?' asked her father.

Tiana knew her parents would never force a decision on her. They had always told Sid and her that the decisions they would make for themselves would motivate them to follow through on them as well. Whereas, a decision made *for* them would only bring about a half-hearted attempt from their side. She knew that they wanted her to say yes, but they wanted her to mean it too. She should go to Bombay not under their pressure but with a will to perform well.

'Yes, I'll go.'

Four

'Be kind to unkind people. They need it most.'

—Ashleigh Brilliant

With much to consider, Tiana went downstairs again. She wanted to discuss everything her parents had said with Sara, but she had left. In fact, most people had left. Some of Sid's friends were still hanging out in the drawing room. Leila was there as well, talking to Sid and Karam. Normally, Tiana would have discussed whatever was happening in her life with Leila, but everything had changed between them. Tiana had witnessed a streak of jealousy within her old best friend and didn't trust her to give good advice.

Aliya was the only person from her old group who had tried to help Tiana and not betrayed her. Aliya was the only one she could trust and so Tiana went looking for her. She had to talk to someone. Anyone except Karam. She didn't know how to break up with him again, that too so soon after kissing him in front of everybody. Unfortunately, Aliya was nowhere to be found. Tiana had given up when suddenly Bella appeared in front of her out of nowhere.

'Hi, I've been waiting for you,' smiled Bella.

'Why?' frowned Tiana.

'Are you free now? I need to talk to you,' asked Bella.

'Not really. I'm looking for Aliya,' said Tiana.

'Oh she left, but I'm here,' said Bella earnestly.

Tiana was amused by this because Bella was the last person she could trust. Additionally, Bella's sudden friendliness was disconcerting because she had been nothing but bitchy to Tiana since the start of the previous term. They had once been good friends. Things had changed ever since Bella's house had been ruined during a party. Bella had held Tiana responsible for it because she had expected Tiana to look after everything. Then there had been the situation with Ronit and the final straw had been when Tiana was selected for the exchange programme instead of Bella. All this had made her betray Tiana. So, for Bella to come and say those words to her was hilarious.

'*You're here,*' said Tiana, raising her eyebrow.

'I know. I know, Tiana. I just want to say that I am truly sorry. I really mean it. I have been filled with so much guilt that I couldn't even sleep after you left. I really want you to know, I had no idea you would get suspended,' said Bella.

'Bella, that happened because of you and the photo you posted! Everyone turned against me—parents, the school board, alumni, teachers and students—they all saw it online. I was used as a scapegoat for your mistake. It sucks even more because I was the only one who *left* that night when I found out what was going on,' said Tiana bitterly.

'Tiana, I don't know what to say.'

'If you wanted to get me in trouble, why didn't you just show the picture to the senior mistress? Then I would have got detention like the rest of you,' said Tiana.

'I wasn't thinking, T! I was just angry that, as usual, you were walking away from the problem so easily while the rest of us couldn't. First that accident two years ago, then my party, then 25 of us got caught except you! You are always at the centre of things and yet you always escape unscathed. Do you know how annoying that is?' asked Bella.

It suddenly became clear why their friendship had hit rock bottom. Bella envied Tiana's ability to make quick decisions.

'My god! I'm sorry that my power to say no is such a problem for you. I got saved from the accident because I refused to get in a car being driven by a drunk person. I got support at your party because everyone saw that I was right. I didn't get caught when 25 of you did because I walked away as soon as I found out what was going on. I asked you all to leave too but you didn't, that was your *choice*! Stop blaming me for your bad decisions,' burst out Tiana.

Now that Tiana could finally see Bella's point of view, she saw her in a new light. It didn't seem as if Bella was jealous. Leila had been her best friend, whereas Bella was just a frenemy. She had expected Leila to stop Bella from posting the photo but Leila hadn't, and that really hurt her. Tiana had had no expectations from Bella and now she felt that all Bella wanted was to express herself better to both Tiana and the rest of her world, but she just didn't know how to do it. That inability made her behave in negative ways and she genuinely seemed full of guilt over her actions.

Suddenly, it became hard for her to stay angry at Bella. As soon as Tiana felt empathy, that's *all* she felt. This was one of her qualities which Tiana was starting to recognize slowly. She could not hold her anger for too long if she understood the other person's point of view. Her anger sort of fizzled out after that.

'I hope we will be able to move past this,' said Bella earnestly.

At this point, Sid's friends increased the volume of the music playing in the background significantly, so Tiana had to pull Bella into the guest bedroom so that they could hear each other better. The moment they entered the room, they saw Ronit standing in front of the bathroom door, half-naked with wet hair and just a towel wrapped around his waist. It was awkward for all of them. More so for Tiana because she had wanted to talk to Bella about Ronit. She instinctively covered her eyes with her hands and turned around.

'I'm so sorry! I forgot you were staying in this room,' said

Tiana, quickly backing out through the door and pulling Bella along with her.

'That was so embarrassing!' exclaimed Tiana with her hand covering her mouth and her eyes wide open.

'I do not regret seeing that. Say what you will, but the boy is hot!' exclaimed Bella, bursting into laughter. It was so infectious that Tiana couldn't stop herself from laughing as well.

Tiana then took Bella out on the porch. It had emptied out by then. They sat on poufy chairs and things seemed almost normal between them.

'What about Ronit? He was causing a lot of problems between us too,' said Tiana.

'I was, and kind of still am, extremely jealous that Ronit likes you. I still have feelings for him. Even though he was using me to make you jealous, I still fell for the guy.'

'Yeah, he has a way of making you like him even when you hate him. I've been through it myself when he kissed me while he was dating Tea,' admitted Tiana.

'But, I'm not going to let that affect our friendship again. I promise I'm done being mad at you for his mistakes,' said Bella.

'I'm sure you know, I'm not even interested in Ronit anymore.'

'Yeah, I saw you and Karam.'

'Actually, I need to break up with him again. I just don't know how to do it,' said Tiana sheepishly.

'Why!? Oh God, T, not again. Poor guy.'

'Don't say that! I feel horrible as it is, but I can't pretend either. I don't have the right feelings for him. On top of that, my parents also think that it's not a good idea for me to be dating anyone right now.'

'Then just do it tonight. There is no need to prolong this disaster. Rip off the Band-Aid,' said Bella.

'Thanks for the advice and by the way, you should know

that you all got caught that night in school because of Tea. She knew what was going on in the clearing behind the building. She pretended to faint on the staircase leading to the clearing and tricked me into getting a teacher over there to help her. That's how you all were caught. She confessed about it to me. She wanted to create a rift between my friends and me because she too has feelings for Ronit, and didn't like him dating you and talking to me. Or some such nonsense. When I got suspended, she felt guilty and told me everything.'

'That sneaky little witch! Is she mentally unstable or what?' asked Bella angrily.

'God knows,' shrugged Tiana.

'I had to sit in detention every Sunday for four weeks because of her,' said Bella grumpily.

'She's obsessed with Ronit.'

'Jeez! What is wrong with Ronit? He just complicates and messes up everything no matter where he goes!' said Bella.

'Welcome to my world,' laughed Tiana.

Five

Ronit

As if his relationship with Tiana hadn't been awkward enough, she had now also seen him in nothing but a towel. That too with his ex-girlfriend being present. Ronit got dressed while debating whether he should go and talk to the girls. He didn't want any more weirdness with them. He left his room and bumped into Tiana's friend Savera. She invited him to a blood donation drive taking place the next day at her home. He didn't know if it would be wise to get into another social situation where he would be surrounded by Tiana's friends.

He was hurting. Every time he saw Tiana, he got angry with himself for screwing up matters with her. She kept asking why he was always ruining everything for her, first with Tea, then with Bella, and in all honesty, he didn't know who to blame except his own impulsiveness. That was his problem, acting without thinking. It was true that he had known Tiana and her cousin his whole life. Tea lived in the same building as him in Bombay but Tiana was always visiting. Three years ago, his friendship with Tea had turned into a light-hearted crush and they had started secretly dating because Tea's parents were very strict.

But that summer when Tiana had come to visit her grandparents, he couldn't help himself from falling for her. His connection with Tiana had developed so suddenly and strongly that when Tiana confessed her feelings to him, he told her he liked her too without thinking. Tiana had not known that he was dating her cousin when she fell for him. That was his first mistake.

Not telling her the truth. Then he had shared a phenomenal kiss with Tiana. This was his second mistake. He hadn't known that it was Tiana's first kiss and that he was ruining it for her by lying. He had behaved like an idiot. Then his third mistake was that he tried to make her jealous by showing an interest in her friend Bella. Finally, his biggest mistake was not helping Tiana when she had asked him to stop Bella from posting that picture.

As he was staying in her house, he was constantly reminded of Tiana. He was surrounded by her parents, her friends, her cousins. He needed some separation from her since she had chosen Karam over him. He was looking forward to returning home to his family in Bombay in a couple of days. He looked around the house which was mostly empty and found Tiana and Bella sitting together on the porch. It was surprising to see them sitting and talking so calmly. When they turned and saw him, they looked at each other and began giggling.

'All right, all right. I'm glad you both are finally talking and not fighting. In fact, I don't think I've ever seen you both hanging out like this,' said Ronit light-heartedly.

'Yeah, our problems started even before you joined the school. I think we can work it out though,' said Bella, looking at Tiana, who nodded in return.

'So I hope there won't be any weirdness about what just happened in my room,' said Ronit self-consciously. He was looking at Tiana but she was not returning his gaze, instead both she and Bella began giggling again.

'So you can laugh at me but not speak to me?' asked Ronit looking at Tiana.

'Hey! I was speaking to you when we were with Sid,' said Tiana raising her hands. 'You were the one who walked off, but I won't be rude like you. So, where is your towel?' she finished with a laugh.

'Dropped it somewhere?' grinned Bella.

'Oh yay! Had I known you were going to be so *grown up* about this, I wouldn't have worried that you saw me half-naked,' smirked Ronit.

'You *what*? You saw him naked?' asked Karam, who had suddenly shown up behind Ronit.

'No, half-naked. Bella was there too,' said Tiana casually.

'Somehow that doesn't make me feel better,' replied Karam while giving Ronit the stink eye. They had taken a dislike to each other since the beginning of last term.

'Relax. It was by accident,' said Tiana, frowning at Karam.

Karam instead turned to Ronit and very threateningly added, 'Stay away from her, jackass.'

'How am I supposed to stay away from her if I'm staying in her house?' asked Ronit flatly.

'I ...' Karam launched towards him.

'What are you doing, Karam? Calm down,' said Tiana irritatedly. It was this side of Karam that made her want to break up with him. This overly possessive and controlling behaviour was a huge turn-off for her. Bella was right, she just needed to rip off the Band-Aid.

'Ronit!' called a voice from inside the house.

'I think that's Tiana's mom,' said Bella.

'Oh look, her mother is calling *me*,' Ronit said to Karam sarcastically before walking into the house.

Ronit had wanted to punch the guy for butting in like he always did. Karam had found out that Tiana and Ronit had a past and had made his life miserable ever since he had joined the school. Just because he was the head boy, he had enough power to keep giving him physical drills. As Ronit was a year junior to Karam, he had been told by his batchmates to take orders and not question them. Mercifully, the summer holidays had begun and he was out of that claustrophobic school.

Six

'Do not lean on anyone, and let no one lean on you.'

—Elbert Hubbard

'I'm going to give you guys some privacy. Tiana, see you tomorrow at Savera's house,' said Bella, getting up from her chair.

'Why would I be at her house?' asked Tiana.

'Oh, don't you know? Her parents have organized a big shindig for the students, parents and many teachers. I think even the headmaster has been invited and he might just come. It's like a big blood donation drive and charity garden party sort of thing,' replied Bella.

'Her parents want her to be head girl next year and they are trying to show initiative on her behalf. They have invited some people from the media and it's supposed to be good publicity for the school,' said Karam.

'Who are her parents trying to impress now? Savera already got selected for the exchange programme, didn't she?' asked Tiana.

'I know,' laughed Bella. 'Anyway, good night! And, Tiana, remember, Band-Aid,' she added, miming ripping off Band-Aid from her arm as she walked away. Tiana rolled her eyes in response.

'What did she mean by that?' asked Karam, looking confused.

'Nothing. I need to discuss something with you.'

'Sure, but first can you tell me why you are hanging out with Bella instead of Leila? I mean, I don't get it. Bella is the one who posted your photo online. I don't think it's in your best interest to be friends with her.'

'And Leila is the one who knew what Bella was going to do and didn't stop her. At least Bella was upfront, unlike your sister,' said Tiana.

Karam didn't say anything.

Then Tiana told him about the conversation she had had with her parents about going for a summer workshop in Bombay. Karam didn't seem very excited about this idea. In fact, his jealousy was quite evident.

'So you will live in the same building as Ronit for an entire summer?' he asked, raising his eyebrows in disbelief.

'That's not even the point, Karam. This is important. Look how much Savera and her parents are doing to get her in everybody's good books. They are trying to buy good publicity for her and I don't even know what else they will be doing. I need to do something as well. I'm not going to Bombay for Ronit. I'm going for myself and if you can't even see that, then we should not be together,' said Tiana.

'What?' asked Karam narrowing his eyes.

'I feel like we rushed into this,' said Tiana quietly.

'Excuse me? Did we not kiss just an hour ago?'

'Yes. In that moment, I wanted to kiss you. I was just not prepared for everything that has followed,' said Tiana.

'Like what?' Karam asked angrily.

'For starters, your controlling behaviour. I don't need you to tell me who I should be friends with because I can decide for myself. I also can't deal with this possessiveness.'

'I can't believe you are doing this to me again, Tiana. Do you enjoy embarrassing me or something?' asked Karam, narrowing his eyes.

'Of course not! But, Karam, there was a reason we broke up in the first place. We didn't resolve those issues. They are still there. Besides, my parents also don't think it's a good idea for me to be dating anyone right now. They want me to focus on myself.'

'You're unbelievable,' said Karam quietly, and they fell into silence.

Seven

'Pack your own parachute.'

—T.L. Hakala

'My name is Rishi Jain and I will be your instructor for this workshop for the next eight weeks. You can call me Rishi. This class will meet twice a week and will run for four hours because I want to focus on all of you equally. Don't worry, I will give you a 15-minute break in between. I urge you to not miss any class; it's for your own benefit. Now, before I explain how the class will work, I want you all to tell me your name and one thing that makes you interesting,' said the instructor.

Tiana felt the panic creep in. What made her interesting? How was she supposed to tell a room full of people why she was interesting when she didn't know the answer herself. However, after the initial panic, the more she thought about it, the more irritated she became at the question. She didn't like being put on the spot like this in front of random people she didn't even know. She was quickly thinking of ways to answer this question without actually having to answer it.

It had just been three days since she had broken up with Karam and it was her first day at the summer workshop. She had decided to go ahead with her parents' suggestion to try the public speaking course. She was staying with her maternal grandparents in Bombay for the summer. Her uncle (her mother's brother and Tea's father) lived on the floor below them. Tea was spending the summer at Tiana's house. Tiana's mother was a senior journalist and the editor-in-chief of a local magazine and Tea had decided to intern for her. Tiana was glad that she wouldn't have to see Tea for the rest of the summer. After what she had done, Tiana needed all the distance from her cousin. Ronit's family lived in a penthouse in the same building; however, Ronit himself was travelling for the summer with his friends from his old school. So, Tiana didn't expect to see Ronit until the new term began.

This was good because it meant she would have no distractions. She wanted to focus on the course, which she was quite worried about it. She was in a new city with no friends, and on top of it, she was feeling intimidated by the thought of speaking in public. She was usually quite vocal and had never faced any trouble while expressing her thoughts. But that level of candidness she shared only with her family and close friends. Beyond that circle, she was kind of shy and an introvert. The thought of not being able to perform well and disappointing her parents on yet another front was adding to her anxiety.

There had been about 20 people already in class when she entered the room that morning. At first glance, she saw nobody her age. They were all much older than her. Tiana sat awkwardly on the first bench.

As her instructor looked at her, expecting her to answer, Tiana cursed herself for taking the front bench. Her anxiety was at a peak. Yet, she decided to answer calmly and put across her point of view.

'I think this question is a set-up and I don't know how to answer it,' said Tiana, glad that she couldn't see the faces of the rest of the class.

'Interesting. Why do you think it's a set-up?' asked Rishi, with an amused expression. He was leaning against his desk with his arms crossed. Tall and smart, he seemed to be in his 40s. What struck Tiana was that it was the first time she had been in a class where the teacher was dressed so casually—sneakers, black jeans and a black t-shirt.

'Because you asked us to define what makes us interesting but what interests a person is very subjective. So, the very reasons for which I may think I'm interesting, you may think I'm not,' she replied.

'Maybe I will find you interesting, but I can't judge until you open up,' said Rishi.

'That's why I feel this is a trick question. There's always a hidden agenda or some judgement behind such questions. It's like I'm supposed to put myself out there, but only for others to dissect my feelings and experiences as soon as I open up.'

'I feel like you may have opened up to people in the past and it hasn't gone well for you. Has anyone ever asked you this question before?'

'Yes. I once returned to school after the summer break and my history teacher asked us to tell her something interesting we did during the holidays. That summer, I had sat in an airplane for the very first time and so I told her that. She said that people travel by air all the time and it was not very interesting, and everybody in class started laughing at me. I felt horrible for opening up in the first place,' said Tiana. She had put this memory away and hadn't thought about this in the longest time but suddenly it came to the forefront and here she was describing it all over again. It must have affected her subconsciously because apparently it was still haunting her.

'How old were you when this happened?'

'I was 10.'

'How old are you now?'

'I just turned 17.'

'Oh! I think you are the youngest in my class. But first, that teacher seems like an idiot. Getting on an airplane for the first time is a very exciting experience for a person, especially for a 10-year-old. Second, you can't let something like this block your personal growth. You had a bad experience at 10 but you didn't let it go, and for the past seven years, it has probably affected your growth. Maybe it turned you into an introvert. Maybe it has made you overly cautious. It's not your fault. But now that you have recognized a problem within yourself, you should do something about it. Now tell me, do you want to try now? Try telling us what makes you interesting,' said Rishi.

Everything he said made sense. But she was still unsure about her answer. He paused and said slowly, 'It's okay. Even though you didn't answer my question, I still have my answer. What makes you interesting is that you are assertive. You're not afraid to express your point of view. That is a great quality for public speaking and also for this class, where we are all going to constantly question each other.'

Rishi turned to the rest of the class before continuing, 'This is a public speaking class but what is public speaking in the first place?'

'About expressing yourself,' said a girl who was sitting behind Tiana.

'Yes, but to whom are you expressing yourself?' asked Rishi.

'To the people who are listening to you,' the girl replied.

'So, that makes it a kind of one-sided conversation, right? It's a different form of communication but it is, nonetheless, communication. In many ways, this class is a communication workshop and before you can communicate with other people, you have to learn to communicate with yourself,' said Rishi as he turned to look at Tiana again.

'I'm sorry, I still don't know your name.'

'Tiana.'

'Right. So, Tiana, now tell me, have you faced a situation in your life where you have felt like you failed yourself by not communicating properly? Or perhaps by not standing up for yourself because you didn't speak up with the force and strength that the situation demanded?'

The answer was obviously yes, so she nodded her head.

'Can you tell us about it?'

Even though it was deeply personal, Tiana told everyone about getting suspended from school, and how and why it happened.

'Wow! Now that was fascinating, wasn't it? You're turning out to be one of my most interesting students, Tiana. For someone so assertive, I'm surprised that you let yourself get scapegoated like this,' said Rishi.

'I'm surprised as well.'

'So you are currently suspended from school?'

'I'm allowed to return after the summer holidays.'

'Tell me, what have you done so far to earn back the respect? What have you done to change your circumstances?'

'What can I do?' asked Tiana.

'Plenty. The first of which is to use your voice. Speaking up and taking charge of the situation. Yes, teachers are your elders and you should always respect them, but that doesn't mean keeping mum when they are not treating you right,' he told Tiana before addressing the rest of the class, 'Speaking up does not mean being disrespectful. Take a stand, but do it politely, without yelling or screaming. When you make valid points calmly, the other person will immediately be more receptive. That's the first rule of good communication.'

Tiana had been put on the spot for a while during the class, but she now wanted to think about everything that Rishi had said to her. It all made so much sense and, suddenly, she was glad that to be part of the class.

'Hopefully, by the end of this workshop, all of you would have learnt how to communicate well. This skill will help you in many situations in your life. Our two main goals will be learning how to make valid points and how to speak with dignity,' said Rishi.

The other students started to introduce themselves and spoke about what made them interesting. Tiana had been right, everybody was much older than her. Everyone except one boy. His name was Krish, who was 17 and in his final year of school.

After class, Rishi called Tiana and Krish to his desk. Then he introduced Tiana to Krish.

'I'm sure you don't have many friends here, Tiana. This is my son Krish. I think, since you are the youngest in this class, maybe you can be a support system for each other.'

Krish and Tiana smiled at each other awkwardly. It had been a while since an adult had tried to fix a playdate for her. Although, as it turned out, Krish was quite easy to talk to.

'My dad is super impressed with you already,' said Krish as they walked out of class.

'Why do you say that?' asked Tiana, surprised by this statement.

'He loves it when he meets someone unconventional. When people ask a lot of questions and don't give regular answers, it makes him very happy,' he said as he smiled.

Tiana was beginning to notice that Krish was actually quite cute. He was tall just like his father and had tousled brownish hair. Then it dawned on her that developing a crush on the boy who was her only acquaintance in the city was not a good idea.

'So... I'm on my way to a party. Would you like to come? You can meet my girlfriend there.'

'Oh! I don't want to ruin your date.'

'Don't worry, it's not a date. It's actually a farewell of sorts for my girlfriend. She's leaving for a summer internship, her mom lives in London and she wants Niti to move there. In fact, Niti will only return to give the final exams at the end of the term. Anyway, we have kind of broken up already because the whole long-distance thing doesn't work. She is leaving soon and her friends decided to throw this party.'

'Oh. It's not weird between you guys?'
'Not really.'
'Okay. I guess I'll come,' said Tiana.

Forty-five minutes later, they entered the restaurant where the party was taking place.

'I can't believe you have come to your girlfriend's farewell with another girl,' said a boy as they entered.

'Ha ha ha. Tiana, meet my friend Vir,' said Krish drily.

Vir smiled as he shook Tiana's hand, 'I'm sorry, don't mind that. I was just joking.'

Tiana smiled and shrugged. In hindsight, she realized that, of course, that's what it looked like. Krish had in fact shown up with a completely random girl. She felt stupid for coming along and, for a moment, wondered if Krish was trying to use her to make his ex jealous. Tiana was in a good mood and for a change, wanted to meet new people, thanks to the class she had attended. She ended up having a great evening.

Krish's ex-girlfriend, Niti, was very sweet to her as well, 'You and Krish are in the same summer workshop, right?'

'Yes. It's a great class. His dad is a great teacher.'

'Krish just told me that you study in a boarding school. How do you manage it? I could never live away from home.'

'See, living away from home is not at all scary for me because I've been doing it since I was 10. Being in a boarding school is amazing. It's tough, but it's amazing,' said Tiana.

'It sounds horrible,' said Vir.

'It's not. I have seen kids in regular schools who are nothing but brats. *That's* horrible. My cousin, Tea, is from Bombay and she struggled when she joined my school last term because she was not used to doing anything for herself. But my friends and I have been making our own beds, polishing our own shoes, studying on our own, looking after our health and making sure we do everything our prefects and teachers ask us to do since the age of 10. We get to bathe only for five minutes and it's actually timed by a person standing outside our bathroom. We are not allowed to use phones or any electronics, and every minute of the day is accounted for. I think it's great that I was raised this way,' said Tiana.

'Why is it great?' asked Vir.

'If I can survive this strict lifestyle, I can adjust anywhere. After this, everything seems easier.'

'Why is your school so strict?' asked Krish.

'It's an old British school and at its inception, it was intended for the children of the British Indian Army. So, the school has always had a military-inspired way of living. In the morning, we don't just walk from our dormitory to our classrooms. We march. To go to the chapel for our morning assembly, we march past the World War I and II memorials on the grounds; back in the day, the training from school was said to be so good that students would go straight to war. The names of those who were martyred have been inscribed on the memorials. Marching has become as normal as walking for me. My school's history is also so rich and unique. It's one of the world's oldest co-educational boarding schools. It started with seven boys and seven girls. It was never sexist but the teachers have made it so,' explained Tiana.

'Wow! I don't think I've ever met anyone who is so proud of their school,' said Vir.

'That's because most schools are so blah. But what Tiana is describing is epic. I bet your school is very pretty too,' said Niti.

'It really is. It's so surreal, situated on top of a hill with stone buildings and wooden floors and red roofs. You won't even feel like you are in India when you are in my school campus,' said Tiana.

'So, what's the routine of your regular day in school?' asked Krish curiously.

'Vir, I think you might start crying if you hear the entire routine,' laughed Tiana.

'I will laugh tears of joy that my parents didn't send me to this torture school,' replied Vir with a wink.

'So the usual daily routine is: wake up at 6.00 a.m. Out to exercise by 6.10 a.m. Return to the dorm by 7.00 a.m. In class by 7.40 a.m. Breakfast at 9.00 a.m. Assembly at 9.40 a.m. In class till mid-morning break at 12.30 p.m. Back in class till 2.00 p.m. Lunch till 2.30 p.m. Sports and hobbies till 5.00 p.m. Bath time till 6.00 p.m. Study hour till 7.30 p.m. Dinner till 8.00 p.m. Night study hour till 9.45 p.m. Lights out at 10.00 p.m.'

'I feel like crying for you now,' said Vir.

'You seem to be quite proud of your school even though they suspended you,' said Krish.

'Wait, you got suspended? You don't look like someone who would get suspended,' said a visibly shocked Vir.

'Looks can be deceiving. I learned that from my friends who got me in this situation in the first place. I'm still proud of my school because the problem is not the institution, its history or its routine. The problem is the current teachers and their way of doing things,' said Tiana, sadly.

Eight

*'All the people like us are We,
And everyone else is They.'*

—Rudyard Kipling

During the next class, Tiana found herself defending her school once again. Rishi had asked everyone to speak for two minutes about what they thought about boarding schools and the kids who attended such schools. Many of the grown-ups had ridiculous ideas about what went on in boarding schools. Particularly a woman named Anita, who was in her 30s and had two children. She talked about how spoiled kids became in boarding schools and that teens were always drinking and doing drugs in such schools. She said that they had such an example right there in class. After all, Tiana had told them herself about how in her own school, teens had been caught drinking. She concluded that she would never send her kids to a boarding school.

'Tiana, I'm curious to see how you would respond to Anita,' said Rishi.

'First, I would like you to know that it's next to impossible to drink alcohol in school, much less do drugs. The teachers watch us like hawks. Even dating is not allowed in my school. Second, it's far easier for kids in regular schools to get "spoiled", drink alcohol and do drugs. They have phones and can sneak out of their houses at night and get into all sorts of trouble. The one time people tried to drink so openly in my school, they got caught. We don't have phones or cash. We can't sneak out at night because our dorms are locked from outside. We don't shop or have birthday parties. We are not allowed to wear make-up or jewellery. And, certainly, no one has access to drugs. It's not so easy to get that stuff into school. By far, boarding schools will make your kids more disciplined in life than you ever could. At least, that's how it is in my school. You should know, your teen will try to sneak a drink no matter where they are. It's harmless and a part of growing up,' said Tiana.

'This is a great discourse. I'm glad we have so many differing opinions in this particular batch. My previous batch was extremely dull. This is the one plus point of having youngsters in class. They are always ready to stir the pot,' said Rishi smiling at Anita.

Tiana smiled internally. Stirring the pot was her specialty.

'Now, to be a good public speaker, one thing is extremely important. What is it?' asked Rishi.

'Confidence,' said a man called Pradeep.

'Absolutely. I can't actually teach you how to speak well. That has to come from within. I can however give you the right tools to practise in order to become a better speaker. Confidence is indeed important, but how does one "get" it?' asked Rishi.

Nobody answered.

'The answer is simple. Confidence comes from knowledge. When you are sure of something and know in your gut that you are right, that is when confidence surges through your body in the form of your words which reach and touch the people around you. Trust me. People respond to confidence. It can be incredibly powerful and *will* draw people to you. Most leaders are charismatic and communicate almost effortlessly. That is why people believe in them and follow them. Am I right?'

Everyone nodded.

'So in every class, going forward, we are going to discuss a topic and I want you to read and research that topic beforehand.

I want you to come prepared so that you can make valid and convincing points.'

⁂

As the weeks went by, the class began to grow on Tiana. Every week, they discussed new issues and ideas. Soon, the class had naturally divided into liberals and conservatives. People who were always defending the old ways or supported bans on various things were, of course, the conservatives. People like Anita fell in that category. Then there were liberals who supported free speech and new ways. Surprisingly, Tiana found herself to be somewhere in the middle. Some of her opinions were liberal, yet some were conservative.

When they were discussing the unconstitutional Section 377 and how it criminalized the LGBTQ community, the conservatives in the class came up with views you would expect from a traditional person.

Poonam, from the conservative side, said, 'I think this is a wrong step for our country. India is getting too influenced by the West in opposing Section 377. This means the end of Indian civilization as we know it. I'm not okay with it. What will our future generations learn? It will ruin them. What will be the future of the "Indian family"? This whole thing makes me sick.'

Then Rishi asked Krish to respond to these opinions.

'Why are you not okay with this? Why are you making such bold statements against people who mean us no harm? As long as it's not affecting you personally, we should all try and be okay with other people's way of life,' said Krish.

Rishi then looked at Tiana and asked her if she wanted to add anything.

'I don't agree with either Poonam or Krish,' said Tiana.

'Why is that?' asked Rishi.

'Why do we feel we have the *right* to be "okay or not okay" in the first place? Who are we to give ourselves this power? Do members of the LGBTQ community ever say they are "okay" with people being straight? No. They don't care because they are too busy living their lives. Everybody should be free to be themselves. Nobody should feel like it's their prerogative to be okay with somebody else's lifestyle. Don't say stuff like "it's okay with me that you are gay". That just sounds condescending. They didn't ask for your permission and you are nobody to give it. You might think you are being accepting by saying such things, but the reality is that if you are truly okay with them, you wouldn't even feel the need to say it. You wouldn't even notice any difference between them and you because the reality is that there is *no* difference. We are *all* normal and abnormal in our own ways. All of us have quirks and problems, and we are all trying to live to the best of our capabilities.'

'Now I feel like an idiot,' said Krish.

'Brilliant, Tiana. You have made an excellent point,' said Rishi.

One day when they were discussing youngsters' access to technology, Tiana found herself siding with the conservatives. The liberals thought that the use of phones and internet had made the lives of the current generation much better. There were some issues of overuse but the benefits outweighed the negatives.

'I don't agree. The internet is used for far worse things today than it is for good. Kids don't want to focus on anything other than watching videos and using social media. It's doing much more harm than it's doing good,' said Anita.

'In my boarding school, we are not allowed access to any kind of tech and I think it's the best thing that ever happened to me. To pass our time we read books, listen to music, follow our hobbies and actually have conversations with each other. We don't even get to watch any TV, except on Sundays, because we don't have time. We get internet access for a limited time and only when we need to do research for a project. I think limiting one's screen time is important,' agreed Tiana.

In the next class, they discussed religion and its place in their life. Tiana found herself siding with the liberals this time and when she was done speaking, several people, even from the conservative side, were in agreement with her.

'For a country that is obsessed with religion, I find it strange that most of us have not even read any of our religious books. What kind of religion are we really following, if most of it is hearsay? We hear myths and believe those to be the gospel truth, so to say. In the West, they have Sunday school to learn about their religion but Indian kids get disjointed and fabricated stories about their religion. We don't understand the ideology or the actual teachings of a religion because it suits the pandits to keep us uninformed. They just want us to believe in rituals because that's how they make money. I was raised a Hindu, but for the longest time, I didn't have much knowledge about my religion. To be honest, I still don't. However, what I have surmised is that more than a religion, Hinduism was meant to be a lifestyle. You are supposed to constantly cleanse and look after your mind and body and that's what yoga, Ayurveda and even Kamasutra are meant for. Hindu philosophy traditionally observes four stages of life. How you should act in every stage is part of the dharma theory. Then there is the karma theory. They all deal with living a good, happy and moralistic life. Instead of working towards imbibing these qualities, most people are stuck on the superficial layer, defending things that don't matter... like firecrackers on Diwali. Traditionally, Diwali is a festival of diyas. Firecrackers aren't even an Indian invention,' said Tiana.

'I have to agree with Tiana today. I feel the same way,' said Poonam.

One of their discussions regarding how western influence was ruining India had gone exceptionally well in Tiana's favour. People had actually begun clapping for her when she was done talking. The conservatives had been going on about how Indians were so stupid to think that speaking English was important.

'After all, the Japanese, French, Spanish, Italians and the Dutch, don't speak English and they proudly only speak their own languages. Why can't Indians be like that?' asked Mohan, one of the conservatives.

'Tiana, I want to know what you think about this,' said Rishi.

'I have heard this argument many times before and I find it laughable,' said Tiana.

'Why is it laughable?' asked Pradeep.

'It's simple. All the countries you just mentioned were never British colonies. Why would the Spanish or the French speak English? They were imperialists who were busy spreading their own empires. Why is English spoken in Canada, North America, South Africa, New Zealand and Australia? They were British colonies. Just like we were. We can't whitewash our history just because we don't like it. For 200 years, the British Raj existed in India and as a result, a lot of changes happened in our country, the least of which is the presence of English. I mean, what's the harm? English has connected us to the world and has given Indians several opportunities and made travelling to so many English-speaking countries easy,' asked Tiana.

The class was quiet for a few seconds so Tiana continued.

'I also think we very conveniently pick and choose what we consider to be "western" influence. The British did horrible things and I'll never defend them. They stole from us and set us back by many years. Their Victorian morals actually made us more restricted, but on the other hand, they also brought the parliamentary, judiciary and executive systems. They brought the railway service, postal service and cricket. They established the country's first museum, first stadium and first golf course in Calcutta. They have built UNESCO World Heritage Sites. All these things are technically a "western" influence on our country. How much of it are we willing or even capable of throwing out? There is a huge double standard. For most Indians, the western influence is only limited to women wearing skirts, people eating pizza and Indians speaking in English. We are stuck on clothes, food and language. These things are just on the periphery, they are just the tip of the iceberg of western influence. We are being delusional if we think that changing the names of our cities from Bombay to Mumbai or Calcutta to Kolkata is going to relieve us of the British imprint. It's our history and we can't change it. They were here and they affected us in many ways. We should learn from the past and understand that today's India exists as an amalgamation of different influences from our past. Primarily, those are the western influences from the British and the Middle Eastern influences from the Mughals,' concluded Tiana.

That's when Rishi and all the liberals began clapping for Tiana. Slowly, some of the conservatives joined in as well. Pradeep did not.

'Brilliant. See, you made such good points and put them across in such a simple and straightforward way that it was very easy for everyone to follow your thought process. That is the most important thing—clarity. Knowing what you want to say and then expressing it, including examples from real-life incidents. That makes it easy for people to relate to what you are saying,' said Rishi.

Regardless of whether people agreed with her or not, it was exhilarating to be able to express herself this way. She knew that she had made a mark amongst the people in the class. Nobody got offended over any discussion because Rishi had made it clear that no personal attacks were allowed. They were all having healthy discussions in the class and after class got over, people would come up to her and tell her that she was making a lot of sense. They even appreciated how well she spoke and contributed rational points to the discussions.

Every week, Tiana's confidence grew. She was voicing her opinions and, at the same time, learning from other people's ideas as well. It was a great atmosphere to be in and she was always looking forward to attending the class. Before this, she had never spoken so confidently to any adult other than her parents. Teachers in school were very sharp with anyone who would try to voice their opinions. In school, if a teacher said something to you, that was supposed to be the end of it. You were not supposed to retort, because if you did, you would be accused of 'answering them back' and be told off for not respecting your elders. Discussions were not a part of high-school life. In comparison, Rishi was a completely different kind of teacher. He was constantly encouraging his students to raise questions and always willing to answer them. He didn't mind his own opinions being questioned. He lived for the conversation. Tiana knew she had become one of his favourite students because Krish himself told her so.

~

Over the last few weeks, Tiana and Krish had become great friends too. His company had made the summer a lot more fun. His ex-girlfriend, Niti, had left a few days after the party that Tiana had attended. After that, Krish decided to show Tiana the different historic sites in Bombay. This led to them hanging out a lot. Sometimes, Vir, Krish's friend, would join them as well. They explored the art galleries in and around Kala Ghoda, walked around the old colonial buildings in Fort and Colaba, sat on the steps of the Asiatic Library, happened upon a Bollywood film shoot and drank coffee in the myriad cafes of the city—no matter how many places they tried, somehow more places popped up in Bombay.

While spending so much time with him, she had also developed a tiny crush on Krish. It had happened very gradually and she only realized it because she was always looking forward to meeting and talking to him. They had such similar interests that she couldn't help it. However, she had no intention of acting on it. The last thing she needed was another romantic connection with a boy. She was glad that for once, she had a good friend who was also a boy. She didn't know if Krish had any feelings for her and she was glad for that. All she had wanted was a simple summer where she could focus and learn, and so far it seemed to be going well for her. She deserved to catch a break after the stressful term at school.

∽

Just before the day of the last class, Rishi had asked Tiana if she would be interested in taking part in a Youth Leaders Conference that he was organizing. He wanted her to tell her story in front of the media. She would talk about how she was wrongfully suspended by her school and how schools were making too big a deal about regular teen experiences. Tiana was taken aback that such an opportunity was being offered to her.

'Look, a big newspaper is sponsoring the event so there will be a lot of coverage and maybe that will help you clear your name as well. Think about it,' said Rishi.

When Tiana told Krish about his father's offer, Krish started laughing.

'What's so funny?' Tiana asked in confusion.

'It's just that my parents are so similar that sometimes it makes me laugh,' smiled Krish.

'I have no idea what that means.'

'So I was telling my mom about you and what you are going through, and she said that she wants to interview you for the documentary she is working on,' said Krish.

'Wait, your mom makes documentaries?' asked Tiana, impressed.

'Yeah, she is quite popular on YouTube. Her last short film has over 10 million views.'

'Wow! And she wants to interview me? Your dad must have asked her to talk to me,' said Tiana.

'Oh no, no! My parents are divorced and they don't get along too well. I spoke to my mom about you. She wants to meet you once,' said Krish.

Things were escalating now. Within one day she had been offered two great opportunities and, surprisingly, both came from Krish's parents. Tiana had no idea what Krish's mother was like, he had never discussed her much. Now that she knew his parents were divorced, she began to feel a bit apprehensive because it was starting to feel like she was about to get stuck between the two of them.

Nine

'Freedom's just another word for nothin' left to lose.'

—Kris Kristofferson and Fred Foster

The next day, Tiana reached Krish's house. He had told her that he lived with his mother on most days. She rang the bell timidly, not knowing what to expect from the meeting she was walking into. Krish opened the door.

'Hey, come in.'

Tiana entered the apartment and instantly saw his mother sitting on the couch in the drawing room.

'Welcome, Tiana. Krish has told me such interesting things about you,' said his mother coming up to Tiana. They shook hands.

'Thank you for inviting me, ma'am,' said Tiana.

'Oh, please call me Ina. None of this "ma'am" stuff; it's too formal for my taste.'

Tiana nodded. She followed them inside. Ina didn't look like someone who had a 19-year-old son. She seemed as if she was still in her late 20s and was dressed casually in jeans, t-shirt and slippers. There was a quality of casual and comfortable charm to her. She offered Tiana green tea, and Tiana agreed even though she didn't really have a taste for it.

'Apparently, you've made quite a mark on my son. He talks about the stuff you say in class all the time. I think he might have a crush on you,' smiled Ina.

'Oh God, Mom. Can you please stop…' said Krish, rolling his eyes. He kept his gaze averted from Tiana.

'Relax, relax. I'm joking. Anyway, Tiana, it seems you are a confident girl who is not scared to speak her mind and that makes you exactly the kind of person I'm looking for,' said Ina, getting directly to her point.

'I'm sorry, for what exactly?' asked Tiana.

'I want you to be a part of my documentary,' said Ina.

When Ina saw Tiana's reluctance, she went on quickly, 'Your story is so interesting. A girl who has never even had a drop of alcohol in her life got thrown out of her school for drinking on campus? That's storytelling gold,' replied Ina.

'I want to clarify that I was suspended, not "thrown out" and second, I have sipped on alcohol just so you know,' replied Tiana.

'Yeah, yeah... I'll get all the details right when I interview you but first say yes!' replied Ina.

Tiana shook her head.

'Why?'

'It's just that right now only the people from my school know what happened. So why would I want to broadcast it to the rest of the world that I was suspended? I want to underplay this part of my life, not highlight it.'

'Don't you want a chance to clear your name? That's what I can help you do. Through my documentary, I am trying to peek into different teenage experiences in our country. I'm going to be shooting a series of episodes with teenagers from different social backgrounds, schools and cities, and so far, I have no one from a heritage boarding school.'

'Ina, I'm sure you can find more deserving people. There are a lot of teenagers in boarding schools who are achieving bigger things in life than getting suspended,' replied Tiana.

'Okay, stop this. Stop diminishing your value. Your school victimized you but there is no need to do it to yourself. Your story is interesting because it shows how the current school system failed you. How schools make a big deal about stuff that teenagers are going to do no matter what and then they go on to punish the wrong people for it.'

'What do you mean?' asked Tiana in confusion.

'Look, you are young, so maybe you can't see it. But from my point of view, I can kind of see what your school did.'

'What did they do?'

'Okay first tell me, how many people were there that night?'

'At least 25,' replied Tiana.

'Were any of them boys?' asked Ina.

'Of course, I'm pretty sure they were the ones who sneaked in the booze.'

'Were they senior boys? Possibly with parents who have connections with the school?'

'I really don't know the answer to that. Maybe... But there were seniors for sure,' replied Tiana.

'Well, I have a feeling that I could reach the story buried in here if only you say yes.'

'So that's your angle? You think we are in a movie where I was scapegoated to save a well-connected boy? Seriously?' enquired Tiana raising her eyebrows.

'It could be true. I mean, stranger things have happened.'

'It sounds like a conspiracy theory.'

'If you let me prove it, it won't be just a conspiracy theory; it will be a conspiracy reality.'

Tiana was silent because, for a second, she thought that maybe an outsider like Ina could in fact see the bigger picture. Maybe there were things she had missed and maybe Ina could right the wrong done to her. She was being offered help on a silver platter. Why refuse it? For too long she had said no to things out of fear—the fear of embarrassment, of looking stupid, of being judged. Her life was on a new path now and maybe it required her to outgrow her fears and say yes this time. She needed the freedom to do something new and to truly feel free.

'You owe it to yourself, Tiana.'

'I will need to talk to my parents first.'

'Of course. But are you saying you will consider it?'

'Yes. I will.'

'Good. Now, I know that Krish's father has also offered you an opportunity to speak about your experience at that youth leaders' event. The thing is, I will need exclusive rights to your story. Which means you can't talk about it on a media platform until after my documentary comes out. If your story is old news, then it won't generate interest in my documentary. So you will have to choose between doing my documentary or speaking at that event. The choice is yours but think carefully. My documentary will have a much bigger reach and I will actually come and interview you inside your school and try to get to the bottom of what happened. That's my promise to you. You just have to be completely honest with me,' said Ina.

Tiana had been right. She was stuck between Krish's parents. She didn't know what the right choice for her was. What Ina was saying made a lot of sense but on the other hand, Rishi had asked her first and had mentored and guided her for the past seven weeks. She felt it was unfair that she was being put in this situation.

As Tiana was about to leave, she asked Ina something that was on her mind.

'How will you get permission to shoot inside my school? I mean the school is very strict especially if you tell them that you want to interview me. They are not my greatest fans right now,' said Tiana.

'I'll find a way. You just have to say yes first.'

Krish walked her to the elevator. 'I'm sorry that you have to choose between my mom and my dad. Suddenly, it feels like your life has become like mine. Stuck between them,' laughed Krish.

Tiana smiled, 'It's okay.'

'If I'd known that it would lead to this, I wouldn't have said anything to my mom.'

'Oh no. I'm grateful that you did. I mean it would no doubt be a great opportunity for me,' said Tiana.

'Also about what my mom said… you know, about me having a crush on you—'

'Don't worry,' interrupted Tiana, 'She was just being a mom. I know it's not true.'

Then Krish took a step closer to her, half smiled at her and then looked away consciously. And suddenly Tiana understood that he was trying to tell her *was* true. Tiana looked up at him and she knew that he wanted to kiss her. She didn't step back either and that's when he leaned in and they kissed. When they broke apart, it was awkward. The kiss itself felt a little anti-climactic. Maybe she didn't really like Krish that much because the kiss didn't make her feel anything. Maybe she was just fond of him and nothing more. Besides, she was leaving in a week and she still had confused feelings for another boy, a rather idiotic one but still, she did. Apparently, Krish felt the same way.

'Wow, that felt strange. Let's pretend that didn't happen,' said Krish sheepishly.

'So we are friend-zoning each other then?' asked Tiana, extending her arm for a high-five.

'Yes. Friend-zoned for life,' replied Krish as he returned her high-five.

∾

Eventually, Tiana decided to do Ina's documentary. During her last class of the workshop, she thanked Rishi for everything that he had taught her. Before she could even tell him her decision, he told her that he knew Ina had asked her for exclusivity.

'Tiana, I understand. It's a better opportunity and you must do what's best for you. This is not the first time Ina has stolen a story or a project from me. Trust me, I'm used to it. Just make sure that you get what you want from this documentary. Don't let her force you into anything you are not comfortable with. Remember, it's your story and she's just telling it. Don't let her control you.'

'I don't understand,' said Tiana, confused by Rishi's warning.

'I just mean that if, at any point, you feel you don't have control over the story or you don't like the methods, you should speak up. When you return to school, use the strength you have shown in this class in the past eight weeks. Okay? I expect great things from you in the future,' said Rishi and patted her on the head.

Tiana felt bad for not choosing Rishi's project. After all, she didn't really know Ina so well. On the other hand, she realized she didn't know Rishi that well either. Maybe they were just playing games with each other and Tiana had been caught in the middle of it all. Either way, the decision was made and she would have to make peace with it.

Ten

'A black swan, a white raven.'

—John Clarke

Sitting at Bombay airport, Tiana was at the end of her summer adventure. Her time in the city had led her to some surprising self-revelations. It had broadened her vision, made her more confident and even slightly selfish, expanded her capacity to think and exposed her to a world outside her comfort zone. Some experiences are profound from the very beginning, and you expect your world to change immediately. This hadn't been such an experience. It was a slow change. The kind where you do, see, read and watch new things, hear and speak to new people, and gradually, the world begins to fall into order and you begin to understand your place in it. Yet, you don't realize this shift in yourself. Over time, such situations arise that would have spiritually incapacitated you but now you can't contain your bubbling energy and you refuse to remain inauthentic. It's at this point that you realize how much you have truly changed. However, Tiana had not reached that point yet. She had gone through the highs and lows of a profound experience, without even knowing that it had been profound. The realization would come much later.

For now, Tiana was dreading her return home because in two days, her glorious freedom would be taken away from her and she would be back in her boarding school. School is really something, isn't it? Especially in India and furthermore at the elite boarding schools that are considered to be among the best in the country. Hill View High was more than a school; it was an *institution*. The school really did take itself seriously, which is why everybody else did too. The alumni association, the board of directors and the teachers were constantly telling the students how lucky they were to be in such a school. They had the heritage of a colonial school and the architecture, facilities, food, academics, sports and the extracurricular activities were one of the best in the country. Only a handful of other schools had similar qualities. So, yes, for the most part, they were indeed fortunate but *those* are not the parts we are going to focus on. Tiana had defended her school to outsiders, but even she couldn't ignore the realities.

In the end, what is the point of having the best of everything when what you are *inherently* learning is something being taught even in the remotest of village schools? Getting a high school diploma is necessary. Doing that in a great atmosphere is a true blessing but the question here is what kind of people are teachers training the kids to *become* as they grow older? In the widest sense, it's the difference between education and knowledge. At Hill View High, bookish education was held as an ideal while teachers freely imparted their prejudices to the students. There was hardly any real growth amongst the students. The capacity to question and think, and be gracious and magnanimous didn't exist either in the teachers or in their students.

Is it constructive, when in math class, the teacher asks the entire class to stand up and solve a problem in one minute? And if you can't solve it, you have to keep standing while the rest of the class gets to sit as soon as they are done solving it, and on top of that, the teacher calls you an idiot repeatedly, day after day. This is a prolonged sort of torture because you can't escape the humiliation. You know it is coming and yet you have to walk into the classroom filled with dread, every single day. This was when she had first begun to lose confidence in herself. As a result, she had also developed a minor case of social anxiety. Tiana felt that when seniors and teachers saw her, they could only see all the things she couldn't do and she felt she had nothing to contribute within the world of her school.

There was constant pressure from the house mistresses and house prefects who wanted their respective house to win The Study Cup, The PT Cup, The Athletic Cup, The Running Cup and, at the end of the year, the Cock House Cup. It was a legacy that the prefects wanted to leave behind and so they pushed everybody under them to perform. The school still followed its original British house system from the time of its establishment. The system was meant to encourage a sense of community amongst the students while giving them a reason to perform better at competitions. Undoubtedly, pressure is essential for youngsters while they are growing up. They need to push themselves to be better, that's how school works. But without any positive reinforcements, it can actually be detrimental to the growth of a person.

Tiana gave it her all for the first two years in Hill View High. She tried to qualify in sporting events because each student added points to their house total by qualifying for cross-country running and athletic events. She scored above 80 per cent in her exams, but no matter how well she did in the other subjects, mathematics and science always pulled her total score down. By class seven, she knew that she was neither a runner nor a long jumper, nor capable of solving trigonometry and certainly not capable of doing a handstand. Yet, for some reason, her teachers and seniors could not understand that about her. When she was unable to perform, they mocked her and made her feel useless, adding to her inferiority complex. They told her she had nothing to contribute to the house, that she was a burden, a dead weight which the real performers had to carry on their shoulders.

School wanted everybody to excel at exactly the same things. It was called being an 'all-rounder'. How could they think it was possible? Did they *actually* expect everybody to get 99 per cent marks and also excel in sports and other extracurricular activities? Surely not all the parents and teachers could have achieved such distinction when they themselves were in school. And if they had turned out to live successful lives despite not being manic 'all-rounders', then why couldn't they give the current youngsters the same benefit? Yet, they turned a blind eye to the limitations of the students. It was about time somebody realized that such an approach to education was useless.

Why didn't the school have a Dance Cup, a Writing Cup, a Debate Cup, a Singing Cup, an Acting cup, a Photography Cup or a Film Cup? There were other talents in which students could contribute to their house and school. But nobody was ever going to think beyond studies and sports.

This time at the start of the new term, Tiana was set on getting noticed on her own terms. Unlike the last time, when her story had been in other people's hands, this time *she* wanted to control the narrative. She was done being taken advantage of by her teachers and friends.

For Tiana, it was the betrayal from her friends that broke her ability to trust people. Betrayal and loyalty are difficult concepts for teenagers to understand and, much less, to follow through. Tiana constantly felt that people only cared about themselves, and maybe that's something everyone learns in their own way as they grow up, but she had been jolted rudely into this reality. Friendship had come at a cost and she had paid the price. She didn't intend to pay again.

The sting of betrayal is a gnawing pain. She had felt a deep unhappiness which had begun to diminish her confidence, but the time for wallowing in self-pity was over. She had decided to be a good friend to the people she liked but she would never blindly trust anyone again.

Eleven

*'Personally I feel happier now that we have no allies
to be polite to and to pamper.'*

—King George VI

Her first day in school after the summer break was filled with awkward encounters. She had avoided contact with almost everyone during the summer. Sara was the only one with whom Tiana had exchanged a few messages during the holidays, but for the most part, she had cut herself off to focus on the workshop and on herself. She had left the hallowed halls of her school amidst rumours and gossip. Now, she was back under similar circumstances. She was still the girl who had disgraced herself. Everywhere she went, she noticed people stopping to look at her, some even doing a double take. People were acting like they were seeing her for the first time. In a way, they really were seeing her in a new light. To most of the students in school, Tiana had seemed prim, proper and boring. This new notoriety had finally made her interesting.

The day she had got suspended, she left without saying bye to anyone. Everybody had been in class and as soon as they got out, the rumour had spread that Tiana had been asked to leave the school premises immediately. She had vanished so suddenly that she had left a sense of mystery behind her. So now, when people were finally seeing her again, they couldn't help themselves from talking about her. Of the girls, the juniors were excited to see her, whereas the seniors gave her dirty looks. Tiana had no idea why they were being so hostile but then again, she had never got along with the seniors because she had always rejected their authority. In any case, she was the topic of conversation for a lot of people and the awkwardness was only starting to build up.

There were many uncomfortable exchanges waiting to happen. She had not spoken to Karam since their break-up. Ronit had been travelling and neither of them had tried to get in touch with the other. Her cousin Tea had deliberately got Tiana and her friends caught during the secret party, so she was just one more person Tiana had avoided. Then, of course, there were Leila and Savera, and there was no way in hell that Tiana wanted to talk to them either. Strangely, Bella had been the only person Tiana had sort of forgiven. She was the first person Tiana saw as soon as she entered her dorm.

'Welcome back, T! Come, take the bed next to mine, I've saved it for you,' said Bella, grinning and giving Tiana a hug. Bella had chosen the beds at the further end of the dorm. 'This is the most private area in the dorm, so I took it,' she said.

'Thanks, but what about Lilly and Celia? I'm sure they would want to have their beds next to you. Are you sure they will be fine with this?' asked Tiana.

'I don't care. They'll get over it,' said Bella.

'Is everything okay between you guys?' asked Tiana, sensing some tension.

'Lilly began dating Parth during the summer. He's a senior who caught drinking with the rest of us that day. Apparently, he and his friends don't like me. So Lilly has suddenly become a supreme bitch,' said Bella, rolling her eyes.

'Why doesn't he like you?'

'Who knows? Boys are weird,' said Bella.

Since Tiana agreed with that statement, she didn't pursue the topic further.

A few minutes later, Leila and Savera entered the dorm together and when they saw Tiana and Bella being friendly and hanging out, they just exchanged strange looks with each other. Tiana ignored their existence completely and they didn't try to come and talk to her either. For the past four years, Tiana and Leila had taken beds next to each other. This term, however, things were going to be very different. By taking the bed next to Bella, Tiana was sending a clear message to Leila about how she felt and Leila had enough self-respect to not question this decision.

Just as Tiana had begun unpacking, her dorm matron sent a message that her house mistress wanted to speak to her. So, she stopped unpacking and went to her house mistress's house, which was a two-minute walk from the dorms.

'Welcome back, Tiana. I'm so glad to see you again,' said Mrs Puri, her house mistress.

'Thank you, ma'am. It's good to be back,' replied Tiana.

'Tiana, regarding what happened last term, I think it would be best if you tried to stay out of trouble now. You have always been a well-disciplined girl, unlike your friends. I was shocked that you of all people were involved in all that drama. I will be keeping an eye on you and so will the senior mistress. Just don't give her a chance to complain to me about you, okay? That's the last thing I need, for her to find fault with any girl from my house, especially you. Be sensible and behave well and keep Mrs Banerjee off both our backs. Promise me, no more trouble,' said Mrs Puri.

Tiana nodded even though she knew that one way or another, there would be trouble. It couldn't be helped.

'Also, no dating, Tiana. I don't want to hear that you are dating any boy. Some junior girls told me that you broke up with our head boy Karam and I was glad to hear it. Now, focus on your studies and enough of this boy nonsense.'

Tiana wanted to retort sarcastically to this condescending conversation, but she knew nothing would come of it except detention, so she bit her tongue and nodded again, 'Yes, ma'am.'

As Karam and Tiana had not spoken to each other since their second break-up at the start of summer holidays, Tiana had no idea what to expect from him on the first day back at school. They had been friends before they started dating, but things could never revert to that stage of comfort between them. It would've been foolish to expect that, so she didn't, and when they finally came face to face in the corridor of the main building, Karam walked past her without a nod of acknowledgement. To ignore her existence was juvenile and Tiana had expected him to be better than that.

'Wow! He just walked past you. Isn't that silly? He could have at least given you a smile or something,' said Sara.

'Forget it,' said Tiana dismissively. She did think it was silly but wasn't going to let this slight affect her. She had made the right decision of breaking up with him and Karam's grumpiness couldn't change how she felt. They were hanging out in the corridor, waiting for the lunch bell to ring, when a few moments later, she heard Ronit call out her name. She braced herself and turned to look at him.

'Hey, Tiana. Can I talk to you about something?' he asked.

'Okay.'

'Umm... can you come into the classroom? I don't want to talk here,' said Ronit, opening the door of an empty classroom and beckoned her to follow him.

'I think he doesn't want to talk in front of me. So, go ahead,' said Sara, walking away to find the rest of their friends.

Tiana entered the classroom. She leaned against a desk, looking at Ronit intently. He seemed different, maybe it was the tan from his summer in Europe or how his hair was slightly longer and dishevelled, but he looked older than she remembered.

'I know that you know everything and I wanted to request you to not tell anyone about it,' said Ronit.

Tiana just smiled knowingly. That made Ronit blush and he

couldn't help himself from grinning.

'You are such a liar,' smiled Tiana, shaking her head condescendingly.

'A part of it was true okay.'

'Please!' said Tiana, rolling her eyes at him.

'A very small, tiny part. You never believed me so it shouldn't matter anyway.'

'I almost believed you at one point but in the end, I really didn't,' agreed Tiana.

During her time in Bombay, Tiana had discovered something about Ronit's past and why he had actually joined Hill View High last term.

Since Ronit's family lived in the same building as Tiana's grandparents, one evening, at the start of the holidays, Tiana had been invited to Ronit's house for dinner along with her grandparents. She had expected to see him at dinner but he had left for his trip by then. In his absence, Tiana finally learned the real reason why Ronit had joined her school. He had given Tiana the impression that he had followed her to her boarding school because he liked her and missed her and felt bad about how he had treated her. Tiana knew better than to fall for such tall tales, but Ronit had stuck to his story. In reality, he had been caught breaking several rules in his old school—smoking on campus, kissing a girl he was dating and stealing a question paper. His school in Bombay had given his family an ultimatum—to withdraw him from school with dignity or else the school would expel him.

'I was so worried about him. I didn't know what had gotten into him. No matter how hard I tried to reach him, he didn't show any interest in talking to me,' Ronit's mother had told Tiana's nani.

'When we had to finally find him a new school, he asked us to enrol him in your school, Tiana. He said he wanted a change, to take a break from the city. He wanted to be in a boarding school because you had said it was the best thing,' Ronit's father had told Tiana.

Tiana had just been trying to process all of Ronit's lies as quickly as she could. He had lied and omitted a lot!

'We're happy we listened to him. He's doing so much better at your school. His marks have improved and he's not getting into trouble anymore. I'm sure it's your good influence, Tiana,' his mother had told her.

'Aunty, I'm not a good influence at all. You know what happened with me, right?' Tiana had replied uncomfortably.

'Yes, we know. Ronit told me that he thinks he could have stopped it from happening and that it was not at all your fault. He feels very sorry about what happened,' his father had said apologetically.

Tiana had just smiled awkwardly.

In hindsight, she realized that perhaps because Ronit had come so close to being thrown out of his old school, he actually felt bad about the part he played in Tiana's suspension. Although that was no excuse for his behaviour, somehow the knowledge that he felt guilty about what he had done, made her feel better.

'Why did you lie?' asked Tiana.

'Why?' asked Ronit, looking up at her.

'Yeah, I want to know.'

'Obviously, because it was embarrassing to tell you the real reason. I mean, so what if I tried a cigarette or kissed my girlfriend or helped my friend steal a question paper? Everybody does this stuff but I was almost expelled and that just sounds so dramatic and intense for something that was done in fun. I didn't want everyone to think I'm a screw up.'

'Turns out you and I have another experience in common. Except in my case, the worst actually happened and everybody does think of me as a screw up,' smiled Tiana.

'This is exactly why I felt so bad! I couldn't explain it before but I understood what it felt like and I felt horrible that you were going through what I barely managed to avoid myself. But, T, people are mad. Don't take anybody seriously; no matter what they say to you,' said Ronit.

'I'm trying.'

'And just so you know, I did really come to this school because of you,' said Ronit.

'Okay, enough.'

'When my parents asked me where I wanted to go next, I really did say Hill View High because I knew you were here. That was no lie. It's true that I didn't randomly uproot my entire life for you and if I wasn't going to be expelled, I would have probably never come here. But when I really needed a fresh start, I thought of you,' said Ronit very seriously.

He had taken a few steps towards her and despite desperately not wanting to, she felt butterflies in her stomach.

'So, you broke up with Karam, huh?' smiled Ronit. At this point, he was standing very close to her and his face was looming over hers.

'There is no need to say that like it is new information for you, Ronit. I'm pretty sure you've known all summer. Sid was travelling with you and he must have told you,' said Tiana.

'I wanted to call you but I didn't know what to say—,' said Ronit.

The door of the classroom suddenly opened and Tea appeared out of nowhere. Tea was a reminder of everything that had gone wrong with Ronit in the past. Tiana had no idea why that boy had such an intense effect on her when they were alone, but as soon as there were other people around them, she was harshly awakened to the realities between herself and Ronit. And currently, between them were Tea, Bella and Karam, and Ronit's own. Upon seeing Tea, Ronit himself took a few steps away from Tiana.

'Hey guys. Tiana, I've been looking for you everywhere. I need to talk to you,' said Tea cheerfully. In response, Ronit gave her a faint smile and Tiana scoffed at her.

'Tea, I haven't forgotten what you did. So please, stop with this fake familiarity,' said Tiana.

'What did she do?' asked Ronit curiously.

'Tiana, please don't,' pleaded Tea.

'Why should I keep secrets about a back-stabber like you? What right do you have to ask this of me?' Tiana shot back.

'I made a mistake.'

'Oh, are you talking about her and Karam?' Ronit asked Tiana.

'What?' asked Tiana loudly.

'Shut up, Ronit!' exclaimed Tea.

'You said you made a mistake, so I assumed you meant Karam. That guy is a mistake for anyone, as far as I'm concerned,' smirked Ronit.

'Tiana, I'm so sorry. I really didn't want you to find out this way,' said Tea.

'Umm... I don't know what you both are talking about,' stated Tiana. She had begun to get an inkling of what was being said, but it seemed so improbable to her that she stopped herself from jumping to a conclusion and, instead, stood there waiting for confirmation of this ludicrous piece of information.

'Tea and Karam apparently became a "thing" during the summer holidays while she was staying at your house,' said Ronit.

Without saying a word, Tiana looked at Tea and she nodded slightly to confirm it.

'Karam wanted to tell you himself and he asked me not to say anything. No one else knows. We wanted you to be the first to know, I have no idea how Ronit even found out,' said Tea giving Ronit an irritated look.

'Karam told Sid, who told me,' said Ronit.

Tiana didn't know how she felt. Yet. Too many details were missing. So she didn't react at all and remained poker-faced.

'Why aren't you saying anything?' asked Ronit.

'Why are you so interested, Ronit? Why did you think you needed to tell me this? It's none of your business, right?' asked Tiana. She couldn't help but wonder why she was always surrounded by so many inconsiderate people. Including her own brother. If Sid had known this, he should have told her himself.

'Why are you turning on me?' asked Ronit in confusion.

'For many reasons, but particularly because you seem to be returning to your games and tricks,' said Tiana.

'I'm doing no such thing. I'm just being a good friend by telling you what's happening behind your back,' he said in exasperation.

'If you really wanted to be a friend, you should have told me as soon as you found out. You could have messaged me or called me because you seem to have known this for a while. You didn't need to wait till we were in school; I could have processed this better if I had known beforehand. Instead, you decided to tell me at whatever time served you best to create drama. Clearly, you are trying to get some reaction from me by telling me this in front of Tea,' said Tiana.

'No! I really didn't think that, Tiana!' exclaimed Ronit.

'I'm sure you *didn't* think. That's your problem. You don't think. If you had, you'd have told me at a sensible time,' said Tiana with irritation.

Ronit suddenly seemed very flustered because until two minutes ago, things had been going great between Tiana and him. They had even been on the cusp of flirting but now, once again, the situation had taken a downward spiral.

'Okay, I agree I could have told you sooner but I'm telling you now because I just wanted you to know what kind of a guy Karam is. He broke up with you and went after your cousin. I want you to be able to move on from him,' said Ronit earnestly.

Tiana and Tea looked at each other; the irony of their situation was too acute. So much so that Tiana couldn't stop herself from laughing and Tea joined her, albeit a little awkwardly.

'You mean, exactly how *you* broke up with me and went after Tiana, who is my cousin?' asked Tea, arching her left eyebrow.

Ronit opened and shut his mouth several times in an attempt to say something, but no words came out. Very conveniently, it seemed, he had completely forgotten about his own actions.

'Turns out, you and Karam have a lot in common,' said Tiana.

'Ronit, can you please leave us alone? I need to talk to Tiana,' said Tea.

'Oh, Tea, don't bother pleading with me again. I already told Bella the part you played in getting everyone caught that night. I'm so glad I told her before I found out about you and Karam because had I told people now, you would have just said that I was being vindictive. Now at least I can avoid that label if nothing else,' concluded Tiana with satisfaction.

'You told Bella? Oh God, Tiana. Why? I said sorry so many times! She will make my life miserable. She will tell everyone. Even Karam doesn't know yet. Now he will hate me for what I did,' cried out Tea.

'What did you do?' asked Ronit curiously.

'She wanted to get Bella in trouble because she was jealous that you were dating Bella. So, she pretended to faint near the secret party that night. I was very worried for her and, like an idiot, brought a teacher to help her out. But the teacher heard the noises coming from the party and she caught all of you. Later, Tea confessed that she wasn't really sick and had done it all on purpose,' said Tiana.

Ronit looked at her incredulously. 'Tea, you are just all sorts of crazy, aren't you?'

'Shut up! Shut up! I opened up to you when I was drunk and out of guilt, but now I wish I had never told you, Tiana,' said Tea sadly.

'That's your problem,' said Tiana matter-of-factly.

Just then, the bell rang and Tiana was glad to finally have an excuse to walk away from that classroom.

Twelve

*'An open foe may prove a curse,
But a pretended friend is worse.'*

—John Gay

During English class, Tiana and Leila were forced by their proximity to finally have a long overdue conversation. They had two consecutive English classes and their teacher was on sick leave, so they were free till breakfast. The entire classroom was talking and yelling in excitement. Any minute, a teacher could come in and give them all detention for being noisy and Tiana didn't want to get into any further trouble on the very first day of classes. Having had enough, she got up from her seat and loudly spoke to her classmates, 'Guys! I don't want to get detention because of the noise!'

'Oh look, who is freshly back from her suspension. I think detention is a step up from suspension. Isn't it, you stupid bitch?' came the crass reply from Jai, a boy from Tiana's class.

'Don't talk to her like that,' said Leila from the other side of the huge classroom, where she was sitting with Savera, Savera's boyfriend Aryan, Lilly and Ronit.

Tiana was surprised both by Jai's gross comment and Leila's sudden solidarity.

'Jai, shut the hell up. And, Leila, thank you very much but I don't need *you* to speak for me,' said Tiana proudly.

'What's your problem? I'm taking your side,' said Leila defensively.

'My lucky day,' said Tiana sarcastically, 'besides, he may be an asshat but he is right about one thing—detention *is* a step up from what I went through.'

Tiana saw that Leila was about to reply but Savera stopped her and whispered something in her ear. After that, Leila walked over to Tiana. The classroom had suddenly got much quieter; they were all waiting in anticipation. Everyone was focused on Tiana and Leila to hear what they would say next to each other.

'Can I talk to you?' asked Leila.

'Do you really need to?' asked Tiana.

'Yes.'

'Fine. Outside.'

They stood in the stone corridor away from the rest of the class. The last time she had had a conversation with Leila, both Karam and Sid had interfered excessively in trying to mend their friendship. Tiana had still not fully processed how she felt at that time, but they had forced her to say she forgave Leila even though she hadn't. This time, Tiana had no intention of holding back her anger.

'I've already said sorry to you, Tiana. Why can't you just forgive me and move on?' asked Leila.

'Excuse me?' replied Tiana, raising her eyebrows.

'Yeah, why are you being such a baby? You're being so rude to me in front of others. I mean, we are supposed to be friends!' said Leila.

'Okay, the only way I could be induced into being your friend again would be if I had been lobotomized. Luckily, that's been illegal since the '50s, so I'm in my complete senses today when I tell you to go to *hell*,' said Tiana with a fake smile.

'What did you say to me?' asked Leila, narrowing her eyes.

'Oh, did that offend you? Glad to know that it did,' grimaced Tiana.

'When I came to your house, you said you forgave me. Since then, there has been radio silence from your end. I even messaged you but you didn't respond. Were you just lying then?' asked Leila.

'Yes! I lied. For the sake of my brother, I lied, but I'm not going to anymore. Your relationship with him is his business and I'm never going to interfere, but I'm not going to allow him to dictate my feelings either. And I think you are a petty, unfaithful friend and someday Sid will see that for himself,' said Tiana.

'How can you blame me for everything? I didn't even do anything. Meanwhile you have forgiven Bella and become friends with her again. She's the one who posted your photo! Not me and not Savera,' said Leila defensively.

'Do you know the difference between Bella and you?' asked Tiana.

'What?' shrugged Leila.

'I expect this kind of behaviour from her. She is who she is. She does not try to be outwardly nice and supportive. If she likes you, she will tell you and if she doesn't, she won't shy away from telling you that either. Bella and I were in a bad place because of the games Ronit was trying to play with me by using her. So yes, I can see why she did what she did,' said Tiana.

Leila was listening quietly.

'I didn't expect you to do what you did, Leila, because I thought we were friends! You knew that Bella was going to post the photo and you didn't stop her or even warn me. Tell me if I'm wrong! Bella is inside the classroom right now, I can ask her to come out and tell you what she told me. That you knew she was thinking of posting the photo. Tell me, right now, that you didn't know,' said Tiana confidently.

'Yes, I knew. But I didn't think she would really do it,' said Leila softly.

'Bullshit. Admit it. Admit that you were jealous that my name had come up for the exchange programme. That you were worried I might become a prefect instead of you. Don't lie to me, Leila. You and Savera had stopped hanging out with me way before this fiasco even happened. Stop lying to yourself and, for once, have the guts to own up to your true feelings,' said Tiana.

'Look, I was a little upset that your name was sent for the exchange programme. I mean, that was always what I wanted, Tiana. I wanted to be selected for the exchange programme. After the car accident, when the teachers found out about my involvement in it, I lost my goodwill with them. The senior mistress lectured me on how I was giving the school a bad name. I had worked for years to be good at studies and sports and extracurriculars and suddenly, because of one mistake, none of it mattered,' said Leila defensively.

'So you decided to ruin my reputation as well,' Tiana said quietly.

'The teachers loved you. They loved that you weren't one of the drunk students in the car that night. When I saw my chance slipping away, I unknowingly wished for you to be like me as well. I never thought that you would actually get *suspended*. I thought you would also get detention, like the rest of us. None of us planned this or wanted this!'

'The reality is that you were just happy to have me as a sidekick. As long as I didn't overshadow you in any way, you were happy to have me as your friend. When that dynamic changed, you changed too. I can never trust you again, Leila. Our friendship, the way it once was, is over. I don't know how we will be going forward, but it won't be the same,' finished Tiana. She turned around and walked back into the classroom.

'That looked intense,' said Bella, glancing at Leila, who had skulked off to her desk.

'It was,' replied Tiana.

'I think Leila is crying. Savera is wiping her face,' said Aliya.

Everybody turned to look at Leila. Everybody, except Tiana.

Thirteen

'The success of an insult depends upon the sensitiveness and the indignation of the victim.'

—Seneca the Younger

On the first day of the previous term, when Tea had joined the school, she had taken Tiana's place at the dining table. When the senior mistress saw Tiana trying to find another seat at the table, she had yelled at her for loitering and had moved Tiana to Sara's table. It had been a blessing in disguise because even though in the beginning Tiana had missed her old table, she ended up becoming friends with Sara, Aditya and Diya.

Now, at the start of the new term, Aliya had decided to change her seating arrangement as well and she moved to Tiana's new table with her new group of friends. Aliya hadn't fought with Leila or Savera but she had still decided to shift away from her old friends because of how they had treated Tiana. It was a very confusing time for all of them. The group had fractured since the incident with Tiana. Nobody wanted to take the blame individually and so, it fell on all of them and that kind of pressure is too much for high school friendships. It had taken a toll on the group ever since Tiana had decided to distance herself from them. Aliya personally didn't like the way Bella, Leila and Savera had treated Tiana. So she had willingly ended her alliance with the group.

Until this point, their friend circle had always stuck together no matter what, but that was no longer true and everybody had noticed this. They had fragmented into various smaller groups.

Leila, Savera and her boyfriend Aryan, along with Lilly's ex-boyfriend, Rehan, had formed a new group. Bella, Lilly and Celia had drifted off from them and formed their own little group. Aliya had chosen to side with Tiana. They had always been stronger together. Nobody would mess with them because a fight with one of them would mean a fight with all seven of them. Nobody ever wanted that. Fighting with seven teenage girls at the same time would be any sane person's nightmare. However, that strength was now lost with the group breaking up and the spell of the 'cool group' was over for good.

Tiana was now the easiest target with nobody defending her or standing up for her. While waiting in line before lunch, she had noticed an excessive amount of name-calling being directed at her. It was meaner than usual, and some of it was abusive.

'Why are so many senior boys calling me a "stupid bitch"? What did I ever do to them?' asked Tiana sourly at the lunch table. This was true. Some of the boys were being aggressively mean to her. Even her own batchmates like Jai were using abusive language with her repetitively in class. She had never had any problems with Jai in the past but suddenly he was being extra rude to her.

'It's because they blame you... Well, me... Actually, us. They blame us,' said Bella. Tiana looked up from her plate and saw Bella's face looming over her head.

'For what exactly?' asked Tiana.

'For all the new restrictions introduced in this term,' said Bella, taking the empty chair next to Aliya.

'What are you doing?' asked Sara, looking at Bella.

'Sitting,' replied Bella sarcastically.

'Why are you sitting here?'

'Because I want to.'

'Tiana, is your entire friend circle going to follow you to this table?' asked Sara.

Since this was exactly what was happening, Tiana didn't know how to answer. So she decided to not say anything. Sara and her friends, Jasmine and Diya, had never gotten along with Tiana's other friends.

'Why are you being so salty, Sara. Chill,' said Bella.

'You've been sitting with us during class and now you're sitting at our table. Why?'

'Why can't I?' asked Bella, rolling her eyes.

'Are *you* okay with this?' asked Sara, looking at Tiana.

'Yeah. Bella and I are good,' said Tiana.

'Why?' Aliya frowned.

Tiana read the expression on her friends' face. Aliya too looked a little confused. Bella was the reason why Tiana had gotten suspended. So Sara and Aliya both found it odd that she was okay sitting with Bella, the very person who had caused her so much grief over the last few months. Tiana explained to them what they hadn't known before.

They didn't know that Tiana had gone through many emotions in that time and she no longer hated Bella for what had happened. There is only so much anger in one person. You can't stay mad at too many people at the same time. It's exhausting. So Tiana had chosen to let go of her anger towards Bella and to direct all her fury towards Leila.

Sara and Aliya still looked confused but didn't argue.

'Where are your minions, Lilly and Celia?' asked Aditya.

'They're too annoying. I can't deal with their constant negativity. I'm trying to change and be more patient and calm in life, and they can't seem to understand why my level of bitchiness has decreased. So I've decided to sit here with you, Tiana. I hope that's okay?' asked Bella.

'Of course.'

'Plus, everybody hates us both right now, so we are stuck in this together,' said Bella.

Tiana realized that just like her, Bella too was an easy target. She didn't have her friends standing by her either. So she had gravitated towards Tiana naturally. They were both coming out of the same scandal. Bella had caused it and Tiana had got caught in it. But at least 25 other people from the school had been involved in it as well. So the school was aware that they had a problem on their hands. After the summer break, they had put strict restrictions on the entire school, but particularly on the senior boys because they were the most likely to sneak alcohol and mobile phones into the campus, which is how their juniors got access to these things.

From this term onwards, there would be surprise raids in the dorms. Nobody would be allowed to lock their cupboards or their trunks and suitcases, which were kept together in the box room. Their weekly allowance for tuck shop had also been reduced. The number of count-ups had been increased, which meant that after 2.00 p.m., when lunch was over, for the rest of the day, everybody had to report to their respective house prefect every two hours to tell them about their whereabouts and the prefects then had to report this information to their respective house mistress or master. This was a lot of extra work for everybody but mostly for seniors who were prefects and had to constantly keep checks on everybody who was under them. If they didn't report on time, they would get into trouble with the teachers. For the seniors, it was their last term in school and they wanted to enjoy it. Instead, they were bogged down with more responsibilities than before. On top of that, if anyone was seen dating, both parties were to be given extra homework to keep them 'busy' because if you are dating, that means you have a lot of free time. So, more homework will make you utilize your free time in a better way than dating.

The anger of all these restrictions could not be taken out on the teachers, so the boys were blaming Tiana and Bella for it. For them, until these junior girls didn't get involved, everything had sailed smoothly. All the wrongdoings in school were under the radar. Before this, even if teachers knew something was wrong, they would sometimes turn a blind eye, especially towards senior boys. But once there was proof, there were photos on social media, the school could not stay quiet either. So now everyone was miserable, but the name-calling was starting to get out of control.

The senior boys had ordered the boys in Tiana's batch to trouble her in class as well. Name-calling was just the tip of the iceberg. Over the next month, this bullying had evolved into pulling of hair, throwing of red ink on her skirt, hiding her school bag and books and other petty things. Bella suffered this treatment in the first week of the new term but after that, it subsided. Tiana went through this on a daily basis, but she kept her cool. Every time anybody misbehaved with her, it made her stronger. It was almost character-building. Somehow, her time in Bombay had given her a different approach to life, now she saw her experience as a human story—something everybody must endure in order to grow up properly. It was just how school worked and she was determined to not let this break her. The one thing her bullies wanted was her reaction and that was totally in her control and she held it with clenched hands. She was not going to react and relinquish her control. After that, it was a matter of patience. Her patience vs. her bullies' patience. Whoever gave up first would win. This is the most basic rule of life.

She was now glad she had agreed to be a part of Ina's documentary. She knew that when it would be announced to the school, it would cause a lot of interest in her again and as she was already dealing with so much, it would only add more drama in her life. That was not necessarily a bad thing in her mind. There was a world of difference between her life from last term to what it was now. She had never thought that people would ever see her as a 'troublemaking outcast'. She had never expected to find herself in the phase she was currently in and so she had decided to treat the whole thing as ridiculously as the situation actually was; this was her chance to reclaim her narrative and give it her own spin. Her bullies didn't know that they were just contributing as minor villains in the hero story she was writing for herself.

Fourteen

'Luck favours the backbone, not the wishbone.'

—Doyle Brunson

It was almost two months into the term when Ina first visited the school with her camera crew and caused many frenzied discussions. Nobody knew what they were shooting and that further led to many speculations. The monotony of regular school life had been broken by the presence of a camera and of a rather glamorously dressed Ina. In Bombay, Tiana had met Ina thrice and had never seen Ina wearing anything other than jeans, t-shirts and slippers. But when she saw Ina in school, for a second she didn't even recognize her.

Ina was dressed in a light pink silky shirt which she had tucked into her light pink palazzo pants. She wore white Gucci sneakers and carried a small nude coloured Valentino sling bag. Her brown hair was done in a messy, high ponytail and she wore huge brown sunglasses. The school was excited by her presence. Ina was different. She was a boss and she came with a camera. Tiana had only seen her from afar. Ina had been talking to many of the teachers and had been going in and out of the school office, giving instructions to her camera operator. Tiana was still uncertain of how Ina had managed to get permission to shoot in school. All through the first two classes of the day, everyone only talked about Ina. They didn't know her name, so they referred to her as the 'camera chick'.

'Yaar! She's so hot!'

'Her hair is so awesome.'

'Her skin is so nice.'
'I wonder what she is doing here.'
'I'm gonna hit on her.'
'Maybe we'll get to be on camera.'
'Is she an actress?'
'I don't think so.'
'She is thin enough to be one.'

Tiana heard all these comments coming from boys and girls from different parts of the classroom and assumed that similar conversations would be taking place in other classrooms as well. It continued all through breakfast.

'Did you guys see that camera chick?' asked Aditya.

'We're not blind, you know,' scoffed Jasmine at her boyfriend.

'Chill yaar, I was just asking,' said Aditya.

'Yeah I know why you were asking,' replied Jasmine grumpily.

Aditya looked at Tiana and Sara helplessly. A week ago, Aditya had asked Jasmine out and she had agreed. However, as soon as they began dating, everybody could notice a change in Jasmine. She became obsessed with Aditya and didn't like it if he spoke about any other girl, much less if he actually spoke to any girl other than her. Jasmine didn't even like it if Aditya spoke to Tiana, because he had asked Tiana out last term, but she had refused because she had feelings for Ronit. They had moved on as friends without any awkwardness but now Jasmine was making everything weird with her unfounded jealousy. Sara looked at her cousin Aditya and tried to signal to him that his girlfriend was unhappy with the attention he was giving to the 'camera chick' and that maybe he should stop. Aditya didn't understand her expression and went on talking about Ina.

'Everyone is asking about her because they are curious about the shoot,' said Aditya.

'I spoke to Mrs Sharma, she said that they are just looking

at the campus today. Maybe they will come back to shoot later,' replied Sara.

'So they won't shoot now? That sucks. I got all excited for no reason,' replied Aliya.

Tiana didn't clarify anything. To be honest, she herself didn't know what Ina was planning. She had been in school for almost four hours now and hadn't tried to contact Tiana yet. If she had come for Tiana, then surely by now she would have asked for her. Good sense prevailed and Tiana decided to observe quietly how the day unfolds.

Before assembly, they were all standing in a squad to march into the chapel. Just as they were about to move forward, Ina walked by and waved and winked at Tiana. Everyone got confused and excited by this gesture.

'You know her?' whispered Aliya.

'Who is she, Tiana?' asked a senior girl.

'How do you know her?' asked Bella.

'QUIET!' yelled their house captain.

Tiana just gave a casual shrug.

During assembly, an official announcement regarding Ina was made to the entire school.

'You all must have noticed Miss Ina Mathur and her team around school today. They will be in and out of school for the next couple of months shooting a documentary on teens and school life. I would like you all to welcome them, be courteous and show them your best selves,' said their headmaster.

After that, it was all anybody could talk about. After assembly, during their economics class the teacher left early and the questions began.

'It's a documentary about teens. That means we might get to be in it!' exclaimed Bella excitedly.

'That would be so much fun!' said Aliya.

'Tiana, how do you know the camera chick?' asked Bella.

'Her name is Ina and she is the ex-wife of my workshop instructor in Bombay. She makes short films and documentaries, and her last two short films have like 10 million views each on YouTube,' replied Tiana.

'Wait. Are you serious?' asked Aliya.

Tiana nodded.

'That's so cool!'

'T, are you going to be in this documentary?' asked Bella.

'I'm not sure what Ina has in mind. I do think I will be in it a little bit though,' said Tiana, underplaying the part she might play in the documentary.

'Oh God, I'm too excited now! If you are in it that means I will be in it!' said Bella, clapping her hands.

Then, during lunch, Ina finally came to Tiana's table.

'Hi, Tiana! I'm so sorry we haven't had a chance to speak yet, but I've been running around getting everything sorted,' smiled Ina.

'Oh, that's okay. I figured as much,' said Tiana, getting up and they hugged like old friends.

Everyone at Tiana's table and the neighbouring tables had stopped eating to look at them. Tiana knew from this point forth, they would all know her connection to Ina.

'Okay, are you done with your lunch?' asked Ina.

'Yes,' replied Tiana.

'Good, because you need to come with me to your senior mistress's office,' replied Ina.

Tiana's heart sank. Every time she had been told to go to the senior mistress's office, it had always been the most unpleasant experience. And the last time she went there, she had been suspended. She suddenly got overwhelmed by a flood of bad memories and feelings and it must have shown on her face.

'Tiana, it's okay. You aren't in any trouble. I promise,' said Ina gently.

'I know. It's just that a certain memory threw me off,' said Tiana, gaining back her composure.

'I get it,' Ina smiled knowingly.

As they made their way out of the dining hall, Tiana saw everyone from her old table staring at them. Leila and Savera averted their gaze as soon they caught her eye. She also saw Karam and Ronit looking at her. Everybody was wondering what she was up to now. If only she knew what she was about to walk into.

Drama. As usual. That's what she walked into.

The office was filled with people. Senior mistress was sitting behind her desk. Senior master and three other department heads were there too.

Ina entered the room and began speaking, 'I think we can start now. I would like Tiana to assist me with the documentary and she will also be one of the students I interview.'

'Why her? I'm sure I can find other students to help you out. We have some significant high achievers in school,' said the senior mistress proudly.

'I think Tiana is very significant and a deeply thoughtful and creative girl. I've interacted with her many times during the summer and my ex-husband was her public speaking instructor. He gave remarkable feedback regarding Tiana's participation in the workshop. She held her own among people twice her age and someone like that is worth interviewing on camera. Besides, it was through her that I found out about this school and I have taken all the permissions to be here from the school administration and your alumni committee and I have permission from Tiana's parents as well. For me, everything is in place,' replied Ina confidently.

'Look, Tiana is a great girl but she has had a rough year in school and we don't want any more bad publicity. If you interview her, then things will come up which really don't need to be dug up,' replied Mr Johnson, the senior master.

'Mr Johnson, one way or another, Tiana's story will be dug up by me. I could do it from outside school too. Now you can decide how you want the school to be portrayed. You want an image of a hospitable school that's trying to correct some things that unintentionally went wrong or do you want to come across as a hostile school that is trying to cover up its mistakes instead of rectifying them? The angle is in my hands. I could use it however I choose.'

There was silence.

Tiana was standing in a corner studying the faces of her teachers. They were all looking at each other. None of them knew how to get out of this catch-22 situation.

'Are you threatening us?' asked the senior mistress testily.

'Mrs Banerjee, if you think the truth is threatening, then I don't really know how to respond. All I can say is that I'm trying to cover different teen experiences in our country, and Tiana is just one of many who will be in my film. I hope to find some more interesting stories from Hill View High, and I plan to interview many more students.'

'Yes, you must. We have some perfect students in the school. Toppers and super achievers. You should talk to them,' said the senior mistress.

'Mrs Banerjee, you should understand that I'm not looking for perfect students because they don't exist. I want real stories. Not made-up perfect stories. There is a big difference between the two,' replied Ina.

Both the senior mistress and senior master looked at Ina silently.

Tiana could tell that they didn't understand. They wanted to use the documentary as an advertisement for Hill View High. They wanted to showcase the intelligent and athletic students and show the country how good the school was and how well the students were doing. Ina had a completely different vision. She wanted to talk about the realities of teen life. The pain behind a topper's perfection. What it feels like to fail a math exam. The pressure that teachers put on students. This was her angle. She was not making an advertisement for the school. But Ina was smart and quickly understood that in order to get what she wanted she would have to make the school believe that she was doing exactly what they wanted.

'However, it would be great if you give me a list of your preferred students. I can use the list as a guide to the student body. I will gladly talk to the students on the list first,' smiled Ina.

Somehow, this statement reassured everyone in the room and everybody began nodding vigorously. It was exactly what they had wanted to hear.

'Tiana, be helpful to Miss Mathur but don't let it interfere with your schoolwork,' said the senior mistress to Tiana just as she was about to leave.

'Yes, ma'am.'

Once outside the office, Tiana gave Ina a full tour of the school.

'This campus is so beautiful! Though it's massive and feels like a maze. I would never be able to find my way,' said Ina.

'You'll figure it out in a couple of days. By the way, good job shutting everyone up in the office,' said Tiana.

'Mrs Banerjee was so condescending. She actually said, "Why her?" when I said I want to interview you. Seriously, what kind of a teacher would try to diminish a student's confidence this way?' scoffed Ina.

Tiana smiled, 'We are all used to being spoken to this way by the teachers.'

'It's wrong.'

'I have to ask, why are you dressed this way? I mean I thought you were a strictly jeans and t-shirt type of girl,' said Tiana looking at Ina's clothes again.

Ina started laughing, 'Jeans and t-shirt is my off-duty style. But here, when I need to grab attention and want people to talk to me, I need to dress differently.'

'Oh, you accomplished that for sure. The entire school has been talking about you,' said Tiana.

'Perfect. That was my aim. To get people talking about me is what I'm here to do. Now when I approach people to interview them, they will feel privileged over the rest and that will make them willing to speak up,' laughed Ina.

'Wow! Those are *some* mind games,' said Tiana, wondering if Ina had played such tricks on her as well.

'Can't help it.'

'My parents are still hesitant about me being in your film. They think I might make the school even angrier and that if my story becomes national news, then the entire country would judge me,' admitted Tiana.

It was true. Her parents had left the decision to her but they had made their apprehensions pretty clear to Tiana.

'Really? They didn't say anything to me when I spoke to them yesterday,' said Ina.

'Oh, they know that I have made the decision to be in the film, so they wouldn't say anything to you,' said Tiana.

'Look, don't worry. We will create something great together and I'm positive my film will end up helping you in some way,' smiled Ina.

'How did you manage to get permission to shoot in school?' asked Tiana curiously.

'I told the board I will present the school as the top boarding school in the country and bring it national recognition. Nobody says no to free publicity, especially if it's made to sound profitable.'

Fifteen

'No one becomes a laughingstock who laughs at himself.'

—Seneca the Younger

As they were almost two months into the term, their Founder's Day practices had begun. The entire school was in a festive spirit and even teachers were at their creative best because they were busy supervising dance rehearsals for different batches or were involved in the school's play production. About 120 boys and girls from classes 10, 11 and 12 were put together to perform a fusion dance of jazz and salsa. A choreographer had been hired from Bombay to come and direct the dance. As class 11 students, Tiana and her friends were a part of this massive production. They would all meet for rehearsals every evening on the sports field. Handling and teaching dance to 120 teenagers at the same time was not easy for the choreographer and that's why over 10 teachers had been deployed to keep everybody in check during rehearsals, which was proving to be difficult because the students were too busy having fun. Every time the choreographer, Mr Patel, taught them funny looking steps, the boys would begin laughing and imitating him.

Ina came back the very next day and her camera operator began recording Tiana and her friends during the rehearsals. Everybody noticed how much attention Tiana was getting from the camera chick and they couldn't understand why Tiana had been chosen for the documentary.

Mr Patel noticed that the students were too busy talking and looking at the camera instead of dancing. 'Focus, everybody!

Dance well because now you are getting recorded as well. If you don't dance well, you will look like fools on camera.'

'We look like fools anyway,' said Parth, a senior who was Lilly's boyfriend.

From the corner of her eye, Tiana saw Ina gesturing her camera operator to record Parth and Mr Patel's conversation.

'Why?' asked Mr Patel turning towards Parth.

'What's with all this twirling?' responded Zoravar, another senior, who was Parth's friend.

'What's the problem?' asked Mr Patel.

'These steps are so gay. That's the problem,' laughed Parth.

'Excuse me?' asked Mr Patel incredulously. Mr Patel had been staying in school as a guest teacher for the past two weeks and everybody assumed he was gay. It was just his mannerisms, they were gracefully effeminate. Even though that is no yardstick for someone's sexuality, how do you stop small-minded teenage boys from talking? He was tall and fit and in his late 20s. He had been a dancer with a famous company for a while and had recently become a choreographer. Maybe because he was a dancer, when he moved he seemed like he was flowing. The girls loved him and all his Bollywood stories; however, the boys had taken a typical approach and begun disliking him. They were often heard saying derogatory things about him while imitating his mannerisms.

'Young man, I will not tolerate such intolerance amongst my students. You have no right to say such things. You think it is cool but all you manage to do is sound like a bigot,' said Mr Patel.

'Why do we have to dance like this anyway? We should be doing bhangra,' said Zoravar proudly.

'You are more than welcome to leave. I don't want either of you here to ruin the atmosphere for the rest. You are excused, goodbye,' said Mr Patel promptly.

Zoravar and Parth made some more homophobic comments and walked away laughing loudly at their own jokes.

'Anybody else have any problem with the dance?' asked Mr Patel haughtily. Nobody said anything and the practice continued in silence. For the salsa portion of the dance, Mr Patel assigned partners to everyone. Tiana was paired with Aditya, Bella with Ronit and Karam with Jasmine.

During dinner, Jasmine's possessive behaviour towards Aditya erupted again and she asked Tiana to speak to Mr Patel to change her partner.

'Jasmine, it's just a dance,' said Bella.

'Yeah, but I want to dance with my boyfriend,' said Jasmine.

'In that case, why don't you ask Mr Patel yourself? I'm not the one with a problem here. I don't want him to think that I'm creating trouble with his choreography,' said Tiana simply. It was unfair when people behaved in such a way. If Jasmine had a problem, she needed to speak up herself. She needed to be upfront and deal with the consequences. It wasn't fair that she wanted something for her own benefit yet wanted Tiana to bear the onus of what would come as a result from it. Tiana wasn't going to let anyone use her again.

'You don't have a problem with it? That's funny,' said Jasmine sarcastically.

'Why is it funny?' asked Sara, giving her friend a strange look.

'She should have a problem dancing with somebody else's boyfriend,' said Jasmine.

'Geez, Jas. It's just a dance,' said Aditya, feeling very conscious of the eyes on them.

'Nobody got to choose their partners, okay? I got paired with that idiot Jai. He kept stepping on my foot,' said Sara.

'Yikes. I'm glad that Ronit is my partner, he's a good dancer,' said Bella happily.

Jasmine continued to look grumpy. Tiana was glad that she didn't have to defend herself for once. Later, Aditya told her that he was sorry, but Jasmine was forcing him to ask for a partner change. Tiana didn't mind. Whether Aditya was her dance partner or not, was a non-issue for her. She was preoccupied with other thoughts. All she could think about was that no matter who ended up being her dance partner, it wasn't going to be Ronit. She wanted to kick herself for wishing that he was her partner. She was constantly drawn to him despite wishing to move on. Her attempts were in vain. The simple truth was that she had a massive crush on Ronit. And it was crushing her. The wise words of Molly Ringwald's father from the film *Sixteen Candles* came to her mind. In it, Molly's character, Sam, confides in her father that having a crush was hurting her. Her father responds by saying, 'That is why they call them crushes. If they were easier, they'd call them something else.'

For a little while, her feelings for him had dissipated but over the past two months, they had returned. The feelings were as new and fresh as they had been when she had first fallen for him three years ago, before he had broken her trust. They'd never really had a fair chance with each other. Something always went wrong. Even now, she was never going to admit her feelings for him, though she suspected that he might reciprocate them. He was constantly trying to flirt with her but something stopped her from opening up. So, when Bella and Ronit were paired up, it affected her.

However, she could not admit it to anyone. She didn't want to sound or behave like an obsessed weirdo, the way Jasmine was behaving around Aditya. In the end, she felt she was utterly confused. She liked Ronit but didn't want to tell him and yet wanted his attention but still didn't want to date him. She didn't want to be his dance partner nor did she want him to dance with anyone else. In her own mind, she sounded like a maniac and that's why she decided to never open up about her feelings for Ronit in front of her friends because it would unleash the

Pandora's box of her insane thoughts.

The next day, before rehearsals, Tiana was answering some questions on camera about Founder's Day; Ina had made a habit of following Tiana wherever she went after classes were over. Rehearsals, hobbies and sports—Ina was everywhere and it had begun to feel like Tiana had her own reality TV show. That's when Aditya came to her with some annoying news.

'Tiana, hey! Mr Patel allowed me to swap partners and dance with Jasmine. Though this means that you will have to be partnered with Karam,' said Aditya sheepishly.

'Oh no no no,' said Tiana, raising both her hands in defence.

'What's wrong?' asked Ina.

'Karam is her ex-boyfriend. Tiana dumped him recently. Then he started dating her cousin,' said Bella, looking at the camera.

'Do we need to record this part?' asked Tiana, looking at Ina and the camera.

'Very much so, yes! This is a real teen experience, after all,' said Ina. She was standing behind Ram, her camera operator who was recording everything. Tiana just shook her head. She went up to Mr Patel to ask for a partner change and Ina followed her. However, before she could even reach Mr Patel, she saw Karam talking to him.

'Are you Tiana?' asked Mr Patel when he saw Tiana approaching him. Karam was standing next to him but he didn't look at Tiana. Instead, Karam was focused on the circus behind Tiana which included the camera operator Ram, hidden behind his camera, and Ina and Bella, who were standing next to him.

'Yes, sir,' said Tiana.

'Is this camera always going to be around you now?' asked Mr Patel, looking directly into the lens.

'For some time, yes,' replied Tiana.

'Great, I love it!' exclaimed Mr Patel, waving at the camera.

'I only know your name, Tiana, because two boys have come

up to me telling me they don't want to be your dance partner. I find that very strange. First, Aditya and now this young man here also doesn't want you as a partner. Why is that?' asked Mr Patel, pointing at Karam.

'Sir, I just want to dance with my friend Tea,' said Karam still avoiding Tiana's gaze.

'Your *friend*. I see. Why can't you dance with Tiana? Hmm? I'm sure you are friends too,' laughed Mr Patel.

Karam responded with a non-committal shrug.

'Okay, okay. You can dance with Tea and send her partner to be Tiana's partner,' said Mr Patel.

'Tea missed the dance rehearsal yesterday. She wasn't assigned a partner,' said Karam and then he walked away.

'I guess you will not be dancing with a partner then Tiana. Unless someone drops out. I'll give you some different steps that you can do alone on the side when everyone is dancing with their partners. Now go back to your position,' said Mr Patel.

Wonderful, among 120 dancers, it was just her luck to be the loser with no dance partner. To top it all, this humiliating experience had been recorded for Ina's documentary. Tiana realized that the price of being heard was that people would hear everything about her, not just what she wanted them to hear. She looked at the camera that was still recording her and in an attempt to not come across as pathetic, tried to be sarcastic.

'Yay! Now I'm going to do salsa *alone*. This just sums up my life,' said Tiana drily, looking right into the lens. This made Ina and Bella laugh out loud.

'That was perfect, Tiana!'

Sixteen

'All looks yellow to a jaundiced eye.'

—Patrick Boyle

Over the past two months, the initial wave of anger and resentment against Tiana had died down. The boys who had blamed her for everything had cooled down and moved on. The bullying had sort of stopped and even the interest in her had reduced. However, as soon as Tiana became the subject of the documentary, the dormant feelings towards her and against her were invoked, and the name-calling, bullying and pranks began again.

Before mealtimes, the entire school would line up in the corridor, according to their houses, before filing into the dining hall. During one such fall-in before breakfast, as Tiana was standing in line, she heard her name being called out. It was none other than the senior mistress. She was inspecting Tiana's house. All the boys and girls around her were now looking at her as well.

'What's that on your skirt?' asked the senior mistress loudly.

Tiana looked at the front of her skirt.

'No, at the back,' said the senior mistress.

Tiana tried to look and saw red ink splashes all over the back of her skirt. The ink spots were on her calves as well. Undoubtedly it was the work of the boys of her class. They must have used their ink pen to splash ink on her during the first two classes. She hadn't realized it. To be honest, since the beginning of term, it had happened so often that she had stopped bothering with such trivial things.

'Priya, come here, look at this,' said the senior mistress summoning Tiana's house prefect, 'What is this? How are you running your house? Is this the standard of girls from Austen House? To turn out shabbily?' asked the senior mistress.

Tiana could hear some boys sniggering and laughing.

'No, ma'am. I'm sorry, I will make sure this doesn't happen again,' said Priya, looking flustered and gave Tiana an angry look. Getting scolded in front of people because of a junior girl before even eating breakfast was clearly not fun for Priya.

Tiana saw her house mistress walking towards them.

'What happened, Mrs Banerjee?'

'Look at this, Mrs Puri.' The senior mistress grabbed Tiana by the shoulders and turned her around roughly. 'Look at her skirt.'

'What happened, Tiana?' asked Mrs Puri.

'Ma'am, some boys from my class did this and I didn't realize when it happened. They do this often,' replied Tiana.

'Why would they do such a thing?' asked the senior mistress.

'I think that *they* think it will embarrass me. As if red ink splashes will somehow look like blood. I mean, even if I had stained my skirt with blood, I wouldn't be embarrassed by it. Periods are natural and sometimes blood stains happen. It won't be the end of the world. But I guess it's a difficult thing for boys to understand,' replied Tiana casually.

Senior mistress, house mistress and Priya looked aghast and others within Tiana's earshot looked shocked. None of them had expected Tiana to respond in such a ballsy way in front of so many people. Tiana was satisfied with their reaction, if senior mistress could pick on her in front of people, then Tiana could answer back in front of the same people. Bella was standing in front of Tiana in the line and Tiana could hear her sniggering.

'I don't need you to tell me how teen boys are, Tiana. I also know how teen girls are and it's very easy to pass the blame.

How do I know you didn't start the fight with them yourself?' asked the senior mistress seriously.

Of course, it was always the girls, mistake according to her. The senior master didn't defend the boys as much as the senior mistress did.

'As soon as you are done with your breakfast, I want you to go back to your dorm and ask the matron to give you a new skirt,' said the senior mistress, walking away.

During breakfast, Bella told everyone about how Tiana responded to the senior mistress.

'You actually said that? I mean I saw her picking on you but I couldn't hear what you said. I wish I had heard it live!' exclaimed Sara.

'Oh, it was epic! Banerjee's mouth was hanging open and for a few seconds she didn't know what to say,' said Bella

'You were talking about periods when surrounded by boys and teachers? Didn't you feel awkward?' asked Diya.

'That's the whole point. As girls, we ourselves give the power to the boys and allow them to make us feel embarrassed about such a natural thing. By not talking about it around boys and keeping this side of our lives so secretive, we encourage them to think that periods are meant to be a dirty secret. If we start talking about it and normalize it, they won't think its something to hide either,' replied Tiana.

'I agree. Think about it, why do boys think that they can embarrass Tiana by splashing red ink on her skirt in the first place?' asked Sara, looking at the group.

'Tell us, Aditya?' asked Bella. All the girls turned to look at him. This didn't faze him and he answered confidently.

'Maybe, because you girls make a big deal about it yourselves? I mean, even I have overheard so many girls asking each other to check if there's a stain on the back of their skirts,' answered Aditya honestly.

'Exactly, boys learn this behaviour from us only. We need to change ourselves first. If we stop getting embarrassed about harmless blood stains and hiding our sanitary pads, then the boys won't make such a big deal about it either,' said Sara.

As a sign of personal defiance, Tiana wore the same skirt for the rest of the day to show the boys of her class that she was far from embarrassed. During the lunch fall-in, the house prefect, Priya, yelled at Tiana for not changing her skirt and punished her with a physical drill of running 10 rounds of the field.

Seventeen

'Whether we can afford it or no, we must have superfluities.'

—John Gay

'Why her?' was the most asked question among the teachers and students when they realized that Ina was only interested in interviewing Tiana and no one else. Nobody could understand why she was being given such an important role in representing the school. The general feeling was that instead of Tiana, *anybody* else deserved it more. Teachers from the Science, English, Mathematics, Social Studies and Hindi departments wanted to put forth the best performing students in their respective subjects to be interviewed by Ina. Sports coaches wanted their star athletes to be in the documentary. The senior mistress and senior master had their own agenda of promoting the students they liked best and the ones they wanted to make prefects next year. All the senior students in class 12 were quite pissed off with Tiana as well. They thought that Tiana was stealing their chance to represent the school one last time since it was their last term and they would leave school soon. After all, if anyone deserved extra attention it was them.

Tiana overheard the same conversation again and again.

'She should just say no. She doesn't even deserve it and she knows it,' said a senior girl named Joy, to her group. Despite her name, she was quite a grim personality. She said this and then looked at Tiana, who was walking past them. Tiana knew that they had wanted her to hear their esteemed opinions.

'Yeah, she's the last person they should interview,' joined in one of Joy's minions.

'Why don't the teachers do something about it?' asked another.

Then during class, she heard some of her own batchmates talking about her.

'I really think our seniors should be interviewed, ya. I mean, it's their last few months in school. If I was in my final term at school and some juniors tried to steal the limelight, then I would be SO pissed off!' said a girl called Arushi.

In the line for lunch, Tiana heard more.

'Like, she's not even good at sports, you know, and she is okay types in studies. You deserve it more, Siya. You got like 98 per cent last time. People like you should be interviewed.'

'Yeah but what can I do? Teachers decide this stuff you know.'

'So unfair.'

'She got suspended; why are they even interviewing her? Didn't the teachers tell that camera chick that she can find better students?'

'Maybe they will. I'm sure someone will put an end to it.'

Then, after lunch Tiana heard the following conversation.

'So Mrs Khanna spoke to senior mistress and, apparently, Tiana knows this camera chick from Bombay and that's why Tiana is in the documentary.'

'Are you serious? So Tiana needs to have *no* talent? She's just going to be interviewed for no reason?'

'Is she related to that camera chick?'

'I'm sure she is! This is like nepotism!'

The nepotism rumour soon spread like wildfire.

'Now it makes sense!'

'This is why Ina chose her!'

'Of course!'

'Tiana is taking unfair advantage.'

The teachers were no less in adding fuel to this fire. They were discussing and spreading this rumour just as much as the students.

'I told the senior mistress that we should do something. Who will listen to us teachers? Only senior management can take a stand against nepotism like this,' said Mrs Dua to a group of junior girls.

'We simply can't allow such nepotism-type practices in our school,' said Mr Bedi, the hockey coach, to Mr Singh, the basketball coach.

'That's right. My boys won the Inter School Tournament last term and should represent the school,' replied Mr Singh.

'Yes, we should highlight our sportsmanship,' agreed Mr Bedi.

Tiana didn't respond to any of these conversations because no one had said anything to her directly.

Tiana had no intention of engaging with these people. She didn't want to give anyone the satisfaction of knowing that they were bothering her. She felt that if everything went right with the documentary, then all of them would get their answers after watching it. No matter how much they all thought they were above it, they would all watch it. She was just glad to have supportive friends even though they could not do much to help her.

'I think being featured in a documentary is super exciting, T,' said Sara during lunch.

'Yeah, I hope I get to be in it,' said Bella.

Tiana smiled and said, 'I'm sure you will be. Ina likes interesting people and that's what you are.'

'Don't let others bother you, okay?' Aditya said reassuringly.

'Are you really related to Ina?' asked Jasmine.

'No, I'm not. Tell anyone who asks you, that I'm not related to Ina.'

'Then why is everyone saying that you are? I mean rumours

don't just start randomly,' said Jasmine.

All of them, including her boyfriend, scoffed at Jasmine.

'Rumours do start randomly, Jasmine. Especially, when it comes to Tiana. You know how people have been behaving towards her since the beginning of the term,' said Sara.

'Right. Sorry.'

Even before the entire dance partner switcheroo, Jasmine was acting weird around Tiana. It wasn't a discernible change but it was there none the less. At first, Tiana had thought that she was imagining it, but now it was starting to become obvious to the rest of them as well. Every time Aditya spoke directly to Tiana or was nice to her, Jasmine would find some excuse to either become irritated or say something stupidly annoying.

As the bell rang to mark the end of lunch time, Ina showed up at their table with the camera in her hand. Her camera operator Ram wasn't with her.

'Ready to shoot, T?'

'Shoot? Like now?'

'Yeah. Hey everyone,' said Ina, looking at everyone sitting at the table, 'if you don't mind I would like to have your permission to shoot you guys at your lunch table. Is it cool?'

'Yeah, okay,' said Sara, but Ina had already begun recording them.

'Are you telling me I'm on camera right now, without any make-up on?' asked Bella dramatically.

'Are you allowed to wear make-up to school?' asked Ina as she turned the camera towards Bella.

'Umm, we are in an Indian boarding school with a military history. Of course we aren't allowed to wear make-up to school. Even if our ear studs are any colour other than gold or silver, our senior mistress yells at us in front of 500 people and tells us to take them off,' scoffed Bella.

'Meet my friend Bella, she's not afraid to say what's on her mind,' laughed Tiana.

'Girls!' came the senior mistress's voice suddenly.

'Speak of the devil,' said Sara under her breath.

'Lunch is over. Why are you all still sitting here causing a ruckus?'

'We were just talking, ma'am.'

'Hello, Ina. I would like to request you to not disturb the girls during lunch or anytime during their classes.'

'Mrs Banerjee, I came after they were done eating.'

The senior mistress gave a painful smile to Ina and walked away.

'You see what we have to deal with? All we are doing is sitting here calmly after finishing our lunch, and she comes to yell at us for "causing a ruckus",' said Bella.

'I think we *are* causing a ruckus,' said Tiana, looking around their table.

Ina's camera was rolling, causing much excitement among the students seated at the surrounding tables. Usually, when the bell rang at the end of lunch hour, the students would walk out of the dining hall quickly, making way for the cleaning staff. Today, however, over 50 people stood enveloping their table out of sheer curiosity.

'I have to say, your presence has excited the entire school,' said Aliya.

Ina smiled.

They walked out together but Jasmine and Aditya went their separate way. The rest returned to their classroom to pick up their school bags and to show Ina where they sat in class. They were the only ones there. They took their places at their respective seats. Ina began recording them.

'I see, you guys are backbenchers then?' asked Ina.

'Always!' laughed Sara.

'So, all of you are in the same section?'

'Actually, Jasmine is not in our section. Aditya is. He is Sara's cousin,' said Bella, pointing towards Sara, who waved at the camera.

'Oh, this reminds me, Tiana, have you noticed that Jasmine is being very weird around you?' asked Diya.

'Of course, she is,' said Bella.

'Yeah, I *know* that. What I would like to know is why?' asked Tiana.

'Isn't it obvious?' asked Bella matter-of-factly.

'Why is it obvious?' asked Aliya.

'It's Tiana's luck,' laughed Bella.

Tiana rolled her eyes.

'So last term, I was the one who was behaving the way Jasmine is behaving now,' said Bella.

'Ooh!' said Tiana, Sara, Diya and Aliya in unison as if they suddenly understood.

'If that's true, then it's very silly,' said Tiana.

'Why?' asked Ina.

'Aditya is Jasmine's boyfriend now but he had asked Tiana out last term. But she had said no. After the summer holidays ended and we came back to school, Aditya and Jasmine began dating. So now, for some reason, whenever Aditya talks to Tiana, Jasmine feels threatened or something. I felt the same way last term because my boyfriend Ronit kind of had a past with Tiana, and so every time I saw them being friendly or talking to each other, I would get uncomfortable and angry,' said Bella.

'Why do you think this happens between girls so much?' asked Ina.

'I don't know. All I do know is that I hated being that person. In fact, I did something horrible in that anger, for which Tiana suffered badly,' said Bella.

'Maybe the problem is that we don't actually talk about what's bothering us. We keep assuming the worst and that kind of becomes a problem over a period of time,' said Aliya.

'The thing is that problems between Bella and I were coming from a real place of jealousy. I had a history with Ronit. I had known him, liked him and kissed him before he ever met Bella. We had a strange history because he was my cousin's boyfriend and I didn't know about it when I kissed him. Bella knew this story, so when Bella began dating him, she knew he was capable of cheating on her. I could understand Bella's jealousy because I too was jealous of her. However, with Jasmine it's completely different. I don't like Aditya, never have. I've never given her a reason to be jealous. It's true that Aditya and I've been friendly since he joined school last term but I've always looked at him as my friend's brother. That's all. Jasmine has no right to be jealous or snarky. She was always nice to me before she began dating him. This is what I don't like, how girls totally change and become needy and whiny as soon as they get a boyfriend,' said Tiana.

'True. You and your boyfriend had friends before you were dating. You should value and respect those friends,' said Diya.

'So, Tiana, this means that, unintentionally, you have become a part of this love triangle?' asked Ina.

Tiana started laughing. The rest of her friends joined in as well.

'Why are you guys laughing?' smiled Ina.

'If only it were one love triangle,' said Tiana laughing and shaking her head.

'As Tiana's luck would have it, she's a part of two love triangles,' said Sara.

'Are you mad? Have you forgotten how to count?' asked Bella.

'Why?' asked Sara.

'As luck would have it, I'm part of four love triangles right now. Most of them are not as active as they once were but they exist alright,' replied Tiana.

'Umm, Tiana, five love triangles,' corrected Bella.

'I don't believe you! It's not possible. That's too much even for a teen girl,' laughed Ina.

'How are you counting *five*, Bella?' asked Tiana.

'Okay, I'm going to make a diagram for our benefit,' said Bella, getting up from her seat and taking out a board marker from the teacher's desk. She wrote 'Love Diagram' on top of the board and underneath it she made multiple triangles and wrote Tiana's name in the centre and then on the other points of the triangles, she kept writing more names.

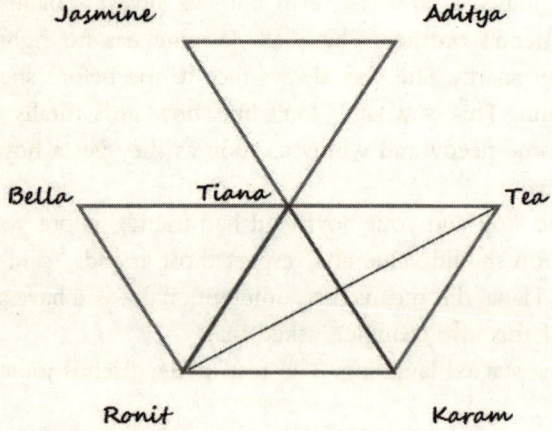

Tiana, Ronit and Tea. Tiana, Ronit and Karam. Tiana, Ronit and Bella. Tiana, Karam and Tea. Tiana, Aditya and Jasmine.

Her love life was a mess and so was her life in general.

Eighteen

'The probability of someone watching you is proportional to the stupidity of your action.'

—A. Kindsvater

The next day brought with it a new set of problems. They had forgotten to erase the love triangle diagram that Bella had drawn on their classroom's white board the previous day. When Tiana and Bella entered the classroom their entire section was talking about it. After they realized their blunder, they knew there was no going back. Sure enough, by mid-day, her friends were coming up to tell her what everyone was saying about her.

'Now they're saying that being in the documentary was not getting you enough attention so that's why you and Bella are trying to make your lives seem more interesting by pretending to be in all these love triangles,' said Aliya.

'Who's pretending?' said Tiana, rolling her eyes.

'Why are they blaming us for spreading these rumours? Why are they assuming we made that chart? I mean, anyone could have done it,' said Bella defensively.

'Apparently, someone from class has your English notebook and they matched your handwriting, Bella,' replied Aliya.

'Damn it,' grimaced Bella.

Many of the seniors suddenly became very possessive about Karam, who was both their batchmate and head boy. His name was very prominently featured in the love triangles chart and when they found out, they didn't like the junior girls, even if they included his ex-girlfriend, making fun of the head boy. If the head boy himself wasn't being respected and revered by juniors, then no senior would be safe and their supposed power in school would be in jeopardy.

Tiana's friends told her about the many conversations their seniors were having about her and Karam. Mostly, they went like this :

'Who the hell is she to drag Karam in all her nonsense?'

'I don't even know what he saw in her in the first place. Thank god he dumped her. He can do so much better.'

'Of course, he can. He's the head boy and she got suspended from school. What a mismatch!'

'I bet she regrets the break-up. That's why she and her friend wrote Karam's name on the board. I bet she wants attention so she can talk to him again.'

'Apparently he is dating her cousin now. She should respect that at the very least.'

'She just wants to make it seem like her life is *so happening* and awesome. What a bimbo!'

Tiana internally rolled her eyes and remained unaffected by all this. At this point, it was more of the same stuff she had already heard about herself. The more it happened, the more immune she became towards it.

However, things were officially weird between her and Jasmine now because Jasmine and Aditya's name was also written on the board. Lunch had been extremely awkward at their table. Jasmine didn't say a single word throughout and Aditya too looked uncomfortable.

Then there was Ronit. He came to their lunch table and announced that he would like to start sitting with them from now onwards. Tiana tried to read Bella's expression when Ronit spoke of his intention. Bella looked both excited yet confused. Tiana remembered that they were dance partners now and were spending time together during rehearsals. She didn't know if

Ronit just wanted to sit with them casually or if he came for Bella or for her. Tiana herself wasn't sure if she was okay with Ronit joining them. She'd routinely avoid him whenever possible and if he began sitting with them at lunch, then avoiding him would become impossible. Who knew what would happen if she began hanging out with him and talking to him regularly? It would open up things that she didn't have the energy to deal with.

'Okay two love triangles can't sit at the same table. Our table is already wobbly and will collapse under this much pressure,' laughed Sara. Tiana kicked her under the table in response.

'Yeah, we are supposed to eat food here, not cause drama,' laughed Aliya.

Suddenly, Jasmine got up and said angrily, 'Fine then. Aditya and I will go and sit somewhere else. That's one less stupid love triangle at this table.'

'Chill, we're joking,' said Diya, but Jasmine simply walked away.

'Aditya, what's wrong with her?' asked Sara.

'I don't know. She's just a little pissed off I guess,' said Aditya.

'Why?' asked Bella.

'Tiana, do you really think that I still like you? Is that why you included me and Jas in your love triangle chart?' asked Aditya, looking directly at Tiana.

'I don't think you like me, Aditya. At all. That chart was just a joke. It meant nothing,' replied Tiana.

'There has to be a reason,' said Aditya.

'The reason is that Jasmine has become weird with me. Until last term, she was my friend but now every time you talk to me, she becomes agitated,' replied Tiana.

'That's not true!' exclaimed Aditya.

'Actually, it is,' said Bella.

'Yeah, even I've noticed it, Aditya,' said Sara to her brother.

Aditya became very quiet, and he too left the table to go find Jasmine. Ronit slid into his seat.

'So there's room for me now?' asked Ronit jokingly.

There was just something about him. When he wasn't playing games and mind tricks to get his way, he could be easy to talk to and fun to be around. That's how she'd fallen for him the first time. Tiana also knew that Bella still liked him, even though she'd never admit it. It just didn't seem right to repeat the mistakes that the three of them had made last term.

'Ronit, why do you want to sit with us?' asked Bella, slowly turning her smirk into a sarcastic pout.

'I'm sick of the people at my table. All they do is talk about you all anyway, so I thought I might as well join the group that everyone is *so* interested in,' laughed Ronit, winking at her.

'Ronit, please don't lie. You're just jealous because our group is in the documentary and you want to be in it too, but that won't happen if you aren't near Tiana and that's why you came here,' teased Bella light-heartedly.

Great, thought Tiana. Now she would have to witness Ronit and Bella flirting with each other, right in front of her eyes during every single meal. She didn't know if she had the capacity to see them like this without cracking. Luckily, the next words uttered by Ronit took away that worry.

'You got me. That's *exactly* why I want to be near Tiana. For the documentary,' smiled Ronit, looking at Tiana. It was such a naughty yet earnest smile that despite trying her best to keep herself from smiling, she broke into a grin anyway. He was flirting with her. This. This was why Tiana couldn't escape his charms. Perhaps, why Bella couldn't either.

'Tiana, you decide if you're okay with him sitting here,' said Sara.

'It's okay,' said Tiana still smiling like an idiot. To be honest, she didn't have much of a choice. Had she said no, it would have seemed childish and petty.

'Awesome!' said Ronit.

Later, Ronit walked out of the dining hall with Tiana and Bella.

'So, apparently, we're in a lot of love triangles together,' said Ronit, pretending to be serious and glancing sideways at Tiana.

'Apparently, yes,' replied Tiana, matching his fake serious demeanour and tilting her head towards him.

'What are you guys going to do about it?' smirked Bella.

'Luckily, most of those triangles are dead now because Karam is with Tea, and Jasmine is with Aditya, I'm just the useless third wheel. Since Karam is taken, there's no longer a triangle between Ronit, him and me either. So the most screwed-up triangle is the one involving the three of us. After all, it's because of the jealousy between the three of us that I got suspended,' said Tiana, looking at Bella and Ronit.

Suddenly, Ronit and Bella became serious. That was not what Tiana had intended to do, so she started laughing to diffuse the tension and uneasiness.

'Relax, I'm joking,' said Tiana.

'No, you're right,' said Bella.

By now they had reached Tiana and Bella's classroom. As usual, Tiana's school bag was missing and she began looking for it in all the usual spots like the dustbin and teachers' cabinet.

'What are you doing?' asked Ronit, looking confused.

'The boys from my class hide my bag every day. So I have to look for it after lunch,' said Tiana.

'Why?' Ronit asked, confused.

'Oh, they've been doing it since the start of term. First they used to hide mine as well but now all the attention is on Tiana, now that she is in the documentary,' replied Bella.

'That still makes no sense? Why would they—'

Tiana cut him off and explained, 'They blame me for getting

caught. They think that because of me, the school has imposed strict rules on everyone in this term. Some senior boy has asked the boys from my class to trouble and bully me. If they don't, they will get physical drills as punishment. So to save themselves, they're troubling me,' replied Tiana.

'That's horrible and stupid.'

'That's school.'

'Why didn't you tell me you were going through this stuff?' asked Ronit.

'I'm just ignoring it,' said Tiana.

'Ron, don't you know about the whole ink stain thing? She was badass about dealing with that,' said Bella.

Ronit looked clueless, so Bella told him about the incident with the senior mistress.

'Okay, that's actually badass that you didn't hesitate to answer back and refused to change your skirt. Respect,' said Ronit. Tiana rolled her eyes like it was no big deal, but it meant a lot to her that Ronit was a slightly more mature specimen amongst the other boys in school.

'I'll help you look for your bag,' said Ronit.

Bella was getting late for her tutorial class, so she left them. After 10 minutes of searching, they found Tiana's bag outside the girls' toilet.

'I can't believe you've been dealing with this stuff for so long and you didn't tell me,' muttered Ronit, irritated.

'What would you have done, had I told you?' asked Tiana.

'I don't know. It's just that you stopped talking to me and I thought, after you broke up with Karam, that things might improve between us. At the very least, we could be friends. That's all I wanted but then you got mad at me for telling you about Karam and Tea and you just started ignoring me again,' said Ronit, sounding a little hurt.

'I don't know how to be friends with Bella and you at the

same time. The three of us just got out of a messy situation and I don't want to get stuck in another one again!' said Tiana honestly.

'What if I promise to not ask you out again?' asked Ronit seriously.

'Umm, what?'

'I mean it. I'm not interested in Bella that way, not anymore. And I will not ask you out again either. Do you think we could be friends then? I need good friends, Tiana. Most people in our batch are stupid and ridiculous. I could have gone to any other school but I chose to come here because of you. If nothing else, I had thought that I would have a friend in you. Can I have my friend back?' pleaded Ronit.

'I think Bella still likes you,' said Tiana.

'We all have to find a way to move on, Tiana. Including her,' said Ronit.

'Then promise me one thing.'

'What?'

'No more flirting with me,' said Tiana.

'Don't be ridiculous, T. I'm the only boy in this entire school who still wants to flirt with you. Do you really want me to put a stop to that?' smirked Ronit.

Tiana opened and then shut her mouth expressing mock shock at this entirely true statement. Until last term, *three* boys had been all over her, but this term, she couldn't even find one boy to be her dance partner. For Founder's Day, she was literally going to be performing salsa *alone* on the side, while everyone else had a partner. All the love triangles in her life were truly dead and the rest of the boys in school seemed to hate her.

Nineteen

'Most of these love triangles are wrecktangles.'

—Jacob Braude

It was during dance practice that Krish showed up. He walked towards Tiana accompanied by his mother, Ina. For a spilt second, Tiana thought she was imagining him. Then she heard Bella's voice.

'Oh my god! Who is that guy?' asked Bella, her mouth wide open.

'Whoo hoo hoo,' said Sara, fanning herself.

'So you guys can see him too?' asked Tiana.

'Umm... what?' asked Bella.

'I thought I was imagining him,' said Tiana.

'That's just the shock of seeing a cute boy after a long time,' laughed Aliya.

'Yeah have you *seen* the guys in our school. We're so deprived. When we finally see a cute one, it feels like we're imagining him,' joked Bella.

'Excuse me, but *we* are in this school too okay,' scoffed Aditya. Jasmine sulked next to him.

'Yeah, I'm offended on the behalf of the boys in our school,' said Ronit sarcastically. However, Tiana noticed him staring critically at Krish.

'Sorry, Ronit. Last term you were the "hot new guy" but your glory days are over,' said Sara.

'Maybe he's a new student!' exclaimed Bella happily.

By then Krish and Ina had reached their group and he walked

straight towards Tiana.

'How are you?' exclaimed Krish, giving Tiana a warm hug.

'I'm great... How are *you?*' laughed Tiana, returning the hug. When she turned to look at her friends, she found them all standing still and staring at her and Krish. Ronit in particular looked irritated.

'Everyone, meet my son, Krish,' said Ina.

Krish smiled and waved and Ina took him to meet the choreographer, Mr Patel.

'Tiana, explain!' said Bella, jumping up and down.

'Krish was in my public speaking workshop during the summer. His dad was our instructor and Krish introduced me to his mom because she found my story interesting,' said Tiana.

'How is it that *every* time you go to Bombay, a cute guy follows you back?' asked Bella grumpily.

'Yeah, next time, I'm going with you to Bombay,' said Diya, winking at Tiana.

'Relax. He hasn't come for me. I think he's here to help his mom with the documentary,' assumed Tiana.

'Oh, are you really telling us that *nothing* happened between you and him during last summer?' asked Sara.

'No, nothing...' trailed off Tiana, breaking into a conscious smile.

'I knew it! You're blushing! Spill it!' said Aliya excitedly.

'Okay, maybe a little something. It was just a crush. But I promise as soon as we kissed, it ended. The feelings sort of fizzled away,' admitted Tiana.

'You've kissed him?' asked Ronit incredulously.

'T, I can't believe this! You had a summer romance and didn't tell us?' asked Bella.

'I didn't have a summer romance. All we did was go to museums and old buildings in Bombay, and try different cafes and hang out,' said Tiana.

'That sounds exactly like a summer romance,' frowned Ronit with his hands folded defensively. Going by his face and body language everybody could tell he was irked.

'Yeah, after all you kissed him,' said Aliya.

'We kissed once. That's all and it made us want to leave things as friends. Nothing more. Besides, nothing could have happened anyway. I mean, he lives in Bombay and I live here,' said Tiana.

'Yeah, but he's here now. So you never know,' teased Sara.

'Time to start a new love triangle between Tiana, Krish and Ronit,' teased Diya.

'Haha, perfect! Two boys from Bombay and Tiana,' laughed Sara.

'That's not funny. I'm not interested in being a part of any more love triangles,' said Ronit gruffly, walking away.

'Hello! Where are you going? We still have to practise!' yelled Bella, however Ronit didn't turn back.

'He looks pissed as hell,' said Aliya.

'Guys, please. Don't make this a thing,' begged Tiana.

Ronit returned grudgingly after a few minutes, only because Bella had forced him to finish the practice, but he continued to look annoyed throughout the dance routine. After practice was over, Krish returned to meet Tiana. Most of her friends had left, but Bella was still with her.

'You were right. Your school is very pretty,' said Krish.

'Thanks. What are you doing here though?' asked Tiana.

'I'm assisting my mom. She wants me to get on-field experience and all. I thought it would be interesting and, of course, I knew I would get to see you again. Come on. Give me a tour of the school,' smiled Krish.

At that moment, something clicked in Tiana's mind, she was going to try her hand at matchmaking.

'I'm sorry, I can't. I have to meet Mrs Puri,' lied Tiana, 'but,

Bella, if you're free, maybe you can show him around?'

Bella was caught off guard by this request, but she agreed.

'Wait. You are *the* Bella. The one that—' trailed off Krish.

'Yes, yes. I'm the one who got her suspended. I'll tell you the whole story, let's go,' said Bella, rolling her eyes.

Satisfied with her work, Tiana turned to leave when some of the boys from her batch came up to her and pulled her hair, removing the scrunchie from her ponytail.

'What is your problem?' said Tiana through gritted teeth.

'You bitch,' said a boy called Ravi while his friends stood behind him laughing like hooligans. That's when they noticed Ina and Ram recording this particular incident from a few steps away, which sent them scurrying away.

'You recorded that?' asked Tiana.

'Yeah. Thankfully we did. How often do you go through this type of nonsense?' asked Ina.

'All the time and it's not just me. A lot of girls have to deal with this crap but they particularly hate me right now,' said Tiana.

'Does nobody teach these boys how to behave with girls? There are so many monkeys living on your campus and they seem more gracious than the boys in your school,' said Ina.

'Oh, the monkeys are far better behaved than the boys,' replied Tiana.

'Why do they hate you?'

So Tiana explained everything.

'That's dumb.'

'Welcome to my world,' said Tiana to the camera.

Twenty

'Leadership involves finding a parade and getting in front of it.'

—John Naisbitt

One day, Tiana decided to carry her school bag with her to lunch so that the boys in her class couldn't hide it. It was irritating to spend 20 minutes after lunch every single day to look for her bag. As a result, she was always late for the sports sessions that followed lunch and the coaches would yell at her for tardiness.

'Smart,' said Bella when she saw Tiana with her bag on her shoulders during the lunch fall-in. Tiana nodded because Bella knew what Tiana was going through. However, the senior mistress didn't and, true to her nature, made a big deal out of such a small thing.

'Why are you carrying your bag, Tiana? You know very well that you are supposed to leave it in class. Go, put it back on your desk.'

'Ma'am, I'm carrying it because boys from my class always hide it by the time I return from lunch. Then I have to spend 20 minutes looking for it and I get late for other activities. That's why I've decided to carry my bag with me to lunch from now on,' explained Tiana.

'Nonsense! Why would they behave like this for no reason? What did you do to provoke such behaviour?' asked the senior mistress.

'I didn't do anything to them,' said Tiana and then she saw Ina walking towards her with her camera ready.

Ina was only allowed to film Tiana after classes were over. So usually, she would show up right before lunch. Her timing couldn't have been more perfect.

'You have to ignore this sort of stuff and after a while it goes away. Behave like a sensible young lady,' said the senior mistress.

'Why can't the boys behave like sensible young gentlemen?' asked Tiana.

Luckily, Ina was now standing right behind the senior mistress.

'Excuse me? What did you say?' said the senior mistress angrily.

'Teachers constantly expect the best behaviour from the girls. You are always encouraging us to behave like young ladies. Girls should not use swear words, should always speak softly, we should never be rude to a teacher or answer them back. Meanwhile, the boys, especially senior boys, are running wild, bullying girls, teachers and junior boys and using abusive language. If girls don't speak in English, we get yelled at by our prefects because they have instructions from you that girls should only speak in English. Meanwhile, the boys speak freely in Hindi and Punjabi, and nobody cares about that. Why don't we have the choice to speak in whatever language we want? Why does the responsibility of making the school appear *classy* fall on the girls alone? Why aren't the boys being groomed to be gentlemen the way girls are being groomed to be ladies?' asked Tiana boldly but calmly.

'That's enough, Tiana,' said the senior mistress testily. Then she turned around and realized that Ina had been recording this interaction.

'I did not give you permission to record me, Ms Mathur,' said the senior mistress haughtily.

'I was recording Tiana, Mrs Banerjee. The angle was over your shoulder, so your face is not going to be visible,' said Ina innocently.

'Enough! Both of you follow me to my office.'

Ina and Tiana smiled at each other and followed the senior mistress.

Once inside the office, the senior mistress almost began snarling at them.

'Do not overstep the boundaries of acceptable behaviour. We are being very hospitable to you, Ms Mathur, and it would do you well to remember that. I can easily revoke your right to shoot on campus,' said the senior mistress angrily.

'I didn't realize what I was doing was wrong. I was just doing what I have done since I have come here. I'm recording real teen experiences,' said Ina.

'This doesn't feel real. It feels like a manufactured experience. Tiana, just because there is a camera on you it doesn't mean you can speak disrespectfully to me. You were not like this until last term. I can see a streak of arrogance in you and I'm assuming it's because you think you have become very important as you are constantly being recorded,' said the senior mistress angrily.

Tiana didn't know how to explain to the senior mistress that the change in her hadn't come because there was a camera on her. It had come because all summer she had been encouraged to speak up truthfully. Her public speaking experience had opened the floodgates of her thoughts. If she felt that she had something rational to say, especially in her own defence, then she had to say it. She did it exactly how Rishi had taught her in class. When she had spoken to the senior mistress, she hadn't raised her voice, she had kept calm and used examples and made a sensible point.

However, to teachers like Mrs Banerjee, any kind of disagreement, even if done respectfully, meant disrespect. She couldn't accept that students, who were much younger than her, could present a counterargument or have the courage to say what was on their mind. Her ego couldn't take such a challenge. Of course, the senior mistress preferred the meek version of Tiana from last term who had allowed herself to be scapegoated and had not raised her voice against the injustice being doled out to her. She wanted to blame the documentary for giving Tiana the confidence to speak up.

'With all due respect, Mrs Banerjee, Tiana was making some valid points regarding how the boys behave in school. I'm an outsider and even I've noticed bouts of aggression, homophobia and the use of vulgar language. And it's all coming from the boys, not the girls,' said Ina in Tiana's defence.

'Well, I can't help that. I'm in charge of the girls. Not the boys. Tiana, I will not tolerate this behaviour any further. You can leave for lunch now and, Ms Mathur, I would like to speak to you in private.'

Tiana left them alone. She'd lost her appetite after all the excitement and decided to skip lunch and wait in the corridor for Ina to get free. After 10 minutes, Ina came out looking irritated.

'Banerjee is forcing me to interview 50 students who she thinks deserve to be in my documentary. If I don't, then she says she will revoke my permission to shoot on campus,' said Ina.

Tiana started laughing and they walked towards the school bell.

'Oh, by the way, the footage is coming out wonderfully, especially the conversation between you and your friends in the classroom. I just edited that scene yesterday and I'm definitely putting it in my documentary,' said Ina.

'Really? The whole five love triangles idea looked interesting? I'm shocked!' mocked Tiana.

Of course, Ina was going to put that scene in her documentary. She was on a hunt to find unique stories and Tiana knew that her life may not be perfect but it was certainly interesting.

'I got into so much trouble over that love diagram,' said Tiana.

'Why?' asked Ina, looking confused.

'Because we forgot to erase it. My classmates saw it as soon as they entered the classroom the next morning. Pretty soon, my entire batch knew and then everyone else knew. There were so many jokes after that,' replied Tiana.

'Oh God, I'm so sorry. Did they bother you a lot?' asked Ina.

'Oh, they tried but honestly, I think I've really become immune to people talking about me. I expect it now,' Tiana replied matter-of-factly.

'That's my girl!' said Ina.

'So when are you supposed to interview the students from the senior mistress's list?' asked Tiana.

'I'm trying to shorten that list as of now. Fifty is too many! She said they are the best students to represent the school in a documentary *about* the school. I've explained to her so many times that I'm not shooting a documentary on her precious school. It's a documentary on teen experiences in school. But it's like she can't understand me.'

'She can't understand you. Teen—'

'Wait,' interrupted Ina, 'let me turn on the camera. Whatever you're going to say I want to record it.'

After a couple of minutes with Ina's camera recording her, Tiana spoke her mind.

'The reason my senior mistress can't understand that this particular documentary is not about the school but instead about teen experiences *in* school is because the "teen experience" is the last thing she thinks about. For her, it's all about her authoritarian approach to controlling the girls under her command. Most teachers in our country are like this. As students, we are supposed to do exactly what the teachers say and not use our brains or raise our voice against their regressive ideals or have any feelings or emotions whatsoever.'

Tiana continued to relay the entire school bag incident and how such a small thing was twisted and turned against her.

'The boys are hiding my bag, yet Mrs Banerjee found a way to blame me for it. She said I must have done something to the boys and that's why they were retaliating. I can't help but think of how much of our youth is moulded by such regressive ideas about gender and behaviour that our teachers tend to pass on to us. For example, a boy scores 100 marks in maths, but mistreats a girl. Is that okay? Or alternatively, a girl scores 99 per cent in her boards, yet her teacher monitors the length of her skirt, is this okay? What is education in the end? Is it just about numbers on a paper or should it also include emotional growth and the ability to think rationally and to question the existing system if it's not working?' finished Tiana.

'Are the lengths of your skirts monitored?' asked Ina.

Tiana smiled, 'Before our socials or house parties, our house mistress asks us to lay out what clothes we will be wearing for the party on our beds. Then she walks from bed to bed approving or rejecting the outfits. In the end, we can only show up to the party wearing the approved outfit, or else we will be sent back to the dorms. In class seven, I was once sent back because my top had a cold shoulder design.'

'Wow.'

'Why can't teachers go bed to bed in the boys' dorms, telling each boy to never comment on a girls' clothes instead of dictating what a girl can or can't wear? They spend so much time being regressive instead of progressive.'

It seemed that a few teachers overheard Tiana's and Ina's conversation, because before the dance practice, her house captain came up to Tiana and told her to miss practice and meet the senior mistress instead.

'Again? What did you do now?' asked Bella, looking at Tiana.

'Honestly, who cares?' replied Tiana.

A few minutes later Tiana again found herself sitting across from Mrs Banerjee in her office.

'I've heard something very troubling from some of the teachers. They overheard what you were saying on camera about the school. I'm asking you clearly, is it your intention to ruin the image of the school through this documentary?'

'No, ma'am,' said Tiana.

'Really, young lady. Do not try me. As it is, you are on thin ice. Instead of trying to earn back your good graces after damaging the school's image, you are further set on ruining it.'

'I really don't think I need to earn any good graces. I wasn't wrong before and I'm going to make sure everyone knows it,' said Tiana confidently.

'So that is your intention, you want to start brewing trouble again,' said the senior mistress, narrowing her eyes.

'I'm just going to tell my story and clarify some facts about myself,' said Tiana.

'Fine. You can leave.'

As it was bound to happen, pretty soon everyone knew that Tiana intended to speak about her suspension and the incident around it. Tiana was surprised that people hadn't figured this out sooner. What did they think Ina's documentary was about after all? It was about Tiana and, therefore, about the incident that caused her suspension. Of course, she was going to speak about it. It caused some panic amongst the students who were involved in the incident but not faced any real consequences so far. The first person to come and talk to her about not going through with it was Savera.

'Tiana, can I talk to you?' asked Savera stiffly.

Tiana was sitting on her bed. She looked up and knew exactly why Savera had come to her.

'What?'

'Are you really going to disclose the names of everyone present at the party that night in the documentary?'

'Excuse me?' asked Tiana.

'That's what everyone is saying. The seniors are freaking out and they've asked me to come and talk to you about it,' said Savera.

'Really? And they thought I would listen to someone who used to be a friend but decided to stab me in the back?' asked Tiana, tilting her head sideways.

'Please, Tiana. I'm really sorry about everything. Please don't say my name on camera. You know my parents are very strict. They already know what happened and they've barely forgiven me, but if my involvement becomes public, then they will take me out of school,' pleaded Savera.

'Save it. I'm going to do what suits me, the way you did what suited you. You stayed quiet. Nobody came to my defence. Nobody put up a united front when I needed it. So, if I have finally found someone willing to tell my story, then I'm going to tell it,' said Tiana.

'Do you just want revenge? Leila and I made a mistake but please you don't need to keep dragging it on. We'll do anything you say. Please don't say our names on camera,' pleaded Savera.

'Bye, Savera,' said Tiana.

After Savera walked away, Tiana realized how superficial some of her friendships had been. Besides, she had no intention of naming anyone from that night; it would solve none of her problems and, more importantly, she had no proof to back her claim. Without proof, no one would even believe her. However, she was glad that she was causing all of the remaining 25 people to worry about their image, even though they were in no real harm.

Many of them came to plead with her to not say anything about that night. Until now, nobody had thought that Tiana was capable of going public with her story. Now, they were really freaking out. A lot of them had gossiped about her and then bullied her, but now they wanted her to spare them. Suddenly, there was a change in the school's dynamic because for once, Tiana had the power.

Twenty-One

'No revenge is more honourable than the one not taken.'

—Spanish proverb

Soon, Pia, who was the head girl, summoned Tiana to her cubicle where Pia sat surrounded by all her friends. All of them had been caught that night as well. Now just like Savera, Pia too was worried that Tiana might name her on camera. However, unlike Savera, Pia was hostile to Tiana and didn't request or plead. Instead, she tried to intimidate Tiana.

'Tiana, I swear to god if you say my name, my boyfriend Zoravar's name or any of my friends' names on camera, you will have a lot of shit to deal with. I promise you, we will make your life hell, you better watch yourself,' sneered Pia.

'How will you make my life miserable? Who are you?' asked Tiana boldly.

'Excuse me? I'm the head girl and I'm your senior, show some respect.'

'Respect must be commanded, not demanded,' said Tiana. She was quoting something she had read on social media. It was something she had wanted to say to teachers like Mrs Banerjee for a long time now, but saying it to the head girl, who was an extension of the teachers and their systems, was the next best thing.

'Shut up! You have no idea what Zoravar and I can do to you. Who do you think has been arranging to hide your school bag every day? Huh?' sneered Pia.

'*You* are behind that? How petty and pathetic are you?' asked Tiana.

'You are the reason why teachers are so bloody strict with all of us! I wish the school had expelled you. That's what Zoravar's dad had demanded along with the other parents. The school was too easy on you. You should have been expelled but the school didn't think it was fair because others were involved as well, so Zoravar's dad forced them to at least suspend you,' said Pia angrily.

'What did you just say?' asked a stunned Tiana.

'Are you deaf now?'

'Zoravar's dad *demanded* my expulsion? Who is he to demand this?' asked Tiana through gritted teeth.

'Oh, you will find out who he is, don't worry. If you say my name or Zoravar's name in your stupid documentary, then you're done. His dad will make sure you get expelled this time. You will be taken care of,' said Pia, smiling at her minions who began laughing.

'Okay, first, calm down wannabe school mafia. Second, you've done all you could and now it's my turn. Now I will take care of you. I had no plans of taking your names, but you were dumb enough to confess all this to me. This stupid scare tactic that you just tried on me has only made me more determined. If Zoravar's father is really responsible for my situation, it means he did it to protect his son which means his son's name is now mine to bring down with me,' said Tiana coolly.

'Nobody will believe you anyway,' said Pia, a little less confidently.

'I don't care. Even if 10 out of 100 believe me, that will still be more than how many currently believe me. So I'm going to do what feels right to me. Plus, I won't name you. Only him. I will tell him that you confessed to me about what his dad did so that I keep your name out of the documentary, that it was a bargain. That way, he will hate you even more,' said Tiana, walking away.

'Don't you dare! I'm not scared of you! Zoravar will never believe that anyway!' yelled Pia.

'You sure sound scared,' yelled back Tiana without turning back and returned to her bed.

Bella was waiting for her, 'That was intense.'

'You heard all that?' asked Tiana.

'Yeah, everybody in the dorm heard it. It was quite dumb of her to tell you all this,' said Bella.

'Yeah!' said Tiana, shrugging.

'Are you actually going to take everybody's name on camera? That's what everyone is worried about, even Sara. They were scared to ask you. We just don't know what to expect,' asked Bella.

'Honestly, Bella, I had no intention of getting more people into trouble. That wasn't this documentary's purpose. The point was to clear my name and show how ridiculously strict the school can be with people who don't deserve it. Now, I'm confused as to what to do. People like Savera and Pia have put this idea in my head themselves. They are so scared of getting into trouble that they are sort of digging their own grave. So, honestly, I don't know what I'm going to say during my interview. It will either come out naturally or it won't but don't worry, I won't name you or Sara or any of our friends.'

Bella just nodded. Then she got up from the bed.

'Well, I'm off to give my interview now. Ina wanted me to sit down properly and talk about some stuff. I hope that's okay,' asked Bella timidly.

'Of course. It's Ina's film and these are her decisions. It's all good,' smiled Tiana.

'Cool.'

'Best of luck.'

Twenty-Two

Bella

'Comparison is an act of violence against the self.'

—Iyanla Vanzant

'You've had a rivalry with Tiana for a while now. You confessed this yourself. Are you friends with her now?' asked Ina.

'Yes, we are friends,' said Bella, looking into the camera. She was finally sitting down for her interview with Ina and they were filming in one of the empty classrooms. She knew that the questions were going to be personal and she intended to be as real as possible.

'Was it easy to move past your history?'

'It was very difficult. I'm the one who screwed up. It was difficult for me to accept what I had done and what kind of a person I was becoming. I caused so much pain and anger and I did it not just to one person but to an entire family. Tiana had to forgive me and the one who forgives always comes out looking better than the one who has to be forgiven.'

'I'm sensing you still have a competitive streak.'

'Aren't we all always competing with each other? It's just how it is. Whether we want to or not, we can't help ourselves. We want to be the best and have the best. Everyone is like that, they just don't say it,' shrugged Bella.

'But you aren't afraid to say what you feel.'

'No, I'm not.'

'Would you admit that you're still trying to compete with Tiana?'

'I get competitive with other people but with Tiana, its completely different. It's difficult to explain...' trailed off Bella.

'How's it different from others?'

'How can I compete and win and come ahead of a girl who is not even trying to compete with me and yet manages to overshadow me at the same time? How is that fair? Tiana doesn't ask for it and yet she is always the centre of attention. Until last term, people were always placing her on a pedestal. Parents, teachers and even boys. The annoying part was that she didn't even seem to want this attention. On the other hand, I was craving the attention and not receiving it. It made me so angry. In that anger, I made some decisions that I now regret,' admitted Bella honestly.

'You mean the photo you posted online?'

'Yes, but also how I mistook pettiness for competition. I had to take a step back after that and throughout the summer, I tried to re-evaluate who I am and who I want to become. I don't want to compete with Tiana. Instead, I want to learn certain things from her. Especially her honesty and ability to express herself without stepping on other people's feelings and how to keep a calm attitude no matter what life throws at me,' reflected Bella.

'Moving on to how the school decided to suspend Tiana, do you think it was justified?'

'Of course not. I love her, but Tiana is one of those annoying students who are incapable of breaking the rules. It doesn't matter if it's off campus or on campus, she doesn't drink alcohol. She read an article a few years back about how consuming alcohol damages brain cells, or something like that, and since then has stayed away from drinking. So the fact that she got suspended for it is ridiculous,' replied Bella.

'Do you know anything else about the incident?'

'Yes, I do, but I can't really comment on the details without stirring up trouble for a lot of people,' said Bella.

'Even if it will help your friend?' asked Ina.

Bella hesitated. In truth, she had thought about speaking up about that night many times. But she had been scared of getting suspended as well. She was expecting Tiana to make the entire incident public for the documentary. So she had been mentally preparing herself to accept the consequences. After all, Tiana had the right to do and say whatever she wanted to. Unlike Savera, Bella had no intention of trying to stop Tiana. However, Bella didn't have the guts to confess on her own either. Especially since her father had just forgiven her for the drunk driving incident from her past. Things were finally good at home for her and if her father were to find out about the campus drinking, then it would ruin her relationship with him even further. So she was stuck in a rather awkward position where she wanted to help her friend on one hand and herself on the other.

'I can sense that you want to say something but you're stopping yourself,' said Ina.

'For now, I can't,' said Bella.

'Does that mean in the future you could?'

'Maybe.'

'So you *do* have the means to help Tiana in the fight to clear her name? She's doing it all alone. Maybe your help could change things for her,' pushed Ina.

'I know, but there's a lot of other things at stake here as well,' said Bella.

'If what you said earlier was true and you really want to learn Tiana's honesty, then you should try by being honest about this. It could change your friend's life.'

'I've already been thinking about how I can help. I just need a little time,' replied Bella pensively.

'Okay, moving on to a lighter note. How's the love triangle between you, Ronit and Tiana?' asked Ina.

'There isn't one anymore. Ronit likes Tiana. Everybody knows that and she likes him back. They have to figure it out themselves.'

'So you mean to say that you don't like him at all? If I'm not mistaken, he was a major cause of your rivalry with Tiana?'

'That's one thing I'm most embarrassed about. Imagine getting competitive with your friend over a *boy*. That's so petty. For this, I'll never forgive myself.'

'For being petty?'

'For being a cliche.'

'That was great, Bella! Let's take a break and next we'll do a joint interview with you and Ronit,' smiled Ina.

'Oh, do we have to do it together?' frowned Bella.

'Yeah, trust me, it's going to be better this way. Ronit will be here in five minutes,' replied Ina.

Twenty-Three

Ronit

'When you invite trouble, it's usually quick to accept.'

—H. Jackson Brown Jr

Ronit was already there. He'd been standing unseen outside the classroom listening to Bella's interview. He'd been surprised by Bella's capacity for introspection. Bella had seemed vapid to him until then, but today he'd seen a completely new side of her. Was this really her? He didn't get time to figure it out because he got distracted by Ina mentioning his joint interview with Bella.

When Ina had asked him to come for the interview, he'd assumed he would be alone. He wasn't prepared to sit with Bella because she could be unpredictable. He took a deep breath and entered the classroom.

'Hey! Right on time. Come, attach this mic and sit. We'll start soon,' said Ina, smiling at him.

Bella waved at him casually and Ram, the camera guy, came to help him with the mic.

'So, Ronit, I want to interview you and Bella together for the next segment,' said Ina.

'Umm, why?' asked Ronit.

'Why not? You both are a big part of Tiana's story after all,' said Ina.

Ronit was unsure of proceeding with the interview but he

didn't know how to get out of it at the last minute without seeming rude. So, he went and sat next to Bella.

'Don't look so nervous, Ron,' said Bella.

'I don't think I should be giving this interview. I really have no idea what to say.'

Before Bella had a chance to respond, Ina came back and started giving instructions to them. 'Just look at the camera and not at me when you're speaking. That way, it will look more personal. Okay, ready? Ram, turn on the lights and roll the camera.'

As soon as the lights and camera were turned on, Ronit felt very self-conscious and nervous. He kept fidgeting, touching his hair and shifting his weight from one side to another. Then Ina began asking personal questions and apart from the literal spotlight, he felt as though he was under a figurative spotlight as well. He couldn't focus on what he was saying or doing. His self-consciousness kept making things worse.

'Ronit, I need you to stay still when you answer,' said Ina.

'Oh okay, yeah. Sorry,' replied Ronit.

'Okay, start your answer again,' said Ina.

Ronit couldn't remember what he'd been saying and he realized that he didn't even remember the question that Ina had asked him.

'I'm sorry, can you repeat the question please?'

Bella was looking at him like he was a moron, 'She's asked you the question like three times already. Just chill.'

'No no, it's okay. Happens all the time. Ronit, I was asking you how you got stuck in a love triangle between Bella and Tiana?'

'How the hell was he supposed to answer such a question? No wonder he kept messing up,' Bella thought to herself.

'I don't really know. Sort of just happened, I guess,' said Ronit, looking at Ina.

'Okay, Ronit, you need to look at the camera and not at me. And I need you to elaborate on your thoughts a bit. I mean your answer is barely an answer. I need some honesty,' said Ina patiently.

'I don't feel comfortable talking about this,' said Ronit.

'Try, please. This is important for the film.'

'How is this love triangle important for the film? How will this help Tiana clear her name? I don't think I can answer these questions.'

'It will help because it will make the film more interesting to watch. More views mean more power to this film. I need to cover all aspects of Tiana's life, and you and Bella are important,' said Ina calmly.

'Can you ask me something else, please?' asked Ronit.

'Okay, tell me this, Bella has just admitted that she was jealous of your connection with Tiana and that in part led her to posting that photo online. How does that make you feel?'

'Horrible.'

'Can you elaborate?' pushed Ina gently.

'I regretted coming here. It made me wish that I had never transferred to this school. My presence ruined so much for both Bella and Tiana. I came here because I knew Tiana but then I ruined everything.'

'You came to this school because of Tiana?'

'I needed to leave my last school for some personal reasons and when I had to choose a new place to go, I decided to come here because Tiana was here,' admitted Ronit.

'Have you known Tiana a long time then?'

'Since we were seven years old. We're childhood friends.'

'When did it become more than friendship for you?'

'About three years ago. We were meeting after a while and things were different. We both liked each other. Two years later, I came to this school.'

'Then what happened?'

'Well, it didn't work out with Tiana, and I began dating Bella and the rest you know.'

'What do you regret?'

'My behaviour towards both of them. My rashness. I guess, I was just... I don't know,' trailed off Ronit.

'What do you mean?'

'It's just difficult to say these things. I mean, I was wrong and I know it, and I feel very sorry but it's still difficult for me to talk about how I behaved.'

'You mean how you pretended to like me to make Tiana jealous and then when Tiana asked for your help, you didn't help her out?' added Bella plainly.

'I sometimes look back at that time and I can't believe that my actions had so much power. When I realized the damage I had caused, I didn't know how to deal with it. My guilt would keep me up at night. I couldn't sleep for weeks,' said Ronit sadly.

'It's not all on you. When you joined school last term, Tiana told us that she still liked you. She was angry at you but she still had feelings for you. I kind of knew that you also liked her. When you asked me out, I should have said no but I didn't because just like you were trying to hurt her, so was I. I was already fighting with her and somehow you just walked into the middle of it. But the problem was that what started out as a casual trick turned real for me and then I started getting jealous of Tiana whenever I saw you two even talking to each other. I'm so embarrassed about that and about how I posted her photo online. I shouldn't have taken it all out on Tiana. That part is my fault. So you really shouldn't feel that guilty. We share the blame,' said Bella emotionally.

As he processed it, he realized that both of them had made big mistakes and had been making up for them. At this point, there was not much else to do except to own up to their actions and to hope to be better in the future.

'I'm really sorry, Bell.'

'I'm sorry too, Ron.'

Instinctively, both of them got up and hugged each other. It was a gesture to absolve all the negativity between them for good.

'Aww… that's so sweet! But Ram wasn't prepared for you both to get up and hug. We were set up for a mid-shot. So, Ram, zoom out and both of you sit down and get up again to hug and this time, we'll record it properly,' said Ina, looking into the camera's digital screen.

So Bella and Ronit sat down and got up again to hug, although this second one was an artificial hug and in no way held the same gravitas as the original. The real hug had been for them alone. It wasn't entertainment. It was the culmination of their real feelings and emotions. It had been a marker for their growth.

Twenty-Four

'Vanity made the revolution; liberty was only a pretext.'

—Napoleon

'We have a breakthrough! Finally!' exclaimed Ina.

'What do you mean?' asked Tiana, looking up from her book.

Ina came and sat beside her on the bleachers of the basketball court where Tiana sat reading after making a health excuse while the coach made the rest of her classmates run under the hot sun.

'So during my interviews with the staff and other students, I've been slipping in questions about what happened with you and why, and all that... Just to pick their brains about what they think of your situation... Usually, people would become uncomfortable and refuse to comment. However, some were sympathetic and thought that it could all have been avoided.'

'Who said that?'

'That's the thing. It has to be off the record because they are worried they will get in trouble with the administration if they speak up openly.'

'How is this a breakthrough if people won't speak up?' asked Tiana.

'It is because even if no one wants to speak up openly, at least three teachers have separately told me the same story of what actually happened. We at least know the truth now.'

'What truth?'

'Apparently, there is a legacy kid in the school called Zoravar Singh in class 12. His father is a member of the alumni council and is a big donor to the school. He is also closely related to the chief minister of the state. So basically, a well-connected father wanted the entire episode to be swept aside as quickly as possible. He didn't want his son's involvement to become public. Especially because according to one teacher, it was Zoravar himself who sneaked in the alcohol. Apparently, he has done this twice before, but his father always gets him out of trouble.'

'Oh.'

'Anyway, the school's plan was to only give detention to all the students who were caught and end it there but then Bella leaked your photo and the school found out that even you were there that night. After that, local media picked up the story about what was happening in boarding schools. So Zoravar's dad was worried that the whole incident might become national news and his son's name will be dragged in as well, so he wanted to divert the attention away. He rounded up about 30 angry parents and together, they pressured the school to expel the girl who was responsible and your photo was used as proof against you. However, the school knew you weren't at fault completely because they knew it was Zoravar's alcohol, so they decided to suspend you for the rest of the term instead of expelling you. Therefore, all the responsibility fell on you and the school saved its face in front of the media and parents by showing that they had taken strict action and Zoravar and his dad got exactly what they wanted,' finished Ina catching her breath.

'My life has officially become a '90s Bollywood movie,' said Tiana dryly.

'Why are you so calm? Isn't this making you mad?' asked Ina.

'I knew this,' replied Tiana.

'What?' asked Ina incredulously.

'Relax. I found out yesterday. Pia, our head girl is dating Zoravar. She was freaking out that I am about to name everyone who was there that night and she kind of confessed all this to me.

She threatened that if I said anything, then Zoravar's dad would take care of me like he did before. I guessed he was probably behind everything and you have basically just confirmed this theory,' said Tiana.

'Oh my god! You should have told me as soon as you found out, Tiana!'

'Why? What can you do?'

'I can interview her and try to coax it out of her on camera!'

'I doubt she would say all this in front of a camera.'

'You have no idea how much can slip out in front of a camera if you haven't been trained beforehand about what to say. If she comes in without knowing my line of questioning, she would be caught off guard and even if she doesn't say anything, her body language and facial expressions alone would give her away. This is not a court case. I don't need solid evidence. We are making a documentary and insinuation can be enough as well,' said Ina.

'Okay, sorry.'

'Is there anything else you aren't telling me? This is important, Tiana. Any information that can help the documentary is going to help you personally as well.'

'No, there's nothing else, Ina,' said Tiana.

'Are you sure? You won't hide anything from me, right? I have invested a lot of time, money and energy in this story, Tiana, and I need all the facts and pieces,' said Ina very seriously.

This irritated Tiana a little and she answered back a bit more sharply than she had wanted.

'It's my life, my story after all. Why would you suddenly doubt me, Ina?' asked Tiana frowning.

'It may be your life but it's *our* story now,' corrected Ina.

It was at this point that it finally struck Tiana: for Ina, her life was just a story. She was just a subject, not a person. For a second, she doubted her decision to be a part of Ina's documentary but decided to change the topic and not dwell on this sudden ill feeling.

'How was Bella's interview?'

'Oh, interesting. I think she went into a deep self-realization mode for a bit during the interview. I think it's going to be very entertaining to watch. Plus, adding Ronit into the mix made it all the more better,' said Ina happily.

'Wait, you interviewed them together?' asked Tiana.

Ina just nodded.

'Why would you do that? Putting them together, you could only use them for one thing,' said Tiana.

'Yeah, for the drama! Come on! Your love triangle is what caused all this in the first place. I'm just using what you guys are giving me yourself,' said Ina, shrugging her shoulders.

'We already spoke about the love triangle and all that. Why are you focusing so much on that part of my life? I don't want to come across as frivolous. I thought the whole point was to clear my name,' said Tiana, beginning seriously to doubt her involvement in the documentary.

'Tiana, that is still the point of the story. Don't worry about that. You need to understand that even though the fight to clear your name is Plot A, we sometimes need to treat it like Plot B because it can get tedious and boring for the viewers. The masses in India don't have patience for serious documentaries. I need to insert all these love angles and teen fights to make it a watchable story. If there is drama, then I must show it. I'm going to look at *all* aspects of your life. You should have known this before saying yes,' said Ina plainly.

A nerve was suddenly struck. Ina had not mentioned any of this before. Perhaps, if she had then Tiana would've had second thoughts about becoming her subject, so she played nice to get what she wanted and only now the truth of Ina's vision was surfacing. Tiana did not like how much Ina was enjoying the real troubles of her life. Ina seemed to be taking it all as a form of entertainment. She was using emotional tactics on her friends now and Tiana had no control over the twist Ina was going to give the story. After all, she was only a subject and she had no creative control. She hadn't even seen any of the footage yet. Ina had just admitted that she had the ability to manipulate people who hadn't been trained in how to conduct themselves in front of the camera. How many emotions was Ina manufacturing for the benefit of her film? Could Ina use her friends to show them in a bad light for 'drama'? These questions were suddenly floating like banners in Tiana's mind and she had no way of knowing the answer to them.

'Anyway, we have to plan your interview soon because Banerjee might banish me any day now. Let's do it tomorrow afternoon. It's a Sunday and we will have enough time,' said Ina.

Tiana simply nodded, but for the rest of the day, every time she thought about sitting down for her interview with Ina, she would begin to get a headache.

Twenty-Five

'As your life changes, so will your circle.'

—Anonymous

When she woke up on the day of her interview, Tiana was an emotional mess. Her palms felt sweaty, her heartbeat kept rising and falling. She couldn't focus on anything. The night before, she had been so frazzled that she couldn't finish her study work. During her Sunday morning extra class for maths, the teacher, Mrs Yadav, yelled at Tiana because she caught Tiana looking out the window instead of concentrating on her book.

'Enough of your daydreams, Tiana. You might think you are a star because you're in a film but in my class, I expect you to focus and pay attention.'

Everyone began giggling and laughing at this statement. All Tiana could think was why her teachers had to pass such personal comments on students. Why couldn't she just have said 'focus in my class' and left it at that. The constant personal attacks from teachers were horrible.

Just after lunch, she was walking towards the dorms with Bella when an unexpected voice called out her name. It was Karam. This was weird because ever since the term had begun, he had ignored her. Often, he had walked past her without even glancing in her direction.

'Why is he calling you?' muttered Bella under her breath. Tiana raised her eyebrows in response as Karam walked toward them.

'Hi,' smiled Karam.

'Hi...' replied Tiana and Bella warily.

'I wanted to talk to you, Tiana. Just for five minutes. If that's okay?' asked Karam.

'Listen, both of you. My advice to you guys is that no matter what you think and feel, don't start dating again. Please, just don't. You are good for a few days together and after that it's all downhill. So don't go down that path. Please,' said Bella superfluously.

Tiana and Karam looked at her aghast.

'Okay, I'm going!' said Bella.

'What's up?' asked Tiana.

'How are you?'

'I'm surprised we're having this conversation. Why did you decide to *stop* ignoring me?' asked Tiana.

'I felt bad about the entire dance partner scene,' replied Karam.

'Oh. It's fine,' said Tiana, shaking her head.

'I also wanted to talk about Tea. I was avoiding you because I didn't know how to bring it up with you; I didn't know how you would react to us. Then Tea told me you were cool but by then I had ignored you too many times and I didn't know how to break the ice, so I kept my distance,' said Karam sheepishly.

'Karam, I didn't expect you to sit around and wait for me. We had a strange break-up but it was for good and I'm happy you have moved on.'

'Even if I have moved on to Tea?' asked Karam.

'I would have preferred if you had moved on to someone outside my gene pool, but it can't be helped now,' smiled Tiana.

'Very funny.'

'I won't lie. It came as a shock. I would have preferred if you had told me about it instead of telling Sid, who told Ronit, who told me.'

'I only told my sister okay! It's Leila who told her boyfriend.

Then stupid Sid told Ronit,' said Karam.

'Exactly why you *should* have told me. Our lives are entwined in a strange way. Our siblings are dating and now you are dating my cousin, who is also Ronit's ex-girlfriend. I don't want to hear distorted things through the grapevine. We were friends before we began dating. I think the least we can do is offer honesty to each other,' said Tiana.

'I was just embarrassed. I didn't know how to tell you but I promise, going forward, if something is related to you, I will tell you first. You won't hear it through the grapevine,' said Karam.

'Thanks,' said Tiana.

'So, how's the documentary going? It seems exciting,' said Karam.

For a few moments she had forgotten all about the interview. Now panic washed over her again. She checked her watch. It was scheduled to happen in exactly 45 minutes.

'I was excited in the beginning but now I don't know if it was a good idea to say yes to it,' said Tiana.

'Why?'

'I don't know. I feel like my life and all my friends' lives are being put on display, to be consumed as entertainment. I didn't think about this aspect before saying yes and it's beginning to bother me now. I don't know what Ina is recording and how she is going to portray me, or the school and everyone involved.'

'I guess at this point, you can just be honest about yourself on camera and hope for the best,' replied Karam.

'Yeah. I have an interview in 40 minutes and honestly, I have no idea what I'm going to say. I feel so nervous.'

'You know exactly what to say, Tiana. It's your story and no one else can tell it better.'

'You do realize that if I go on record with my side of the story, then I will be getting a lot of people into trouble including your sister, Bella, Sara, Ronit, my former friends and my seniors/

your batchmates,' said Tiana.

'That's why you are nervous?' asked Karam.

A lot of thoughts were troubling Tiana but suddenly she didn't think it was right to have such heartfelt conversations with Karam anymore. There were many reasons for this apprehension. Every time they had such deep conversations, she would end up giving Karam false romantic hope. That's exactly what had happened before the apology party, when they got back together. Besides, he was her cousin's boyfriend now. She had to maintain a sensible distance from him.

'I'll figure it out though. Thanks, anyway,' replied Tiana abruptly.

Karam sensed the sudden change in Tiana's tone. They were instantly aware that their dynamic had changed for good. There was no going back. They were not going to be close friends going forward and it was okay. They had been a phase in each other's life and now they were beginning to move on from their first relationship. It was bittersweet but Tiana felt good that they were ending things well. They wouldn't need to ignore each other in the future and would offer help if the other needed it but that would be it, nothing more.

Twenty-Six

'Hesitation is the death of advantage.'

—V.E. Schwab

Twenty minutes later, Tiana walked into the auditorium where Ina would interview her. Ina greeted her cheerfully. Instead of wearing the casual Sunday tracksuit, Ina had asked Tiana to wear her formal school uniform, complete with the school tie. Ina seemed to really have a flare for the dramatic.

'Put this mic on; I'm going to set up with Ram.'

Tiana went in a corner and fixed the mic. When she turned around she saw Ronit walking towards her.

'What are you doing here?' asked Tiana, surprised.

'Well, believe it or not, Karam actually asked me to come and find you. He said that you needed a friend today,' smiled Ronit.

'Oh, that was sweet of him.'

'If you say so.'

Tiana rolled her eyes at him but smiled at the same time.

'So I went to the girls department and found Bella, who told me you were doing your interview here.'

'Yeah. I guess it's finally time.'

'Are you ready for it then?'

'I'm not sure. I need to talk to you about a few things that are bothering me,' said Tiana, looking at Ronit intently. He nodded and they sat down on the auditorium steps.

'I get it if you are nervous. I don't mean to scare you but for me personally, and to a certain extent Bella, the interview had been a rattling experience.'

'Why?'

'I guess, because it was my first interview ever. I had never really thought about how it would feel to actually sit in front of a camera and talk about my feelings and motives. It's on video and you begin to realize midway that whatever you say can cause people to either judge you or like you. For the first time, I was being asked personal things in such a public way, and didn't know what the right way to behave was.'

'What do you mean?' asked Tiana, frowning.

'I mean, if you seem hesitant, then people might think you are hiding something. And if you talk too much, then they might dislike you for being loud. And if you are too aloof, they might think you aren't taking things seriously.'

'This is not helping me at all! I'm nervous as it is, Ronit!' said Tiana, her hands felt clammy and she kept wiping them against her skirt in anxiety.

'I don't mean to scare you, T. Think of it as prep,' said Ronit gently.

Tiana scoffed.

'I'm telling you this so that you understand that if and when such thoughts enter your mind during your interview, you can disregard them. Overthinking is what got to me. There were long awkward pauses during my interview because I was too self-conscious.'

'That will be edited out you know,' said Tiana.

'Yeah but my awkwardness can't be edited out. That's just who I was on camera that day. I may not be like that in real life but that's how I ended up looking that day. I don't want you to squander your chance, Tiana. Say what you want to, without inhibitions. You need to be absolutely honest to actually *look* honest on camera. We aren't actors; we can't pretend, which is why you have to be yourself. Don't play around with words, just say things the way you would in real life and with full conviction.'

'Ronit, if I speak, I will do so with full conviction. Trust me, expressing myself is not a problem. My problem is that I'm beginning to question if this documentary was a good idea. I don't like the way Ina is treating certain parts of my life. To her, it's just a story.'

'What do you mean?'

'She might be making things too dramatic and probably isn't keeping things real enough.'

'Everyone takes artistic liberties to keep their work interesting, Tiana. That can't be so surprising to you. Just think about what you are getting out of this—a chance to tell your story.'

'I guess, I've been too naive about all this so far and only now am I realizing that what I'm doing is going to leave a permanent mark on my school, my friends and even the people I dislike.'

'That's okay, Tiana. What they have done is also going to leave a permanent mark on you,' said Ronit.

'If I go through with this interview, then people will hate me even more than they did before. I don't know if I have the strength to face all of this again. To be talked about again. Some of them have been so cruel. This interview will start it all over again,' said Tiana.

'Look, you need to have full conviction before you go into this, Tiana,' said Ronit seriously.

'I just feel that this is one of those moments in life that will decide what kind of a person I become in the future. When I will look back at this very moment, I will either regret it or cherish it. The problem of life is that I don't know which decision will lead me to a happy outcome. Honestly, this is worse than solving a maths problem.'

Ronit looked confused as hell. He raised both his hands and dropped them. Twice.

'I know. I know,' said Tiana, acknowledging the fact that he couldn't really help her out. She would have to make up her own mind.

'Will anyone even believe me?'

'Some will. Some won't,' Ronit stated.

Tiana shut her eyes and sighed deeply.

He took Tiana's hand in his own as a comforting gesture but dropped it swiftly.

'Eww! Why is your hand so sweaty? Disgusting,' he exclaimed through his laughter.

'Shut up! I'm nervous, okay? This has never happened before, so shut up,' Tiana yelled back at him.

They broke into a bout of laughter. Strangely, this helped; it released some of the pent-up anxiety within Tiana, and a few minutes later, she was sitting in front of the camera. A strange sense of calmness enveloped her.

Twenty-Seven

'People can be divided into three groups: those who make things happen, those who watch things happen and those who wonder what happened.'

—John Newbern

Ina had set up the camera on the stage, flanked by two big lights on either side. The rest of the auditorium was dimly lit. The lights were blinding her, so she couldn't see anyone else in the hall. Ronit had left the auditorium after wishing her luck. Tiana knew that Ina and Ram were standing right in front of her, but they had become a silhouette to her.

'Okay, Tiana, the first thing to remember is look into the camera while talking and secondly turn on the mic and say something, we want to check the sound,' instructed Ina.

'Um… Hello, I'm Tiana. Mic check.'

'Okay, great. Rolling now,' said Ina.

Tiana nodded.

'Tiana, why are you sitting here today? Tell us your story,' Ina asked as she began the interview.

Tiana was quiet for a few seconds. Then she looked directly into the camera and began speaking slowly and earnestly.

'Before I tell you my story, I need to explain why I need to share it. I had a lot of apprehensions before this interview. On one hand, I was thinking, do I really need to dig up all this stuff? I mean, the damage is done. If I stay quiet, then I won't get any of my friends or seniors in trouble and this way, my school's reputation will also not get spoiled any further. I know I can recover from this. I just have to accept that what happened to me was simply bad luck and I can move forward. All the gossip, the rumours and cruel name calling will die down soon if I keep ignoring them and keep my head down,' said Tiana.

She paused for a few seconds.

'On the other hand, what kind of a person will I become if I don't raise my voice right now? This is the first truly bad thing to have ever happened to me. Not only have I been embarrassed but so have my parents. Everybody is judging them for raising such a *problematic* daughter. When the truth is, they have been such good parents and I have not done anything wrong. I'm facing adversity for the first time in my life and if I do nothing to counter it, then what kind of personality will I have in the future—defeatist or escapist? I asked myself, do I really want to grow into such a meek adult? The answer came quickly. No,' finished Tiana.

'So you have decided to speak up then?'

'Yes, I'm doing this for my peace of mind and for my growth as a person. Many won't believe me or might say I'm doing this for publicity or just to drag down my school and other students for revenge, to get back at people for what happened to me. People are calling me names, being abusive towards me and making up stories about me. But I've decided that because I'm not wrong, I'm not going to be fearful.'

Tiana took a deep breath and paused for a moment.

'So, tell us what happened?' asked Ina.

Tiana did. She explained her side of the story—from how she had accidentally found herself in a secret party with alcohol on school campus. It had been dark and she was handed a beer bottle. Someone had been taking photos because there were a lot of camera flashes briefly lighting up the dark, and before she could put down the beer, someone must have taken a picture of her as well. Unfortunately, it had been a solo photo of her. It was also the only photo that had been posted on social media, the next day by a friend who was jealous. Her other friends had known about it but didn't stop her jealous friend.

Tiana didn't name anyone. She told Ina how there had been people who had felt threatened because Tiana had been fast becoming a favourite of the teachers. These students had wanted to spoil her reputation because they didn't want her to become a prefect in the future or be selected for the exchange programme. So many factors had worked against her. To top it all, after a teacher had discovered the party, everyone there had been given detention. Despite knowing that so many people were at fault, Tiana alone was suspended because a local newspaper had picked up the story and some parents had pressured the school into taking strict action against her. The onus of the entire incident was put on her alone.

'Do you feel you are still suffering the consequences?'

'Conveniently, everyone has forgotten the part they played in the incident. I was the only one suspended, but they know they were there as well and they were all drinking. So they can't blame it all on me. Yet, somehow, my suspension seems to have given them a licence to pin it all on me. As if I sneaked in the alcohol. As if I planned the whole thing. They have erased their involvement in the incident from their collective memory,' Tiana replied.

'What other action has the school taken?' asked Ina.

'The school has become extremely strict this term. The teachers are constantly raiding our dorms and keeping a close eye on everything. So far, they have confiscated multiple mobile phones and a lot of cash. The seniors are accusing *me* for the new rules because I got caught last term. They seem to have forgotten that they *all* got caught. There is one particular senior boy who was closely involved in the incident, but he has been constantly calling me abusive names and has even asked his batchmates to keep bullying me.'

'Do many people bully you then?'

'The boys in my batch have to do everything their seniors tell them to do, even if they don't want to. After lunch, my school bag often goes missing and it takes nearly half an hour to find it. I know that it's the boys from my class who are doing this. All the ridiculous and annoying things they have been doing to me have begun to accumulate over time and hurt me. Some days, they will steal all my pens, some days they splash red ink on my skirt, sometimes they steal my homework and I'm unable to hand it in to my teachers on time, which gets me in trouble with the teachers. While the teacher is yelling at me and calling me lazy and useless, I can see the boys giggling and laughing on the side. It's this kind of bullying that I've had to deal with for the past few months.'

'So, only boys are involved in this kind of behaviour towards you?'

'Not really. The senior boy that I mentioned before has a very popular girlfriend who was also present during the incident. This girl recently boasted to me about the part she has been playing in bullying me. Hiding my school bag was apparently her brainchild and it's being executed by her boyfriend. She has also been instigating other senior girls to spread lies about me. They have constantly been talking about me, in front of me, but then pretend they can't see me. Just like the boys, they have been using abusive words to refer to me. It's this constant stream of negativity that I have to deal with on a daily basis. This stuff might not seem so big, but it affects me a lot. Sometimes, I want to sit and cry but I don't want to give the satisfaction to these people.'

'Why do they all listen to this boy?'

'I guess there is always one senior boy in every school that the entire student body just worships. The junior boys have to do whatever he says or else he will give them physical drills. He can because he's a prefect. The senior girls are his batchmates, and I guess they are united in solidarity. His dad has clout. His dad is also an old student and an important member of the Hill View High Old Student Society. Apparently, he is the one who pressured the school into suspending me, to keep the attention away from his son.'

'How do you know this boy's father had caused your suspension from school?'

'I don't have proof, but the senior girl I mentioned told me this herself. Some teachers have confided that they knew but it's off the record. The teachers are afraid they will lose their job if they speak up. So even though some of them believe I was wrongly punished, they can't really speak up in my defence and against this boy and his father.'

'That seems unfair.'

'Apparently, this boy has sneaked alcohol into the campus twice before but the school has let him off the hook both times due to his father's influence.'

'Do you wish to name this boy?'

'I do, but without proof there is no point.'

'Can you name any of the other students who were at the party, drinking on campus that night?'

'I could but what's the point of calling out people without proof to back up my claims?'

'What about the girl who had posted your photo online and caused your troubles. You don't wish to name her either?'

'No, not really. Like I said before, my intention is not to get more students in trouble. I don't wish to lose my sense of self and become a negative person because of one bad thing that has happened. I've been working on finding myself and who I am over the past three years. I don't want to abandon it all just when life is beginning to test me.'

'What do you mean when you say you have been trying to find yourself?'

'Pink or Black, actually,' smiled Tiana.

'What does that mean?'

'I was very confident as a kid. I remember when I was 10, it was my first year at boarding school and we were having a social for Diwali and all the girls were wearing Indian clothes. I wore a lehenga except my choli had a cut-out detail at the back. It wasn't backless or anything, but for the small-minded girls in my class, it might as well have been. I was sniggered at and whispered about. I was even told to either change my outfit or to cover myself with my dupatta. So there I was, thinking that it was only appropriate for me to wear that lehenga my mom had designed for me. She had packed it for me herself. If my mother didn't have a problem, then these girls were nobody to make me question myself or my clothes. I took a stand and didn't change into anything else or try to hide myself. I was boycotted for my defiance and nobody danced with me that evening. I controlled my tears and after everyone had gone to sleep that night, I went and wept my heart out in the bathroom.'

'Not letting your clothes get politicized. You've been a feminist since you were 10.'

'As a kid, I always stood my ground even to the point of being left out. I felt if someone was worth being my friend, then they would be like me and not be afraid of cliquish behaviour. This ideology made surviving a boarding school very difficult because we had to live with people we didn't like and groupism was rampant in both the dorms and the classrooms. For how long could I be alone? For how long could I eat my meals sitting quietly on the side, or sitting alone during classes? I realized that I needed friends and for that I needed to adapt. So once I became a part of a group, I began to lose my voice and sense of self. By 14, I was so lost that I didn't even know what my favourite food or colour was. Did I like Italian food because *I* liked it or because my *friends* liked it? Was my favourite colour pink or black? That's when I decided to take back control. Be me again.'

'Very few youngsters think about such things.'

'I'm glad I did because it saved my life. Around the time I had decided to be true to myself, my friends and I had started to hang out together during the holidays and they had also started to drink. I had read an article that said drinking alcohol caused neurons to die and I knew enough biology to know that neurons don't regenerate. That had freaked me out. In hindsight, I don't even know if that article was true or not, but it had affected me. I was already quite stupid in maths and I didn't want to lose any more mental capacities and since then, I have refrained from consuming alcohol. Anyway, one day after hanging out, one of the drunk boys had offered to drive everyone home; I refused to get into the car. They made fun of me for being such a "mom" but I didn't succumb to their peer pressure. I decided to wait for my brother while they left and within seconds, my friends' car had crashed into another. They had been speeding while taking a right turn onto the main road. It happened in front of me and I was in shock,' said Tiana.

'That's crazy.'

'What's crazy is that when my school found out what had happened, they put me on a pedestal for not drinking and being a model student. Suddenly, the teachers loved me and could not stop praising me. Cut to two terms later, and I am again made an example, but for all the wrong reasons this time,' said Tiana bitterly.

'So what do you want now?'

'Justice. I want for all the students who were caught that night to be treated the same way. Twenty-five of them were given detention, whereas I was suspended. Either they should be suspended as well or I demand an apology from the school. By that, I mean an apology from the teachers in charge, for blaming me to save their face,' said Tiana.

'Do you think you can achieve this?'

'No, because I don't have proof but I still wanted to tell my story. People may or may not believe it but this is what happened. I wish I could prove it for my parents' sake but that's just going to remain a dream,' said Tiana.

'Final question. Let's end on a positive note. Pink or black?'

Tiana laughed at that.

'Pink, always pink.'

'Tiana, that was fantastic! Cut.'

Tiana had spoken as truthfully as she could. By the time they were done, she was exhausted and emotionally taxed. Reliving everything and talking about it hadn't been easy but she'd gotten through it. Relief was beginning to pour over her. She was no longer concerned about the consequences of her interview. There was bound to be a backlash but she felt she was equipped to handle it by now.

That's when she heard voices cheering out her name and someone hooted loudly. The lights were still on so she couldn't tell who it was but judging by the amount of noise and footsteps scuffling on the wooden floors of the auditorium, Tiana could sense there were lots of people present in the hall. When Ram turned off the big lights on the stage, she found all her friends standing near the front row, looking up at her and cheering her on.

Twenty-Eight

*'Holding onto anger is like drinking poison and
expecting the other person to die.'*

—Buddha

'What's going on?' asked Ina, looking at her uninvited audience.

'We knew Tiana was giving her interview today, so we decided to come and support her,' said Bella.

Tiana was closely observing the group of about 20 people standing in front of her. She could believe that Ronit, Bella, Sara, Aliya, Aditya, Jasmine and Diya had perhaps come to support her. Even Karam and Tea's presence made some sense considering the conversation she had had with Karam earlier. However, the presence of Savera, Leila, Zain, Aryan, Lilly and some other seniors didn't give her the feeling that they were there to support her.

'Really, Leila. That's why you're here? To *support* me?' asked Tiana pointedly, raising her eyebrows at Leila and Savera.

'Tiana, I'm so, so sorry. I mean, I don't even know what to say to you. You had every right to name each and every one of us because we were all there. Yet you didn't name us. I mean, I don't even know how to thank you!' exclaimed Leila with tears in her eyes.

Tiana was taken aback by Leila's tears. She didn't want to say anything to further aggravate Leila, so she looked away but then Savera began thanking her.

'Stop. I didn't take your names because I don't have proof

and getting all of you in trouble was never the point,' said Tiana, cutting off Savera.

'Yeah, we know that now. We came in when you were doing your mic check. All of us heard your entire interview,' said Savera.

'I'm so sorry for thinking you would name us,' said Leila. Behind her, Zain, Aryan and Lilly nodded their heads in unison.

'Tiana, honestly, we came to hear your interview because we were worried. My boyfriend Parth had told me that he and all his friends thought that you were going to name them and get them in trouble. So I had to come and listen to what you had to say. I realized that until I heard you speak just now, I hadn't even thought of things from your point of view. You didn't name anyone. Thank you so much for that,' said Lilly.

'Why does your boyfriend think that I want to get him and his friends in trouble? I have done nothing to make people believe that I would do such a thing,' stated Tiana.

'Didn't you tell Pia that you would get them all in trouble?' asked Lilly.

'Your boy Parth is friends with Zoravar?' smirked Tiana.

Lilly just nodded.

'Pia pissed me off and I snapped at her. I'm in this mess because of Zoravar and his dad. If anyone deserves trouble, it's their group. Lilly, you can do better than hanging out with them,' scoffed Tiana.

'Zoravar is the guy you were mentioning in your interview?' asked Ronit angrily.

'He caused your suspension?' asked Karam furiously.

Tiana nodded.

'Not just that, throughout the term, Pia and Zoravar and their friends have been messing with Tiana. Everything she said in the interview is true. They have been bullying her,' said Bella, filling everyone in about how Tiana's term had gone on so far.

'T, I had no idea you were going through all this,' said Leila in a quivering voice.

'Tiana, why haven't you spoken up about all this till now?' asked Karam, looking concerned.

'That Zoravar and his friends are such asses. We've been dealing with their nonsense for so long as well,' said Aryan.

'They think, just because they're a year older, they have a permanent right to keep bullying us. I'm so done with taking shit from seniors,' said Ronit.

'Karam, they are your batchmates. Why can't you say something to them?' asked Leila, looking at her brother.

'You think I can control my batchmates?' asked Karam, raising his eyebrows.

'You're so proud about being the head boy, aren't you? Last term, you tried to intimidate me because of your title. You can only intimidate your juniors, like me? Can't control your batchmates?' asked Ronit aggressively.

'I'm not delusional. My batchmates won't listen to me just because I'm head boy. Prefects can only discipline juniors because juniors are actually scared of us. My batchmates can only be controlled by the teachers. They don't listen to the prefects. Zoravar won't stop tormenting Tiana just because I ask him to. I've known him since class five and we've never been friends. In fact, we are constantly fighting with each other,' said Karam.

'Really?' asked Bella.

'House rivalries. Every time Karam and Zoravar play a basketball or a soccer match against each other they walk out of it with bruises and muscle pulls. I've helped him ice his shoulders so many times,' said Tiana.

Karam and Ronit stopped and looked at her strangely.

'What? I dated you for a year. I remember stuff. Geez.'

Karam gave her a soft smile, while Ronit and Tea looked uncomfortable.

'I hope you at least won these matches against him,' said Ronit grumpily.

'Every single time,' beamed Karam proudly.

Ronit rolled his eyes in response.

'Oh my god, Tiana!' exclaimed Leila.

'What?'

'Maybe that's why he hates you even more than usual. He hates Karam, and you were dating him. Then you got caught and—'

'And it became worse than ever,' said Karam slowly, realization dawning on him.

'Guys, no,' said Tiana.

'Maybe it's my fault, T. Maybe he actually hates you more than usual because of me, and is using this as an excuse to trouble you even more,' said Karam in an apologetic tone.

'Karam, chill. That guy is a goon. I really don't think it's so premeditated, I just happened to be someone they could all blame for ruining their senior year and they just went with it. Don't make this about yourself,' said Tiana.

'Tell me the names of the boys from our class who are doing this to you. I'll deal with those idiots, at least,' offered Aditya.

'I don't think any of you can really help me out with what I need,' said Tiana.

'What do you need?' asked Savera.

'This idiotic bullying doesn't bother me. It's almost stopped anyway, but the people who caused it are going to walk away from this without any consequences and that really stings,' said Tiana sadly. Suddenly she felt very tired and she sat down on the edge of the stage, her legs hanging over the edge.

All her friends surrounded her. Maybe it was the dejection in her voice and her body language that pulled everyone to her.

'Maybe we can talk to the senior mistress?' asked Leila, timidly looking around the group.

'What will you say to her?' asked Aryan.

'I can't do it alone. But the general idea is that we all speak up together and tell her that we know about Zoravar's dad's involvement and if they don't take action, we can—'

'We can what?' interrupted Lilly sharply.

'Revolt together,' said Leila hesitantly.

'Revolt?' laughed Tiana. She wasn't alone in breaking into laughter; pretty much everyone knew that it was a silly idea.

'We can do *something*,' said Leila, holding her ground.

'Leila, the only thing we can do is confess our own involvement. We have to say that we were all there with Tiana that night. Only then will they take us seriously because they are so touchy about the school's reputation and they won't want this to come out. So do you have the guts to speak up? I do. I'll say I was there if it helps Tiana,' said Ronit.

'That's because you are in love with her. I'm sorry, I would like to help but I'm not confessing about being there,' said Lilly.

'Lilly, if all of us confess collectively, they won't really take any strict action. They can't suspend 25 people together. I mean it's the least we can do for T. She could have ratted us out but she didn't and honestly—'

Tiana interrupted her, 'Leila, be realistic please. You won't manage to convince 25 people to confess for me. The seniors in particular hate me and definitely won't want to help. Even now, nobody around us wants to help and it's okay. I don't expect it either.'

'Hey, come on, Tiana, if it helps, I'll confess too,' said Bella.

'Me too,' agreed Sara, her words echoed by many others including Aditya, Diya, Savera and Aryan.

'If Tea and I had been there, we would have confessed too,' said Karam.

Bella scoffed.

'What?' asked Karam pointedly.

'Your precious Tea was there too,' smirked Bella, looking at

Tea, who turned red.

'Bella, don't. Let it go,' said Tiana.

Bella scoffed at Tea again but raised her hands in resignation.

'What's going on?' asked Karam suspiciously, looking first at Tea and then Tiana, and when none returned his gaze, he turned to Bella.

'Ask her,' said Bella, motioning towards Tea.

'Guys, focus on the real problem please. Tiana, eight of us have already agreed to confess. Maybe some more will agree if we try. Even if 10 of us take a stand, the school won't suspend us. It's worth a shot,' said Leila optimistically.

'Guys, thank you so much for saying you'll do this for my sake but please, it really won't help and you guys could get in more trouble. And the people who should actually get in trouble, like Zoravar and Pia, will still walk away unaffected. So please, let's forget this idea.'

No one pushed for it after that because there was truth in what Tiana had said. Besides, their sense of friendship had prompted them to say that they would help, but no one actually wanted to get into this situation again. Especially having dodged it once already. Most of them had expected Tiana to name them during her interview, and perhaps the relief mixed with a sense of obligation had pushed them to stand up for her. However, it was a deeply flawed plan and wouldn't have made an iota of difference in clearing her name.

Nonetheless, she was touched that her friends had come up with this idea. It was unexpected and this gesture made her feel better. Nothing can compete with the feeling of being loved enough for people to stand with you and support you. Deep within, she had given up on her friends and after months of dealing with bullying on her own, she had begun to feel alone. For obvious reasons, she had kept Ronit at arm's length and even though she had forgiven Bella, she didn't fully trust her yet.

Leila and Karam had been the closest to her for many years and without them, she had felt adrift and alone. Now all of them were here, wishing to correct what had gone wrong. Tiana had held on to her anger so strongly for so long that she no longer had the energy to keep it going. And not when her friends were finally attempting to salvage the situation. Their reputation was the reason why they had turned their backs on her and yet, somehow, now they were willing to put it at stake for her sake.

All of them hung out together for a little while in the auditorium. Tea and Karam had gone off to a corner and were having a dramatic argument, no doubt because of Bella's earlier comment. No one could hear what they were saying, but everyone was trying hard to read their facial expressions. Tiana didn't want to tell everyone why they were fighting. If they all found out that Tea had gotten them caught that night on purpose, then they would have made her life a living hell in school. Tiana, having suffered bullies for so long, understood what a burden it could be and so she didn't tell anyone. If Karam had finally found out about his girlfriend's involvement, then Tiana honestly felt that it was for the better.

Tiana knew that things would always remain formal with Karam but she was glad that with the rest of her friends, it was like slipping into an old pattern. They were all laughing and making plans to get back at Tiana's bullies. It was like old times again. Even better than old times because Tiana's new friends and old friends had finally broken the ice and were actually talking and hanging out happily. This had not been possible until last term, when Sara and Leila were constantly at each other's throat. Today, everyone was getting along. Ina hung out with them as well and found an opportunity to film some candid interviews about bullies.

For some blissful minutes Tiana felt that things finally might get better.

Then they got worse. Much worse.

Twenty-Nine

*'There is in human nature generally
more of the fool than of the wise.'*

—Francis Bacon

They were all climbing down the steps of the auditorium and as they reached the stone corridor Tiana saw a tall man walking towards them. He was an outsider and probably a parent, so the group wished him a good afternoon.

He didn't wish them back and instead asked, 'Which one of you is Tiana?'

'I am, sir. Can I help you with anything?' asked Tiana politely, taking a step forward.

He looked at her scathingly from top to bottom, making sure that even before he spoke, Tiana and the rest knew that he was angry. For what reason, who could say?

'Yes, you can help me with something. Tell me, how can you sleep at night knowing you are ruining innocent lives?' the man asked loudly.

Tiana was stunned, as was everyone else standing behind her. All the parents knew that if they ever had a problem with a student, they were supposed to talk to that student's house mistress or senior master and that it was only in their presence that parents could directly address the concerned student. They couldn't just enter the school and start yelling at students in the middle of the main classroom building.

Tiana didn't know how to react because she didn't know who this man was and why he was talking so disrespectfully to her. Maybe he had confused her with someone else? That's when she saw Zoravar, his friend Parth, Pia and three more of his friends walking towards them only to stop right behind the man. She realized that it was Zoravar's father she was standing in front of and suddenly she was filled with anger, but she forced herself to stay calm.

Zoravar tugged at his father's hand and when his father turned around to look at him, they began to have a frantic, hushed conversation. Tiana was quick as lightning. She turned around and saw Bella right behind her. She whispered in Bella's ear to run and tell Ina to quickly film the conversation secretly from top of the stairs. Bella moved fast without being noticed by the other party.

'Where did you send her?' whispered Leila.

'Shush,' Tiana had already turned back to look at her tormentors and she was trying to piece together what they were saying to each other.

'Dad, you can't talk to her here,' Zoravar was saying to his father.

'Just shut up,' Mr Singh said to his son sharply as he turned around and looked at Tiana again.

By then, the corridor was filled with lots of other students because it was time for their evening extra classes. The students anticipated a spectacle, so they stood there. Soon, a large crowd had gathered around the two groups facing each other. From the corner of her eye, Tiana saw Bella climbing down the stairs and she nodded her head slightly to confirm that Ina was filming. That's when Tiana began speaking.

'Sir, maybe you have confused me with someone else,' said Tiana calmly.

'Oh, you have made sure no one ever confuses you with anyone, haven't you? Bringing shame to your family and school and now you think you can just pass the blame on to my son! I am shocked that you are representing the school in this documentary. You had your interview today, didn't you? Tell me, did you blame your foolish actions on my son? I demand to see the tape,' said Mr Singh.

'Sir, I am only interested in getting justice for myself. I have not—'

'If there was any justice in the world, this documentary would be featured around good students like my son and not disgraceful alcoholic girls like you who have given a bad name to the school.'

'Sir, if there was justice in the world, then your son and 25 other students who were actually drinking on school campus would have been suspended. But we don't always get what we want, do we?' replied Tiana in her most mellow voice. This conversation was a performance for her. She wanted everyone to look at the video later and only see how respectfully and calmly she had conducted herself while talking to a thundering, irrational parent.

'This is too much. Do you have no sense of how to talk to your elders?' said Mr Singh. With every sentence, his voice rose higher, partly in disbelief because he hadn't expected Tiana to respond in such way.

'Sir, I don't understand what is wrong with stating facts. I was just at the wrong place at the wrong time but your son, along with many others, was actually drinking alcohol on school campus,' replied Tiana, maintaining her calm persona.

'Answering back to your elders, spreading lies and being disrespectful. Is this what they are teaching you in school these days?' thundered Mr Singh so loudly that his voice boomed across the corridor.

The juniors standing around them started to laugh and snigger. Zoravar decided to take matters in his hands and stepped in front of his father. He was aggressive and looked as if he wanted to rip Tiana's face off.

Instinctively, she took a step back. Karam stepped forward when he saw her move back. Now, Tiana was beginning to get a bad feeling. These two had gotten into too many fisticuffs in the past, and a physical fight at this point really wasn't going to work in her favour. This wasn't part of her plan. On top on everything else, Ronit pulled Tiana further back and went and stood next to Karam.

'Karam, Ronit, just stop!' yelled Tiana quickly. She was ignored by both of them.

'Get out of the way, Karam. I'm talking to that stupid bitch,' sneered Zoravar.

'Oi! Mind your language!' responded Karam.

Zoravar looked at Tiana and spoke directly to her, 'Why are you hiding now? You think you can disrespect my dad in front of all your friends and these juniors, and then just go and hide? Apologize right now!'

'She has nothing to apologize for, asshole,' said Ronit in a confrontational tone.

'Who's talking to you? Bloody junior, get out of the way,' said Zoravar.

At this point Ronit and Zoravar were nose-to-nose. Karam tried to pull Ronit back but it didn't work. Zoravar's other friends Parth, Rishi and Tarun decided to present a united front and stood next to Zoravar. In response to this, Aditya and Aryan stepped forward and joined Karam and Ronit. It had become a dramatic face-off.

'Why are you taking these juniors' side, huh? What about your batch loyalty, Karam? Why are you supporting this girl? You aren't even dating her anymore. That's probably the best decision you made in your life,' said Zoravar.

'Don't say anything about Tiana. You know that you're the one who's wrong, so watch it,' said Karam threateningly.

'Watch it? What will you do?' laughed Zoravar and then

suddenly he shoved Karam with both hands.

Karam wasn't expecting this so he lost his balance, staggering backwards onto Leila and Tiana.

Leila yelled out as Karam stepped heavily on her foot.

'Guys, stop it! We can talk this out. There's no need to get violent!' shouted Tiana angrily.

'I'm sorry, Leila, but please step back,' said Karam, looking at his sister.

Zoravar and his friends were sniggering now.

'What a loser! He hurt his own sister,' laughed Parth.

'Karam, you're good for fighting with girls only. You kids can't handle us,' said Tarun.

'You're pathetic. Who even made you head boy?' taunted Rishi, joining in the laughter with his friends.

Tiana knew exactly what these boys were doing. They had been doing the same thing to her for the past few months. They had been passive aggressively instigating her to get a reaction out of her but she had taken the high road every single time. She had become good at ignoring the reactionary words uttered carelessly by these aggressive losers. The boys in front of her were not like her. As head boy, it was hurting Karam's ego that his batchmates were talking to him like this in front of his juniors. Tiana figured as soon as Karam had stepped forward to protect her, that Ronit saw it as an opportunity to do the same. Ronit had been competing with Karam ever since the last term and it really was one of his most unattractive qualities. Aditya and Aryan were just doing what boys do, which was to support their friends in case of a fight.

Tiana tried one last time, she ran and stood between the two groups of boys and spoke to Ronit and Karam, 'Please don't create a scene. I'm handling this my way—'

'What are you handling? They are not going to stop,' interrupted Ronit.

'Oh look, Tiana asked you to stop so you stopped? Does she have your remote control, Karam? Huh, can't do anything without someone else pushing your buttons?' laughed Zoravar.

Karam had probably reached boiling point because even before Zoravar could finish laughing, Karam punched his face. Then the corridor turned into a zoo.

In a flash, all the boys began hitting each other and Tiana found herself in the middle of this 'fustercluck'. She felt herself get rammed into Ronit so fast that this time, she was the one who lost her balance and ended up twisting her ankle.

'Tiana, step aside!' yelled Ronit, pushing her behind him.

'Are you okay, T?' asked Bella.

Tiana just nodded absentmindedly, observing the fight but there was a searing pain in her right ankle, so she sat down on the auditorium steps. As she watched from the sidelines, she couldn't help but notice that the fight looked ridiculous. All the juniors who were standing around laughing at the spectacle weren't wrong, the fight was sloppy, messy, funny and unnecessary.

In the movies, fights look like art—a visual, violent art which is performed for the sake of honour. In real life, not so much. It looked like these eight boys were tumbling around in a mosh pit. Lots of hands flailing about and bodies scuffling to and fro, no one seemed to hit anyone because they were all holding each other's arms, trying to stop their opponent from throwing a punch. As a result, they just looked like a big pile of limbs. Tiana almost wanted to laugh at the absurdity of what she was seeing.

'How can you laugh right now?' asked Savera, frowning at her.

Tiana hadn't noticed that she had actually broken into a laugh. 'Well, it's funny.'

'My boyfriend is fighting for you. He could get hurt!' said Savera, sounding hurt herself. She was looking anxiously at Aryan.

'I asked them to stop! I told them I'm handling it.'

'What do you mean "handling it"?' asked Leila.

That's when Ina moved downstairs from her hiding spot.

'She means that I was recording the entire conversation secretly. Quick thinking, Tiana!' said Ina, who was still recording the fight.

'Ina, Mr Singh will take your camera and break it. Look at these boys. Zoravar is insane. Go fast and protect the footage…'

'Oh, but this is just getting good,' said Ina.

'Ina, you have enough. Don't ruin it for us. I can't afford to lose these videos to this insane man and his son,' pleaded Tiana.

'Okay, okay. I'll be back soon!' said Ina, quickly walking away with Ram at her heels.

'So that was your plan?' asked Savera.

'Yeah, I was trying to show what kind of a man Mr Singh is, talking so horribly to a young girl on school campus. I was trying to change the story but now the story is this stupid fight, which doesn't make me look good at all!' said Tiana with exasperation.

Then the booming and angry voice of the senior mistress stopped everybody in their tracks.

Thirty

'Sometimes it is too late to win.
But it's never too late to lose.'

—Tom Watson

'Why am I not surprised that, Tiana, *you* are at the centre of this horrible incident?' said Mrs Banerjee after things had settled.

Tiana just shrugged. The senior mistress didn't like her nonchalance.

'Stand up when I'm talking to you. Do you have no manners?' yelled Mrs Banerjee.

Tiana had tried to rise before but the pain in her ankle had caused her to sit back on the steps. She tried to stand again but couldn't manage it.

'She hurt her ankle during the fight, ma'am. She can't stand. Zoravar pushed her,' replied Leila.

'And whose fault is that?' asked Mrs Banerjee meanly.

'Not mine,' replied Tiana.

'Excuse me?' asked Mrs Banerjee, narrowing her eyes.

'This fight is not my fault,' said Tiana adamantly.

'Do not test me right now, young lady. Two seventh graders got hurt, a *parent* got hurt! Your own friends got hurt. Do you know what it will look like if this incident reaches the media?'

It turned out that a lot of people had ended up hurt by the time the fight was over. Apart from several torn uniforms, Zoravar had a black eye, Karam a cut on his lips, Parth a broken nose, Aditya had a big blue bruise on his cheek and Ronit had bit his tongue badly and there was a lot of blood. Additionally, two junior boys who were watching from the sidelines became collateral damage just like Tiana and suffered some minor scrapes and bruises. Somebody also fell hard on Mr Singh when he had tried to separate the boys. Somebody pushed him back and his elbow went through a classroom windowpane and the glass cut his arm. All of them had been rushed to the school hospital.

Before leaving, Mr Singh had of course blamed it all on Tiana.

'Mrs Banerjee, I'm shocked that such a student is allowed to study at our prestigious school. Really, I have no words,' Mr Singh had said as he shot another scathing look at Tiana.

'Why, Mr Singh, what did she do?'

'She is disrespectful, she is rude and not to mention this documentary that she is using to spread lies about my son. How can you allow cameras on campus like this? The school committee needs to have approval of what is being shot here. How can a girl like this represent the school, especially after the incident that happened last term? And now this fight that she instigated. She is out of control and should be expelled. Innocent people get hurt around her and she doesn't even show any remorse. Look at her sitting there arrogantly.'

Mrs Banerjee had tried to pacify him a little and had sent him to the hospital with his son. Then, she had turned her attention towards Tiana.

'If this reaches the media, I'll be happy for once,' said Tiana, meeting the senior mistress's gaze.

The adrenaline rush she had experienced during the fight had subsided and she'd been left feeling week after the fight. Now the same vibrating rush was again pulsing through her body, her cheeks were burning up in anger. She wasn't scared but she knew she was stepping further into a mess she couldn't get out of easily. Answering back to senior mistress would have serious consequences.

The entire fight had been easily pinned on her. Meanwhile, the people who had actually been fighting were nowhere to be seen. The boys were at the hospital and weren't dealing with the immediate fallout of the fight. Besides, they were all hurt and would end up getting sympathy. Though Ina's video could prove that Tiana had tried to stop the fight, it wouldn't help much because people had gotten hurt.

'Ma'am, it's not Tiana's fault. She tried to stop it,' said Leila to the senior mistress.

'I suggest you keep quiet, Leila, unless you want to be in the same boat as Tiana. I don't care if she tried to stop it. She shouldn't have started it in the first place. Picking a fight with a *parent*, that is absolutely unacceptable! And then talking back to me; I will not stand this much disrespect,' said the senior mistress vindictively. It was enough to shut Leila up.

'But, ma'am...' began Aliya, however she was interrupted quickly.

'I suggest you all pick your friends carefully. Standing up for Tiana is only going to get you all into hot water right now. I will make sure of it,' said the senior mistress, looking at Leila, Bella, Savera, Sara, Lilly, Aliya and Diya, one by one.

'Ma'am, it's not fair to blame it all on Tiana,' said Bella.

'Don't tell me what's fair and unfair. Tiana has gotten into a habit of instigating people and has made it her life's purpose to bring ill repute to this school. You expect me to believe that the head boy, who happens to be one of the most level-headed students in school, just decided to get involved in a fight including juniors and a parent, on his own? I know he was dating Tiana and has a soft spot for her. It's because of her that all this happened. So who should I blame? Tiana, who is always involved in this kind of behaviour, or Karam? Even for that matter Zoravar, Aryan,

Ronit and Aditya have always been well-mannered boys. They have never been involved in this sort of rubbish. So tell me, who is wrong here?'

Tiana rolled her eyes at the senior mistress, 'I think you have forgotten that except Karam, all the boys you just named had been caught drinking on campus just last term. You have started believing the lie that you projected to the parents, the school board and the media. Sure, you put the blame on me, but you can't whitewash the truth. I wasn't alone that night. Very conveniently, you and many others in school have forgotten that,' said Tiana, standing up in anger; however, once again, she had to sit back down because of the pain. She was beginning to realize that she might have really hurt her ankle during the fight.

The senior mistress looked stunned. She didn't know how to respond because she had done exactly what Tiana had said, she had forgotten about the boys' involvement. She opened and shut her mouth a couple of times but said nothing. Seeing this, the girls exchanged looks with each other. In so many years of being at school, nobody had managed to shut the senior mistress up in such a way. Bella smiled at Tiana. Savera mouthed 'wow'. Sara winked and Aliya gave a discreet thumbs up.

Finally, the senior mistress recovered and continued her rant. She completely ignored everything that Tiana had just said and blamed the documentary as a bad influence.

'Your documentary is cancelled this very second.'

'I think Ina was pretty much done. She has some very interesting things to show the world about our awesome school,' said Tiana.

'She will have to take our approval before showing anything about our school,' said the senior mistress.

'Actually, while taking permission from the school administration, Ina made them sign a waiver that the content she shot on the campus would belong to her, that means it's her property and she does not need your approval. This is not her first documentary. She came prepared,' replied Tiana smugly.

'It's all gone to your head, Tiana, if you think you can get away with talking back to a parent and, above all, to me. This nonsense is done. I'm absolutely certain that you instigated this fight today for your own attention-seeking behaviour. There will be serious consequences. I'm going to call your parents and by tomorrow, the headmaster will take a decision regarding your behaviour and if you deserve to even be in this school.' The senior mistress turned around haughtily and stormed off.

'What have you done, T?' exclaimed Leila.

'Finally, I did what felt right,' replied Tiana.

'But now you've made her so angry.'

'So what? It's nothing new. Anyway, I think I need to go to the hospital,' said Tiana.

'Yeah, we should go and check up on the boys,' said Savera.

'I don't really care about the boys, I need to go and get my ankle checked. I can't even stand,' said Tiana.

'Oh, is it bad?' asked Sara.

In answer Tiana stood up shakily and tried to take a few steps but the pain was too intense and she cried out as she sat back down.

'I can't walk.'

'I guess we need a stretcher,' said Bella.

Thirty-One

'What a Day may bring a Day may take away.'

—Thomas Fuller

'The good news is that it's not too serious. You've been luckier than some of the boys involved in that fight. You have a minor hairline fracture in your ankle. We'll fix you up with a splint and you'll have to use crutches for a few weeks to keep the weight off your right foot. Your ankle will heal fully in about 4–6 weeks,' said the school doctor.

Tiana was in the doctor's office. All her friends had been waiting outside. The doctor called them in to help Tiana.

'Girls, come in. Take your friend to the girls' ward and the nurse will fix her up with a splint.'

Using Bella and Sara for support, Tiana dragged herself to the ward. She caught a glimpse of the boys' ward as they were crossing it and she saw Ronit, who rushed out to help them.

'What happened?' asked Ronit. His tongue was swollen and nobody could understand a word of what he was saying. In fact, Bella, Sara and Savera began laughing at him but he rolled his eyes at them and took Tiana to an empty bed in the ward.

'Seriously, are you okay?' asked Ronit, but once again it sounded like gibberish and Tiana joined in her friends' laughter.

'Quiet!' yelled the nurse who had come with a splint for Tiana.

Ronit motioned with his hands to ask what was going on, so Bella filled him in about Tiana's injury.

Ronit didn't say anything for the fear of being laughed at

again but he looked sadly at Tiana to show his concern. Tiana could only manage a shrug and a bland expression in response. Ronit slumped his shoulders and walked away dejectedly.

'Aren't you being a bit harsh to him?' asked Sara.

Luckily, the nurse interrupted them and began giving instructions to Tiana. Finally, she handed her a pair of old crutches. Using them was a very strange experience. Leila laughed and said that Tiana would get used to it in a few days. Leila had experience with crutches because after the drunk driving accident, she had used them for almost three months. The girls finally left the ward, at a very slow pace, thanks to Tiana's restricted movement, and reached the courtyard outside the hospital, where they met Karam, Ronit, Aryan and Aditya—all of them in their wounded glory.

'You got hurt as well. Join the gang,' laughed Karam.

Tiana frowned at him.

'What's wrong?' asked Karam, looking confused.

'What's right?' shot back Tiana.

'I don't understand, are you mad at me or something?' asked Karam.

Tiana just rolled her eyes.

'Why are you being like this? We were standing up for you and helping you out,' said Aryan.

'Oh, is that what you did? Thank you so much,' said Tiana sarcastically.

'Guys, you don't know what happened okay. Banerjee blamed the entire fight on Tiana. She is making plans to expel her,' said Leila seriously.

The four boys looked confused upon hearing this news. Ronit yelled something in anger although it sounded more like a loud jumble of sounds.

'You all had your fight, satisfied your male egos for wanting to look like heroes. Karam, you probably even settled some of your old scores with Zoravar. And after everything was done, you all happily walked away without facing any consequences. The senior master will maybe scold you all for two minutes and then he will say something ridiculous like "boys will be boys" and all will be forgiven. Everybody will believe Mr Singh, who claims that I instigated the fight because he's a parent. In reality, I tried to *stop* the fight and in the end, only I will be left to suffer the consequences, just like last year,' said Tiana.

'We didn't exactly walk away without consequences, okay?' said Aditya.

'Yeah, we all got hurt too for your sake. Look at Karam's lip and Ronit can't even feel his tongue,' said Aryan.

'Am I supposed to feel sorry for you all now? I told you guys multiple times to stop! Did anybody listen to me?' asked Tiana, raising her eyebrows.

'First, you had a problem that we didn't stand up for you and now you have a problem that we did. Make up your mind, Tiana. We did this for you,' said Karam angrily.

'Oh, I was just *waiting* for you to say that. You did this for me, Karam? Seriously? If you wanted to do something for me, then you should have started by listening to me when I told you to stop. That's how I got hurt; because I was trying to protect you all from making a mistake. This fight is not on me. Zoravar pushed all the right buttons to get a reaction from you and you fell for it,' said Tiana angrily.

'Excuse me?' asked Karam.

'You fell for his stupid tricks. He is the one who instigated you and you fell for it, Karam. Ronit, I don't even know why you jumped in. I don't know what you are trying to prove to me or other people, but your rash decisions have created too many problems for me in the past and, yet again, here we are. Aditya and Aryan, you jumped in for the sake of your friends. You could have stopped them but you didn't because the truth is that none of you like Zoravar because he is your senior and he treats you all like shit. You saw this as a way to put him in his place. None of this was done for me. All I get out of this is blame,' said Tiana. She wanted to storm off in anger, but couldn't as she was using crutches. Instead, she walked away limping, and her friends followed her.

Thirty-Two

'The journey is the reward.'

—Taoist Proverb

Could it be so easy? It seemed *too* easy. Surely, big problems in life could not be solved so easily? How is it that something small can suddenly become so big and on the other hand, a big problem can be solved so *easily*? Why was life so ridiculous and so full of surprises? Yet, thank god for those surprises because they made life worth it. They could be an ordeal, a lesson or a reward. And for once, Tiana was getting her reward. She had not thought in her wildest dreams that she would be able to clear her name. She had resigned herself to the fact that her image would always remain a little tarnished as far as school was concerned. In fact, she was probably going to get expelled after how she had spoken to the senior mistress. Now, suddenly, she had a chance at redemption.

Bella was at the root of both these extremes for Tiana. She had caused all of Tiana's problems and now it seemed she had the means to solve them too. Back in the dorms, after the hospital, Tiana had been lying down on her bed. Her intention was to get some sleep but everything that had happened kept her tossing and turning. In her mind, she kept replaying one infuriating scene after another and felt a myriad of emotions. She felt helpless, angry, sad and weak, all at the same time. Nothing felt right and there was nothing she could do about it either. If there was a lesson in here about growing up, then Tiana didn't want to learn it. That's when Bella came and sat on her bed.

Tiana looked at her and Bella saw tears running down Tiana's cheeks.

'Hey! No crying, okay? We'll fix this,' said Bella gently, wiping away Tiana's tears.

'I don't think we can.'

'I know what you mean. This is quite a situation you are in and I don't think there is anything you can say at this point to get out of it. Which is why I'm going to help you,' said Bella.

Tiana smiled, 'Is that right? What will you do?'

'Okay, promise that you won't get mad at me for this,' said Bella.

Tiana sat up on her bed and looked cautiously at Bella, 'What did you do?'

'It's what I didn't do and I guess I should have done it sooner. I'm doing it now only because I see no other way to keep you in school. I mean, even if the boys go and talk to Banerjee and assume the blame, she will still find a way to blame you because at this point she's made it her personal vendetta. She'll keep bothering you until you put her in her place,' replied Bella.

'Easier said than done.'

'It might be easily done. Please, just don't hate me for not telling you before,' pleaded Bella.

'Okay. I won't,' said Tiana curiously.

'Give me your hand,' said Bella.

Tiana put out her palm and on it, Bella placed a memory card and a pen drive. Tiana blinked at the contents on her hand blankly for two seconds and then it clicked. Her heart rate began to rise and her eyes bulged out.

'No way,' said Tiana very slowly.

'Yes,' said Bella.

'You've had all the photos from that night all this time?' asked Tiana in a quickening voice. She sounded a little hurt because Bella had seen her suffer for so long and yet hadn't told her about the photos before.

'I'm sorry, Tiana. I thought about giving it to you many times. It's just... I got scared because my dad has finally forgiven me for the accident last year and things have been good at home. If my parents found out that I was drinking in school, it would have ruined everything. I'm sorry I freaked out,' pleaded Bella, desperate for Tiana to understand her point of view.

'Okay, so what changed? You could still get into trouble,' said Tiana.

'While giving my interview, I realized that I've always been competing with you. That's what caused all the drama with Ronit last year. Even before Ronit, I was jealous of you because everybody liked you more and even respected and trusted you. I wanted to ruin that for you and I succeeded but as a result, I felt horrible. Bringing you down didn't elevate me. People still didn't like me any better. I realized that genuinely being good and not wanting to hurt other people is the only way to gain respect. It's a vibe that you can't steal but have to create for yourself. Tiana, you are like that. You've never actually wanted to hurt people on purpose. You don't lie or cheat. No matter what other people think or say, you stay honest and say what's on your mind. I realized after you got suspended that I can't compete with that. Instead, if that's what I want, then I should aim to become like that.'

Tiana was stunned. This was the last thing she would have expected Bella to say to her.

'Bella, I'm not like that. Trust me. No one is, or can be, good all the time,' said Tiana.

'I know, I know. I don't intend to *always* be good. That would be too boring. But, I'm finally doing what feels right to me by giving you the photos. It's fair. Give them to Ina for her documentary,' said Bella. Then she went to her cupboard and got a camera.

'Here, put the memory card in and see the photos,' said Bella.

There they were. On the tiny screen of the digital camera, Tiana saw all the pictures from that night. They implicated a lot of people. All her friends for sure, several more people from her batch and many more seniors who could clearly be seen drinking on campus in those photos. This was her proof. She could so easily get everyone in trouble. All the gossip and rumours about her would instantly stop because she could provide everyone with a brand-new excuse to talk about the people in the photos instead.

'You think I should give it to Ina?' asked Tiana.

'Well, what else can you do?' asked Bella.

The first thought in Tiana's mind was to give the photos to Ina, who would put them in her documentary. If people and parents saw that 25 others had also been involved that night along with Tiana, then no one would be able to blame her and how her parents raised her. After all, they were just teens being teens. Teens drink sneakily. No matter what school or city or country they are in, teens behave in the same way. The adults don't need to make such a big deal out of these things. It's not the end of the world.

She began to think about the consequences of giving the photos to Ina. Did she really want Bella and Ronit and despite everything, Leila and Savera, to go through what she had gone through? Their parents would also get involved and she didn't want them to feel the way her parents had felt. That wouldn't help her situation any way. She had said during the interview that she didn't want revenge. She had meant it then and she meant it now.

Revenge was a disgusting cycle. If she took her revenge now, then this cycle wouldn't end. Her friends would also find a way to retaliate in the future. She was not scared of the retaliation as much as she was scared of not being better than them. If she behaved just as Bella and Leila had behaved towards her, then it would mean Tiana had not learned anything from her ordeal. She wanted to place herself above such awful high school behaviour. She wanted to be better than the other people of her age. The awful teen age.

At the same time, Ina had been the only one who had stood up for her and Tiana didn't want to betray Ina's trust by not telling her about the photos because the photos would really help in strengthening Tiana's section in Ina's documentary. It felt like Tiana was suddenly stuck in an impossible situation. Something wonderful had happened but now it seemed like there was no right way to proceed with this wonderful new information.

So it was *not* so easy after all. That was a more familiar feeling. Still, she had to act soon because the senior mistress was surely making a case to the headmaster to expel her. This was her time to respond and she was dead set on doing so. What she needed to decide was exactly who did she want to respond to, who had hurt her the most and left her to fend for herself despite knowing that she was not the only one to blame? Who had made the mistake of underestimating her? Who had tried to squash her spirit as much as they could? The senior staff was to be blamed because it knew the truth. Yet, the senior mistress was the one Tiana planned to put in her place.

Thirty-Three

*'The first reward of justice is the consciousness
that we are acting justly.'*

—Rousseau

The first thing Tiana did the next morning was to go to the senior mistress's office. She skipped her first class to do it, but it was important. She knocked on the door.

'Come in.'

'Good morning, ma'am,' said Tiana, limping into the office.

When Mrs Banerjee saw it was Tiana, her face flared up in anger.

'I have nothing to say or hear from you. The headmaster will soon be taking a decision regarding you. Until then, I don't want to see you,' said the senior mistress through gritted teeth.

'Ma'am, I have to discuss something important with you.'

'I'm sure you just want to grovel for leniency. That is not going to happen.'

'Sorry to disappoint you but I'm not here to grovel. I'm here to tell you that I have photos from the night when everyone was drinking in school,' said Tiana promptly.

This made the senior mistress look up from her papers quickly. 'Excuse me?'

'By some strange luck, I have them. It implicates all of the students from that night. Many of them are seniors and their last term could be ruined. Including your favourite, Zoravar,' said Tiana smugly.

'Who gave them to you?'

'That's not important.'

'How do I know that you're not lying?'

Tiana put a pen drive on the table and said, 'You can see for yourself. I have the original memory card and I have them saved on various other pen drives too.'

'Why are you telling me this, Tiana?'

'To tell you my demands. If they aren't met by the school, then I will give these photos to Ina and she will make it national news.'

'Your demands?' asked Banerjee, raising her eyebrows.

'I want the school to officially apologize to my parents for wrongfully suspending me. I want an official letter from the school. I want the headmaster to make an announcement in front of the entire student body during assembly, telling them that the school management was wrong in how they treated me. Additionally, I want you to make a similar statement to the same newspaper that printed the news of my suspension. Ina will get a chance to finish shooting the rest of her documentary.'

The senior mistress stared at Tiana quietly for a few seconds.

'That is impossible, the headmaster will never agree to this. We want to avoid being in the news, Tiana, especially for such things. This is in the past.'

'It's not in my past. It's in my present,' said Tiana.

'Do you really want to embarrass your school like this, Tiana? Have you no respect for this institution?'

'I have a lot of respect for my school and its history. What I don't have respect for is how it's being run today. With all due respect, ma'am, changes need to be made. The way teachers talk to us, either scolding us too much or not saying anything at all to the ones who deserve it, is messed up.'

'You think it's so easy running a school? You think you can teach us? You will teach me? You will teach the headmaster?' asked the senior mistress furiously.

'I don't think I can teach you anything. You should know what's right yourself. If you don't know yet, then no one can teach you.'

'How dare you, Tiana? I will not tolerate this behaviour!' yelled the senior mistress angrily.

'I'm not saying anything wrong, ma'am. I know I'm right and that is why I'm not raising my voice or screaming. I'm not misbehaving. I'm speaking up for myself and for what I think is right. If you want, I can say this in front of the headmaster too. I can stand in front of the entire school and say this proudly. I am right,' said Tiana calmly.

'You know why you were suspended. Your singular photo was put up on social media, and parents and the alumni council forced the school to take some action and make an example out of you.'

'I'm a person, not an example. You dehumanized me by disregarding how it would affect me and how my family and I would have to deal with it. You put the blame of 25 people on me and I have been dealing with it till today. None of those 25 stood up for me. Today, I am changing this narrative.'

'Tiana...'

'I think I will have to take this matter to the headmaster,' interrupted Tiana.

'Tiana, be sensible.'

'If you and the headmaster don't do as I ask, then I will give the photos from that night to Ina. She will include everything in her documentary and she will mention how the school lied about me, how the headmaster and the senior staff are controlled by outside entities like the alumni committee. You don't need to tell me the name of the alumni who forced you because I already know he is Zoravar Singh's father,' said Tiana.

The senior mistress was quiet.

'You should know that Ina's previous documentary was seen

by 10 million people. Compared to that, giving a statement to a newspaper that nobody reads anyway is a much better bargain for the school's reputation,' continued Tiana.

'I need to speak to the headmaster. I will talk to you after I have spoken to him,' said the senior mistress in a controlled voice.

Tiana knew she had her. There was nothing else that the school could do to hurt her. By some miracle, she was in control now.

Tiana was in a daze for the rest of her classes. She'd never been as bold as she was in the past two days. In the beginning of the summer, her instructor Rishi had asked her what she was doing to redeem her reputation. He had asked her if it was important to her, then why hadn't she taken any steps to change her situation. Why was she wallowing like she had no strength? She was happy to finally be doing something.

Teen years are an awful age because crucial realizations about being an adult happen during this time. As a kid, she remembered that when she messed up and made mistakes, they were presented to her as problems that adults in her life had to solve. So at the age of six, Tiana remembered believing that mistakes created problems and adults have to solve them. She assumed that as she would grow older, she too would make fewer mistakes and solve more problems. Realizing that adults screw up and make just as many mistakes as children and that she too would do the same as she grew up was a difficult thought to get accustomed to because it was scary. The teen years are awful enough as it is without having to add such heavy realities into the mix.

Now nearing the end of class 11, she realized that 'finding herself' was a quest that is still continuing and would go on for the rest of her life. She would constantly lose herself and come back stronger than before. It wouldn't always be easy. Sometimes, it would be extremely hard. That was the truth, the awful truth that she was starting to understand about life.

She had faltered for a little while but at least for now that was finally changing. She could feel it. The first step had been to say yes to Ina. Being in that documentary gave her the control she needed. There was nothing more empowering than making a decision and then watching it do wonders for you. Sitting passively and blaming your circumstances was the worst thing a person could do to themselves.

Sometime after breakfast, a junior girl interrupted Tiana's economics class with a message that the headmaster had called Tiana to his office. Everyone in the class 'oohed' and 'aahed' mischievously at hearing this because students were rarely called to the headmaster's office. Usually, the senior mistress or senior master dealt with student-related issues. The headmaster only got involved when parents were involved as well.

'What did you do?' asked Bella.

'You'll know soon enough,' said Tiana confidently.

'Quiet, class! Tiana, you are excused to leave,' said her teacher.

It was the first time Tiana had been to the headmaster's office. There had never been a need before this. It was a huge stone room, one of the oldest and perhaps the coldest offices on campus. The headmaster was sitting behind a massive wooden desk flanked by the senior mistress on his left and the senior master on his right. If the idea had been to overwhelm Tiana, then they had failed already because her confidence was soaring.

'Good morning, Tiana,' said the headmaster in a calm and dignified voice.

'Good morning, sir.'

'Have a seat.'

Tiana sat down.

'Mrs Banerjee told me about what you discussed with her earlier. I am very sorry to hear that you've had to suffer so much because of this situation. I wish it could have been avoided.'

'Thank you, sir.'

'However, I would like you to be reasonable about what you are asking.'

'This is me being reasonable, sir. I could just as easily have gone to Ina first and given her the photos but I'm not interested in revenge,' replied Tiana.

'Please think about your school,' said the headmaster.

'I'm doing that, sir. If photos of 25 of your students drinking on campus were to go public, it would be worse than anything for the school's reputation. I'm trying to avoid doing that because I don't want to ruin the school's image. However, I want to do what's best for me and my parents as well. So, I want an apology letter from the school, from you and the senior mistress. I want an official announcement in front of the entire school during tomorrow's assembly and I want you to give a statement to the newspaper that printed this news last term. Lastly, Ina will get a chance to finish her shoot on campus.'

'I see. You want me to apologize to you.'

'Yes, but more than anything, to my parents. You knew what you were doing when you signed the paper suspending me from school. Just like Mrs Banerjee, you too knew it wasn't all my fault. I also know that as the headmaster, you have to keep members of the alumni committee happy and that means doing them favours, like the one Zoravar Singh's father asked you to do by suspending the girl who had accidentally become the face of the incident that his own son had started,' said Tiana.

'You don't have proof of that,' said the headmaster.

'I don't need proof for that. Insinuation in such situations can work wonders. I have first-hand experience. On top of that, once Zoravar's photos from that night are made public, then everyone will believe your involvement to be true as well.'

The headmaster looked at the senior mistress and senior master who had been standing quietly throughout this conversation. He shook his head at them. Then, he turned to Tiana.

'Alright then. It seems there is no talking you out of this. I will make the announcement during tomorrow's assembly and send an apology letter to your parents and make a statement to the newspaper,' said the headmaster in a resigned voice.

'What about the documentary?'

'Yes, yes, Miss Mathur can finish her film.'

Tiana had never felt more triumphant in her entire life.

Thirty-Four

*'If you don't know where you're going,
you'll end up someplace else.'*

—Yogi Berra

For the rest of the day, her feet weren't touching the ground. In her mind, she was floating from class to class. In reality, she was using her crutches and limping from class to class but even the thought of the fight couldn't bring down her mood. Nothing could wipe the smile from her face. She didn't want to say anything to anyone yet. She didn't want to jinx it. She knew that the headmaster understood how serious she was about the apology. On that, she was immovable. So if he wanted to save the school from another scandal, then he would have to agree to her terms. There was no other way around it. Still, it was her secret to keep until the next day's assembly because that's when even Tiana would know for sure if she was going to get what she wanted.

At this point, she was unsure of what she would do if the headmaster didn't comply with her demand. She didn't know if she would actually give the photos to Ina or not. If she did, it would be disastrous for her friends and the school would forever be remembered in infamy. Her actions could single-handedly ruin the reputation of a 160-year-old institution. Granted, the incident in question isn't even such a big deal, underage drinking and sneaking in alcohol happen almost everywhere in the world but parents and media would make a mountain out of a molehill and they wouldn't let it go.

Tiana could imagine all the juicy headlines the national newspapers would concoct to bring down a 'posh' heritage school. It was why she had decided to not give Ina the photographs immediately because she had begun to feel that for Ina, this was just a story and she didn't care about her school and friends the way Tiana did and it was unrealistic to expect such considerations from Ina. Tiana knew that she was depriving Ina of a fantastic end to her documentary. Ina had been trying to sniff out a scandal since she had come to school and now Tiana herself was keeping a scandal away from Ina.

She felt guilty because Ina had helped her when no one was willing to and now, when it was her turn to help, she was not upholding her end. Tiana had thought of a compromise which she felt would give Ina a good end to her story and wouldn't affect her friends or her school. She just wished that her plan would work and also that Ina would agree to it. Tiana remembered what Rishi had told her in Mumbai at the end of the summer—if she ever reached a point where she felt she was being taken advantage of, then she should do something about it. Being scapegoated once by her school had been a huge lesson and she needed to remember what it had taught her: to never get used again or to at least try and stop it if she noticed it was happening to her again.

By mid-morning break, she had become fidgety and restless from keeping all this information to herself. When she saw Ina and Krish, it became even tougher to hold her tongue but she had to. She told Ina to attend assembly the next day with her camera.

'Why?' asked Ina curiously.

'Stuff will happen. I can't say what.'

'But...'

'Please, Ina. Don't ask me anything, just be there and record it because it's going to be important for your documentary.'

'You can't tell me?'

'I want to be completely sure before I say anything and I

won't be certain until it happens,' said Tiana.

Ina looked perplexed but she knew that Tiana wasn't going to divulge anything, so she gave up and left. Krish stayed back and seemed to be curious about Bella. So Tiana took him to where everyone was hanging out. For the past three or four times that Krish had come to school, he and Bella spent time together, getting to know each other. Apparently, they had clicked the very first time he visited, when Tiana had sent Bella with him to give a tour of the school. It was nice to see them getting along so well. It made Tiana feel less guilty for still having feelings for Ronit because if Bella was moving on, then it wouldn't be so awkward in the future.

Bella lit up when she saw Krish. They went and sat on a bench, a little away from the rest of them and were soon laughing and joking.

Ronit and Tiana exchanged a quick look when they noticed how happy Bella seemed when she was with Krish. At this point, Tiana and Ronit had unspoken mutual feelings for each other. Neither of them had any intention of confessing those feelings or acting on them in any way. A major reason for that was Bella. The games Tiana and Ronit had played with each other last term hurt Bella's feelings as well as theirs. Tiana thought that Ronit had come out of it unscathed, but that wasn't true. His guilt had eaten him up. In any case, neither Tiana nor Ronit wanted to revisit the feelings that had caused all this misery in the first place. Now, finally, it seemed that Bella was moving on and it signalled a change in Tiana and Ronit's dynamics too.

Despite everything, the three of them had somehow formed a friendship. It was strange because all of them had confused feelings; yet, without saying anything, all three of them were finally on the same page. Sara, Aliya and Diya had once asked Tiana how and why she was still friends with Ronit and Bella. Wasn't it awkward or strange? Tiana had told them the truth, which was that she didn't really think about how or why it had happened. She had known both of them independently for a really long time. Despite having differences with both of them, they had always stood with her. How could she then hold on to grudges and anger that had no reason to exist anymore? They were all friends because they were constantly making mistakes and learning from them together. They were growing together.

Having issues with her friends and understanding how to handle interpersonal relationships was one of the most important things that she had learned in recent months. This type of communication was so important and yet there was no class to actually teach this to anyone.

Tiana had learnt how to navigate the opinions of multiple people without taking anything personally. During her summer classes, she had heard such diverse opinions; some had taught her new concepts and some had made her roll her eyes and yet, there were some that had made her reflect on her own thoughts. She had been left emotionally enriched by the end of the experience. Maybe that was why she had so easily recognized that she was not liking the direction Ina was taking with her documentary. It *felt* wrong. She understood that her school's reputation was just as important to her as her own. She didn't want to turn selfish in the name of self-preservation. These two concepts are very different but so easily confused.

Similarly, she had decided to not let go of her friendship with either Bella or Ronit and she was glad that, in time, things had sort of worked out between them. For the most part, the awkwardness was gone and they had moved past their earlier mistakes by not lying or hiding anything from one another.

The look that Ronit and Tiana had just exchanged was loaded with a lot of unsaid feelings. Ronit had looked very strangely at her; he almost looked hurt. Tiana found this very confusing. Was he upset that Bella was moving on? For the longest time, he had maintained that he had no feelings for her anymore. Maybe she was misinterpreting something.

Hoping to keep things honest, she tried to find him later in the day, but Aditya told her that Ronit was staying at the hospital because his tongue was still swollen. He would get discharged in a day or two. He had to attend classes but other than that, he had been excused from all sports, hobbies and Founder's activities.

'It's that bad?' asked Tiana.

'Didn't you meet him today? He couldn't speak at all,' said Aditya.

Tiana felt bad that she hadn't been paying attention. She had been so caught up in her own problems that nothing else had mattered to her. She was excused from her mandatory sports session due to her fracture and she used that time to go meet Ronit at the hospital. Maybe earlier he hadn't been upset about Bella. He had looked hurt because he was in actual pain.

The doctor told her to be quick. 'Don't make him speak too much. He needs rest.'

Tiana nodded and went to find him. She told a junior who was entering the boys' ward to ask Ronit to come outside. A few minutes went by and no one came out. Tiana called out his name and there was no response. The junior showed up again and told her that Ronit didn't want to meet her.

'What? Are you sure you went to the right person?' asked Tiana perplexed.

'The guy with the swollen tongue? I went to him only,' said the junior boy.

'Tell him if he doesn't come out to meet me, then I'm coming in,' said Tiana.

Five minutes later, Ronit came out begrudgingly.

'Why are you being weird?' asked Tiana as soon as she saw him.

Ronit rolled his eyes and pointed to his mouth to remind her that he couldn't speak and motioned to go out into the courtyard.

'Right. Look, I'm hurt too, okay? I had to limp all the way here using the crutches and this hospital is on the farthest edge of the campus. And on my way back to the dorms, I will have to go up the hospital slope which happens to be the school's worst slope. I've reached a point where my ankle hurts less but my underarms are bruised because of the crutches.'

Ronit gave a faint smile but it was soon replaced with a grimace and he just shrugged as if to say that she had come on her own. He hadn't invited her.

'Seriously? All you can do is shrug? Can you write down what's wrong on a piece of paper or something? This is insane. I have no idea why you are suddenly behaving like this.'

Ronit shook his finger at Tiana's question.

'I finally have some good news for once and I haven't told anyone because I'm scared to jinx it, but I still came to tell you because I thought you would genuinely be happy for me. But I guess not, if you are going to be moody, then so can I,' said Tiana. She was hurt at Ronit's sudden and inexplicable change in behaviour.

Maybe Ronit realized how visibly upset Tiana was and before she could turn, he raised his palm to stop her.

'Just wait. I'm coming back with a piece of paper,' said Ronit, except the sounds that came out were nothing like it. Ronit rolled his eyes at Tiana's astounded look and mimed writing on his palm.

'Oh okay, paper, I get it,' said Tiana sheepishly.

Ronit left and reappeared a minute later with a notebook. He sat down on one of the benches in the courtyard and Tiana sat next to him, but Ronit moved away from her to the other end of the bench and began writing. So he didn't even want to sit *near* her. Fine, she thought with determination and moved to her end of the bench, leaving a massive gap between them. She sat there observing Ronit, who was too busy writing to notice her. She couldn't see the page but it was starting to feel like he was writing an essay at this point. What was going on in his mind? Maybe the gap between them on the bench had a bigger significance.

'You don't need to hide it. Aren't you writing to me? I will read it anyway,' said Tiana in bemusement.

Ronit shot her a look from the corner of his eyes and ripped out the page from the notebook, folded it and tore it up and put it in his pocket.

'What the hell are you doing?'

He began writing again and Tiana just sat feeling perplexed. She wished Sara or Bella had come with her and witnessed this behaviour. They could have confirmed if this was actually happening or if she was imagining it. She began laughing quietly at the absurdity of it all.

Ronit handed her the notebook and Tiana read the new page he had written on.

I'm glad you have good news. Hope it works out for you. I'm just going through some difficult things right now and I want to think about things properly before I discuss anything with you. Please don't get offended but I need space to figure things out.

'Umm...You are asking for space? We aren't *dating* Ronit. You can have as much space as you want. I came to check up on you as a friend but clearly that was a mistake. I also need peace of mind and friends who don't get moody without an explanation. So understand that from this point, I will also need space from you, so don't get offended by that either. Take care and goodbye,' said Tiana as she got up to leave.

Ronit quickly began writing in the notebook again but Tiana was done with his drama.

'Don't bother. I'm not going to read it,' said Tiana, limping away.

Thirty-Five

'What you become is more important than what you accomplish.'

—Proverb

Next morning in the chapel, during the assembly, the headmaster finally addressed Tiana's issue and did exactly what she had asked for.

'I would like to make an important announcement today. As you all are aware, last term there was a shameful incident when several students had been caught drinking on campus. Now, I hope such incidents never take place in this school again and to ensure that, strict measures have already been taken in this term. However, I regret to say that the school made a big mistake too because only one student, Tiana, was suspended for the incident. This was not fair to her or to her family and even though she was there, so were many others and punishing her alone was not right. So today, I want to apologize to her for everything she has gone through due to the school administration's decision to suspend her. I don't want anyone to ostracize her any further for this incident. I also don't want any teacher or student to treat her with contempt in regard to this incident anymore. Her parents will receive an official apology from the school office and going forward, I hope we never have to be in such a situation with any student again. So, please, all of you, behave well and respect your school and remember this institution's reputation is in your hands. If you go out into the world and you hear bad things being said about your school, remember they are saying bad things about your upbringing because you are a product of this school. You live here, away from your parents. This is where you are growing up and if you can't uphold the integrity of this institution, then you don't deserve to be here. Behave well and be good to one another. I have asked Tiana to tell me anytime she faces any kind of bullying. Such behaviour will not be tolerated here. Now, please rise for the school song.'

Tiana could sense her friends' excitement and agitation. They couldn't wait for assembly to get over. Bella, who had been right next to her, squeezed her hand tightly. Leila, Savera and Aliya were grinning from ear to ear. From across the aisle and a few pews ahead, Sara, Diya and Aditya kept looking back at her excitedly. Head boy Karam and head girl Pia were standing near the headmaster, facing the students. Karam gave Tiana a discreet thumbs up as Pia sulked. From the pew right behind her, Aryan patted her on the back and she heard a heavy voice say congrats. He still sounded funny. It was Ronit of course because he always sat right behind her. On other days, she would look back and chat with him before assembly but today she did not. Not once, and she wasn't going to either. Without even turning around, she responded to him with an impersonal victory sign.

As soon as the headmaster and the teachers left the chapel, all her friends rushed to hug her.

'OMG! Tiana this is amazing!'

'I'm so happy for you!'

'How did this happen?'

'Did you know this was going to happen?'

'Quiet! You are in the chapel. Go outside and talk,' said their prefect. She then looked at Tiana and added, 'I'm glad it worked out for you.'

Outside the chapel, Tiana told her friends everything.

'So you have photos of all of us from that night?' asked Savera.

Tiana nodded.

'I gave the photos to Tiana. I had them all along. I told her to give it to Ina,' confessed Bella confidently.

'You could have given us a warning that our photos were going to be public, Bella,' said Sara, frowning.

'You were all ready to help Tiana a few days ago. You said we should band together and pressure the school. I had a way to actually do that,' said Bella.

'Okay, relax everyone. I was never really going to give your photos to Ina. I just wanted the headmaster and senior mistress to think that I would if they didn't do as I asked. It was a bluff and it worked for me,' said Tiana.

'So now what will you do with the photos?' asked Leila.

'I won't give them to Ina for sure. You all and the school are more important to me than—'

'Than me and my film,' interrupted Ina.

Tiana turned back and looked guiltily at Ina. This was the hardest part because she had betrayed Ina to get what she wanted. Then she saw Ram standing behind Ina with his camera pointed towards Tiana and her friends. So Ina wanted a scene.

'I recorded your assembly just as you had asked. Is this supposed to be the end to my documentary? This lame apology that came out of no explanation.'

'There is an explanation, but you can't use it. I'm so sorry about this, Ina,' said Tiana softly.

'I helped you out, you know. I mean, Bella had an easy way to clear your name and yet she didn't help. I helped. I realize now that when I was interviewing her, I unknowingly encouraged her to help you out. She gave you the photos because of what I brought out in her.'

'Ina, please don't flatter yourself. I gave the photos to Tiana because I saw that she was in serious trouble after the fight. Everything had been blamed on her again and she really needed those photos to get out of it,' said Bella matter-of-factly.

'Bella, please. You and I both know how much you admitted in the interview. You had many suppressed feelings and thoughts and I made you voice them out. And because of that, you were able to deal with how you really feel and what you really want. Sure, the fight might have triggered you to finally act but you began thinking about it because of our conversation,' said Ina confidently.

'Ina, I'm really sorry, but I just don't like the direction you are taking your documentary in. I had initially thought that you wanted to capture real teen life but you seem to be sensationalizing my relationships with my friends with the entire love triangle nonsense. And you clearly don't care about my school or my friends. You would be happy to throw them all under the bus.'

'Tiana, why don't you understand? I had to make the story interesting, otherwise why would people want to watch a boring film?' asked Ina.

'I get it. You have your reasons and I have mine.'

'How am I supposed to end the film now? I need you to give me those photos to show how the school messed up under the pressure of an influential parent. I can make you look good on a national level, Tiana. Otherwise, all your suffering will amount to nothing. All you got was a lousy apology. Where is the emotional pay off? With my film, I can turn you into a young leader fighting against injustice.'

'Ina, you want me to betray my friends just so I can benefit on a personal level?'

'Isn't that what your friends did to you? They thought you were taking their place in the school, what with the teachers liking you more and you almost getting selected for the exchange programme instead of one of them? They shoved you aside when it was convenient for them and boohoo now, they feel bad but they didn't suffer, did they? You did, so why not get ahead when you are being given a chance?'

'You just said that I could be a young leader but what kind of a leader would I be if I'm not a good person first? Why would anyone want to follow me when they realize who I became for personal gain? Just because my friends behaved a certain way, does not mean that I have to reciprocate in a similar manner.'

Ina wanted to say something but stopped herself. She looked exhausted and irritated. So Tiana decided to tell her the plan she had come up with to help her end the documentary.

'I can't give you the photos of everyone because that would be a huge scandal for the school but I can give you Zoravar and Pia's photos from that night. Just the two of them. Not even their friends. Just them.'

Ina looked up sharply, 'How would that help my story?'

'I'm giving you your dramatic angle,' said Tiana.

'I don't get it. How?'

'With some help from my friends, I think I can instigate Pia and Zoravar into fighting with each other and giving up more information. You can secretly record them,' said Tiana.

'How will you manage that?' scoffed Ina.

'Pia is a loudmouth and Zoravar is temperamental.'

'So?' asked Ina.

'The day of my interview, Zoravar and his dad showed up together to try and stop me. That's how the fight broke out. How did Zoravar's dad show up out of nowhere? It happened because Pia told Zoravar that I was going to name him because that's what I had told Pia. The point is, it's a sensitive subject for Zoravar and his father. They don't want to shed light on the fact that Zoravar sneaked in the alcohol or the fact that his dad forced my suspension.'

'So, it's their weak spot,' said Bella.

'Yes, they become so engrossed in guarding their secret that they don't realize that by doing so they kind of give it away. His dad is guilty and that's why he created so much drama. I have a feeling that Zoravar is just like his dad. If we say the right things, he will erupt in anger and end up revealing the very things he wants to hide,' said Tiana.

'Okay, if you can get him to say something worthwhile, then I *might* forgive you, Tiana,' said Ina.

'Deal.'

Thirty-Six

*'He who sees little, always sees less;
he who hears poorly always hears something more.'*

—Nietzsche

The plan was simple. Ina gave Tiana a small digital camera which could record videos because students weren't allowed to keep phones on campus, but cameras were allowed and wouldn't get confiscated. All her friends agreed to help out. Sara was the one who would be secretly recording everything, but she needed to be surrounded by a lot of people to camouflage her. So Aditya, Diya, Leila, Savera, Ronit and Aryan were going to cover Sara to keep the attention away from her.

The rest was up to Tiana and Bella. They had to act natural because even a trace of artifice would give them away and they wouldn't be able to get the reaction they wanted. They decided to do this during the mid-morning break because Zoravar and Pia usually hung out in one of the empty classrooms when everyone was away at the break area. It was their dating/making out time. It was the perfect opportunity because none of *their* friends would be around to notice what Sara was up to and it was also the only place where Tiana and her friends could talk about Zoravar and Pia and also be 'accidentally' overheard by their targets, which of course *was* the plan. Their window was small because the break was for only 15 minutes.

During the English class, which was right before the break, Bella kept shaking her leg in nervousness.

'Oh God, Oh God… I hope I don't mess it up,' said Bella.

'Calm down. Stop overthinking, otherwise you *will* mess up,' said Sara.

'Yeah, please, you are starting to make me nervous. Just remember that they are annoying stupid people who deserve this,' said Tiana.

'Oh they totally deserve this. Okay. Okay. I'm just going to go through my lines again,' said Bella.

'Just be natural. You know the gist of what we are going to say. For the most part, we aren't even lying,' said Tiana.

'True,' replied Bella.

As soon as the break started, all of them rushed towards the class where Zoravar and Pia were hanging out. A bunch of them, including Sara, stood discreetly near a window that was open, ready to record the scene that was about to unfold.

Tiana and Bella stood a few steps away from the door of the classroom and they began talking. They didn't even need to be too loud because the entire corridor was empty and their voices would carry through into the classroom easily.

'Tiana, you got so lucky that the headmaster said sorry to you in front of everyone,' said Bella.

'It wasn't luck, Bella. The headmaster had to apologize because I made him,' said Tiana.

'How did you do that?'

'I told him that I knew Zoravar's dad had forced him to suspend me because he wanted to keep the attention away from Zoravar's involvement.'

'But how do you know that Zoravar's dad really did it?' asked Bella.

'Pia told me herself that Zoravar's dad got me suspended. She also told me that Zoravar was the one who sneaked alcohol into the school that night and he was the one who was forcing everyone, including her, to bully me,' said Tiana, hoping that this tactic was working on the two fools inside the classroom.

'Pia really told you all this?' asked Bella.

'Yeah and she said that she would help me out because she was scared of Zoravar and his dad. She gave me photos from that night that show Zoravar drinking on campus. She wanted him to get suspended. That way, she wouldn't have to break up with him because she's scared he will get aggressive if she tries to break up. I think I might give the photos to Ina to include it in her documentary. It will help Pia,' replied Tiana.

At this point, Pia ran out of the class and charged at Tiana angrily.

'Why the hell are you lying, you stupid bitch?' yelled Pia angrily.

Zoravar was right behind her looking as angry as he had on the day he had fought with Karam and Ronit. Tiana noticed that the rest of her friends, while covering Sara, had quickly begun moving towards where the confrontation was happening. As Tiana had predicted, Pia and Zoravar were too angry to even notice that there was a camera in their midst.

'Oh no, Pia! I'm so sorry. I didn't know you guys were here. I didn't mean to let slip your secret in front of Zoravar.'

'Tiana, I swear to god! Stop lying!' cried out Pia.

'Pia, just stop it. Stop lying! How does she know that I sneaked in the alcohol? Only you and Parth knew this! *You* told her. Parth would never betray me and you love gossiping! How does Tiana know the details of what my father did? She just dreamt it up? For the longest time, I couldn't figure out how she knew enough to blame me. You have clearly been talking about me and my dad! I told you to never discuss my dad and his connections and what he does with anyone! I told you those things in confidence!' yelled out Zoravar angrily.

'Zoravar, I promise you she is lying! I never said that I wanted to break up with you because I'm scared of you. Never, never!' pleaded Pia.

'Did you tell her about my dad? Don't you dare lie!' said Zoravar through gritted teeth.

'Okay… yes. It slipped out but only by accident when I was trying to stop her from taking our names during her interview.'

'It slipped out? Do you know how much trouble my dad could get into? He helped all of us—you, your friends, my friends and all the rest—by getting the school to punish Tiana and move on quickly. How ungrateful can you be that you just couldn't shut up about his involvement!' said Zoravar, sounding more hurt than angry at this point.

'I am so sorry. That was the only mistake I made and I will admit it but the rest of it is all lies, okay? I never told her that you sneaked in the alcohol. I kept that a secret. I never gave her any photos! She is completely lying about that,' said Pia taking Zoravar's hand in hers in an attempt to gain back his trust.

'Why should I believe you? Why would she lie for no reason?' asked Zoravar testily.

'Because I'm not lying for no reason. I'm lying for a good reason,' said Tiana, smirking.

Ever since Pia and Zoravar had rushed out of the classroom, the scene had played out even more beautifully than she had imagined. Sara had quite openly recorded the two of them because they had been so engrossed in their anger and passion to look at anything but each other. Now Tiana had everything on video. Plus, she had the photos as further proof. Ina would have a fantastic end to the documentary with a good dose of school politics and the resident bad boy getting what he deserved. Bella walked up to Sara and motioned her to hide the camera and then the two of them quickly walked away to hand over the footage to Ina.

'Excuse me?' said Zoravar with narrowed eyes.

'This whole scene that you just performed for me, we have recorded it. You yourself have confessed to everything and it's going to totally go in the documentary.'

Zoravar and Pia were stumped. Before either of them could recover from the shock and start spewing out their hatred, Tiana and her friends walked away. She was done with this chapter of her life. It was over.

Thirty-Seven

Ronit

'Our dilemma is that we hate change and love it at the same time; what we really want is for things to remain the same but get better.'

—Sydney J. Harris

Tiana had just managed to get Zoravar to confess and everyone was stoked about the plan having worked. Ina, who previously furious with Tiana, also seemed to have mellowed down after watching the footage Sara had recorded. They were all sitting behind the tuck shop, Ina was treating them for being a part of her film.

'Wow. You guys really came through for me. This is great. I can use this to end my documentary,' said Ina.

'I'm glad. And once again, Ina, I'm so thankful to you for helping me out. You are amazing and I can't wait till you finish editing and I finally get to see the film,' smiled Tiana.

'Oh, most of it has been edited already. There will be eight episodes for eight different teens, but I think I'm going to start with your story. So, your episode will release pretty soon,' said Ina.

'Wow.'

'Gotta start with a bang! That's what you brought, lots of bang! All of you,' said Ina.

'I've seen some parts of the edited film, it's looking pretty cool,' said Krish.

Bella was standing beside Krish, beaming at him. Ronit had been observing Bella and Krish for a while now and he knew that Tiana had noticed as well. The very first time he saw them hanging out together after the dance practice he had felt a slight pang. He wasn't jealous because he didn't have any romantic feelings for Bella but he knew that she had feelings for him and seeing her move on from him had caused the sudden jolt. He had felt replaceable. First, he found out that Tiana had kissed Krish in Bombay and then he saw Bella's interest in Krish and he couldn't stop himself from getting upset. Now after a couple of weeks, he was used to seeing them together. He loved Bella as a friend and wanted her to be happy.

But his insecurities were very much intact. If Bella could move on so easily, then there was nothing to stop Tiana from moving on as well. She could replace him too. In fact, Tiana had come close to doing just that in Bombay. A lot had been weighing on his mind and then the fight happened. He had just jumped into it without thinking but he had done so with genuine intent. He had just been trying to defend Tiana. When he had felt that she was in danger, he leapt to her side instantly.

He had never imagined that the fight would later get blamed on Tiana. That part wasn't fair but Tiana hadn't been fair to him either or the other guys who fought for her. Instead of appreciating that it had been done with genuine intentions, Tiana had just criticized them without even trying to understand their side of the story.

Maybe all the negative things that had happened to her had turned her negative as well. She couldn't help but see only the negative side to most situations. He hoped this was temporary and now that better things were finally happening to her, maybe some positivity would also return in her life. He wanted to clear the misunderstanding between them because his tongue had healed and he could finally speak without sounding like a mumbling idiot.

'Tiana, I need to speak to you,' said Ronit in front of everyone, which of course made all their friends go 'ooh' and 'ahh' to tease them.

'I wish I could record this conversation,' said Ina.

'But you can't. You have your story's end,' said Tiana, smiling at Ina to soften the blow.

'Yes, mom. Give her some privacy now,' smiled Krish.

'Oh sure. Tiana, enjoy your privacy. You have it for just a few more weeks. As soon as the documentary releases online, nothing about you will remain private. I'm going to do everything in my power to turn your episode into an internet sensation. You should know that it will be marketed as the "real life of an Indian teen girl in an elite boarding school". People will love you and hate you and judge you and along with you all your friends too. You all should prepare for it. And no matter what, don't read the comments section under the video. It's mostly competitors who troll to spread negativity. Genuine viewers don't even write comments. They watch the video and move on. Comments are mostly paid these days, so don't pay any heed to them.'

Everyone was quiet for a few seconds.

'You know I've been so engrossed in making this film that I forgot that people, or rather strangers are going to watch it as well. This is going to be interesting, isn't it?' asked Tiana reflectively.

'You have no idea,' smiled Ina and then she left.

Krish stayed behind to hang out with Bella and the rest of the group.

'Tiana, can we talk now?' asked Ronit, bringing the attention back to himself because Ina had side-tracked him earlier. He noticed that Tiana looked irritated at his insistence. She exchanged a glance with Sara and Aliya and both of them silently mouthed the word 'go' but Tiana was still hesitant. He wasn't going to give up either.

'Please, it's important. I know you are irritated with me but that day I didn't want to write anything down because I knew that if you took it the wrong way, then I wouldn't be able to defend myself. I was in no condition to speak that day. Today is the first day since the fight that I feel no pain, so can finally talk it out. You had also wanted to talk that day and here I am. I can finally do it,' said Ronit, looking straight into Tiana's eyes. He was confident about what he wanted to say and it didn't matter if Tiana agreed with his point of view or not. It was how he felt and he was going to tell her. What would happen between them after that was up in the air.

'Fine,' said Tiana. She got up and went in a corner with Ronit so that their friends couldn't eavesdrop.

'I was, and kind of still am, upset with you,' said Ronit honestly.

'Excuse me?'

'Your behaviour towards me after the fight was horrible. I didn't want you to get in trouble and it sucks that you did but your behaviour towards me and the other guys was unfair,' continued Ronit.

'Unfair? I was unfair?'

'Yes, you were. We did it to show solidarity for you. Just because it went wrong it doesn't mean that our intentions were wrong. At least you could have acknowledged that,' said Ronit.

'That fight was between Karam and Zoravar. It was a new regurgitation of the same fight they have had multiple times over the years. There was no need for you or Aryan or Aditya to jump into it.'

'Maybe, but Zoravar was attacking you. Karam was coming to your defence. I joined for the same reason.'

'I came back to your defence also. I came between you and Zoravar to stop you.'

'I know. I should have listened to you and I didn't. I admit I made a mistake. The fight was a mistake and if we had kept a cool head, it could have been avoided but that still doesn't change the fact that my intentions weren't wrong. You didn't even see that. You just flipped out on us,' said Ronit earnestly.

Tiana looked conflicted and was quiet for a while after that. So Ronit continued.

'I feel like I can never win with you. Last term, I knew what Bella was up to and I didn't help you. Even before that, I kissed you when I shouldn't have because I was dating Tea back then but I just fell so hard for you that I couldn't stop. I ruined your first kiss and you have never really forgiven me for that. Both of those times, you got mad at me and you were right because my intentions were always wrong. But I felt horrible each time and I have been working on changing my behaviour. I am really trying to do right by you. This time, I tried to help you with the best of my intentions and yet you blamed me. It was an epic fail and that hurts me too because I have been trying for months to be better but you aren't even noticing that,' said Ronit with hurt seeping into his voice. He had wanted to keep this conversation simple, so he had been trying to keep both his voice and expressions devoid of emotion. But now, he couldn't help himself.

'I've been dealing with a lot of things too. How am I supposed to notice what you have been feeling *internally*?' asked Tiana.

'If you ever spoke to me, you might have known. But you always avoid being alone with me. We only hang out when Bella and our friends are around us and I can't discuss this stuff in front of them.'

'Of course I've been avoiding you. Getting close to you always messes me up, Ronit. I can't help it if the first instinct I have when I see you is to just run away,' said Tiana defensively.

'Then what are we even doing, Tiana? If we can't communicate or be near each other, then what are we doing? You know that

I have feelings for you. I know you have them for me too. You can pretend but I know.'

'Oh, how do you know?' scoffed Tiana.

'I'm not oblivious to the way you behave around me. Or even the way your friends behave when I'm around. They are always winking at you and pointing at me when they think I'm not looking and on top of it all, the teasing.'

'I'm going to kill them,' muttered Tiana.

'What are we doing? Why can't we get this right?'

'I don't know, Ronit.'

'I have done as much as I can. I have messed up but I'm willing to make up for it, if only you give me the benefit of the doubt and trust me again. You should know how serious I am about this because I *transferred* to this school for you.'

'You're forgetting that I know if you hadn't left willingly, your old school would have expelled you,' said Tiana.

'I didn't need to leave my city and my parents and come to this insane military asylum. I came because I knew you were here,' said Ronit

Tiana was quiet.

'Tell me, do you believe me? What I just said? That I came here for you?'

'I don't know,' shrugged Tiana, trying to escape the question.

'Yes or no. Do you believe me?'

Tiana looked at Ronit, studying the expression on his face and finally she said, 'Yes. I do.'

'Okay, good. Let's move on to the next point then. Have you forgiven me for kissing you that day in Bombay? For ruining your first kiss?' asked Ronit pointedly.

'No, I haven't,' smirked Tiana.

'Yeah, I already know that. I just wanted you to admit it to yourself.'

'Oh, okay. Next you'll ask me if I have forgiven you for—'

'For dating Bella? For not stopping her from leaking your photos? Yeah, that is our next issue. But tell me, Tiana, why did you get angry at me for that? I didn't get between your fight with Bella because she was my girlfriend and you had made it clear that you didn't care about me. You weren't on talking terms with Bella, so as her boyfriend, I too kept my distance from you. What was wrong in that? Tell me, why were you so angry at me for not taking your side?'

'I...I guess...I don't know. I mean because I thought that... Ah, forget it,' stammered Tiana.

'No, let's not forget this. You expected me to drop everything and leap to your side—go against my own girlfriend. Why would you expect that from me? Admit it. You were jealous.'

'Why would I admit that? I just expected you to be a good friend,' said Tiana.

'You said last term that you didn't think I was serious about Bella and that you could have me whenever you wanted. You had implied that I would come running to you as soon as you called,' said Ronit quietly.

Tiana blushed, and Ronit instantly knew that she remembered this particular conversation very well.

'Yeah okay, I said that but only because I was trying to piss you off.'

'You meant it, Tiana. That's why you got mad when I didn't come running to your rescue. You wanted me to keep waiting for you and you were hurt when you realized that I wasn't there just waiting for you.'

'What is the point of rehashing all this?' cried out Tiana.

'I want you to realize how you treat me! You want me to just sit on the sidelines and wait for you and who knows how long you want to keep me there. You said I'm always playing childish games with you but guess what? So are you.'

Tiana looked stunned.

'You're right. I shouldn't have expected you to rush to my side at *my* convenience. I told you to move on and you did. That's fair. I hope you didn't break up with Bella for my sake. I mean if you had feelings for her and you broke up out of guilt, then I'm very sorry! I saw how upset you were when Bella was hanging out with Krish the other day. I can tell you that until recently, Bella still had very strong feelings for you and you guys should figure it out if you want. I don't want to cause more misery to either of you,' said Tiana. She was avoiding Ronit's eyes at this point and mostly she was just staring at her shoes.

'You still don't get it, do you?'

'What?'

'That's not what it's about. I was absolutely wrong and I used Bella to make you jealous. I was a complete jerk and no, I don't have feelings for Bella. I was not upset about her and Krish. And how oblivious can you be, Tiana, to think that I still have feelings for Bella?'

'Then why are you bringing it all up?'

'To make you admit that you wanted me to wait for you!' cried out Ronit.

'Of course, I did!' huffed Tiana.

'I wish you had said this to me. But you never did. I lost your trust when I didn't rush to your side last term and now, I lost your trust because I rushed to your side during the fight with Zoravar. You just want me to do everything according to you without giving me any explanations. I can't read your *mind*. You don't trust me, you can't forgive me and you avoid me. You have no idea how horrible I feel most of the time because of all this,' said Ronit, breathing heavily.

They were quiet for a long time, standing awkwardly and avoiding eye contact. Tiana felt, in equal parts, embarrassed and confused and after having bared his soul, Ronit felt shy. He couldn't help but wonder why he was feeling so emotional but expressing his feelings had made him feel lighter. Although, he felt bad because he could see he had burdened Tiana with a lot of his emotional baggage.

'I'm sorry that I've made you feel so bad. That was never my intention,' said Tiana.

'I know. I hope you know that the fight was not my intention. I just rushed in for you,' replied Ronit.

Tiana nodded.

'I know that we both messed up together where Bella is concerned. Not you alone. I took you for granted and instigated you. I have thought about it many times, but I couldn't bring myself to say this to you,' said Tiana honestly.

'Thanks for saying that now,' said Ronit softly.

'Okay. So, what now?' asked Tiana timidly.

'I don't know, Tiana. This shouldn't be so hard. We can't seem to find our original rhythm. Three summers ago, the time we spent together in Bombay had been so easy and light. We didn't fight or hurt each other like this.'

'Now all we do is hurt each other,' added Tiana.

'I don't think this is healthy and we should try and find a way to move past this without the awkwardness and the mixed signals which we are constantly giving each other. Let's just end the cycle,' said Ronit flatly.

'That makes sense. We've been pretending to be friends till now but friends don't behave this way. So, okay. Let's try to move on,' said Tiana slowly.

'I think the two of you need some extra homework,' said Mrs Pal, their economics teacher.

Tiana and Ronit had been so engrossed in their conversation that they didn't realize how close they were standing or that a teacher had suddenly walked up to them.

'Mrs Banerjee has given us strict instructions to give extra homework to any students we catch,' said Mrs Pal with pursed lips.

'Catch? Doing what, ma'am?' asked Ronit in confusion.

'Dating, what else? Don't pretend now,' said Mrs Pal sternly.

Tiana couldn't help smiling at the sheer irony. Here they were, essentially trying to be *friends* and now they were going to get punishment for *dating*.

'What is so funny, Tiana? Behave yourself. You might think you are some sort of a heroine, but I don't care. In school, you will follow all the rules like everybody else.'

Tiana just nodded but kept smiling.

Mrs Pal got more agitated and gave them both extra homework.

Ronit asked her why she was smiling, but it was too painful for her to be near him just then and she walked away with the smile still plastered on her face.

Thirty-Eight

'Authoritarian organizations are past masters at deflecting blame. They do so by denial, by rationalization, by making scapegoats.'

—Norman F. Dixon

'I know boys aren't robots and they have lots of feelings but those feelings come out in stupid aggressive ways. Like pulling our hair, stealing our favourite chair, saying mean things to us or downright ignoring us. Who knew one of them was capable of *thinking* about his feelings, let alone *expressing* them to a girl!' marvelled Sara.

'Maybe Ronit is a messiah. Maybe *he* can take the species forward,' said Bella.

'Haha, the messiah of high school boys. Nice!' laughed Leila.

'He could always talk about his feelings. It was one of the things that had attracted me to him in the first place. Despite studying with boys all my life, he was the first one I had real conversations with about books, films, people and even feelings,' admitted Tiana sadly.

She had just filled in her friends about her conversation with Ronit. She had agreed to move on but saying those words had broken her heart. Walking away from him earlier had made her lose her breath. It wasn't what she had wanted but it wasn't up to her. So agreeing with him was the only way to not lose face.

He had given her a lot to think about because everything he had said was true. She had been so embroiled in her own drama that she had forgotten to even notice how he was doing. Even though she still believed the fight was stupid, she had to concede that Ronit hadn't meant to cause her harm. In fact, none of the boys had wanted that, but when she had yelled at them, Tiana was at her tipping point. In hindsight, she felt that she could have behaved better. Later, she had apologized to Karam, Aryan and Aditya. They were surprised and forgave her but quickly admitted that the fight was stupid and she had been right to get angry at them. At least this had been easy to solve.

Ronit was an altogether different problem. He had been hurting for a while and she hadn't even bothered to notice. Tiana had actively avoided him and she shouldn't have been surprised that he finally wanted to get out of the limbo they were stuck in together. It was fair. This didn't mean that her feelings had disappeared because despite hurting her in the past, he had changed and this she had noticed. She had just been too scared to admit it because it would have meant taking things forward with him and she was scared that if things got bad again, then she would be too messed up to trust any boy ever. At least not for a long time.

Now, because of that fear, she had lost her last chance with him anyway.

'You still like him though, don't you?' asked Bella, reading Tiana's expression.

'What? No,' said Tiana quickly.

'T, please, it's written all over your face,' said Savera.

'Guys, chill. It's just the end of a chapter in my life. I'm reflecting on it. That's it.'

'Uh-huh,' said Leila.

'And please stop teasing us when he's around. No more winking and pointing or hooting. He has noticed it,' pleaded Tiana.

'We can't promise anything,' smiled Leila.

'Guys, come on.'

Her friends just laughed, winked, pointed and hooted in

response. Friendship is an irritatingly beautiful thing.

Except when it's not. Sometimes friends are just irritating as Tiana found out a week later.

The Founder's Day practices continued in full swing for the rest of the week. Classes had been suspended in the week leading up to Founder's Day. It was the best time during the entire school year because all they had to do was practise their P.T. and marching in the morning and for their dance routine in the afternoon. For the rest of the day, they were free to just hang out and have fun. Tiana was still using crutches so she couldn't dance anymore and had been sitting on the sidelines. She was happy to miss P.T. but she missed being a part of the dance because if nothing else, it would have at least been a good distraction for her.

If having feelings for Ronit and avoiding him was hard, then pretending to not have feelings for him and hanging out with him was even tougher. She had been trying to stay cool and collected around him. Except that there were no classes, and all the friends were constantly hanging out together. Ronit was a part of her friend circle and so there was no respite. She thought she had been handling this well but little did she know that her friends had been undermining all her efforts.

∽

On Founder's Day, Tiana finally got to meet her parents. She hadn't seen them since the summer holidays, although they had spoken after receiving the school's apology letter. They had been overcome with joy and relief, and her mother had cried on the phone. Her mother teared up again when they met.

'I'm so proud of you, Tiana,' said her mom.

'I love you, ma,' said Tiana, hugging both her parents.

'I'll admit, I was hesitant when you told us about wanting

to be in Ina's documentary but you just took that opportunity and made the best of it. I'm so proud of how you managed to get the school to apologize to you and to us,' said her father, patting her on the shoulders proudly.

'I managed it by blackmailing them, dad,' said Tiana.

'Well, they deserved it,' shrugged her father and Tiana started laughing.

'Mrs Banerjee wants to talk to us. She asked us to bring you along,' said her mom.

'Oh God. Now what does she want?' groaned Tiana.

A few minutes later, they entered the senior mistress's office. At first, there was a lot of small talk between Banerjee and Tiana's parents. Tiana was quietly observing the conversation, growing slightly agitated, as she could see a curveball coming.

'So, whatever happened last year was regrettable and I'm glad it's all sorted out now but I have found out that Tiana broke her word. The headmaster agreed to Tiana's terms on the condition that she would not give Ina any photos from that night.'

'Yes, we know that already.'

'Well, the head girl, Pia, told me that Tiana has given Ina the photos and has broken the good faith that the headmaster had shown her,' said Mrs Banerjee seriously.

'Tiana?' asked her father.

'I have given only one photo that shows Pia and Zoravar drinking on campus. I didn't give Ina the rest,' admitted Tiana, looking at the senior mistress straight in the eye.

'Why did you do that? You can't break your word like that,' said her father.

'They deserved it,' replied Tiana.

'Tiana, you have to stop Ina, otherwise you will ruin Pia's reputation completely,' said the senior mistress.

'Excuse me, but where was this concern when my daughter's reputation was at sake? Why didn't you make a case for her in front of Zoravar's father?' asked Tiana's mom.

'Please try to understand.'

'Mom, forget it. Pia is her favourite student. That's why she is the head girl. There were other girls who were more qualified but in the end, the decision was going to be made by the senior mistress and she of course chose Pia.'

'Tiana, behave yourself. I'm still your teacher.'

'You are her teacher, but that doesn't change the facts. Tell us why you want to save this girl so much,' asked Tiana's mom.

'Okay, fine. Pia is like a niece to me. I really...'

'Oh so my daughter's future is not important but just because Pia is like a daughter to you, she deserves better?' asked Tiana's father angrily.

Mrs Banerjee was quiet for a while, then she made her counter-offer.

'I will make Tiana a prefect next year if she saves Pia,' said the senior mistress.

Tiana smiled at the transparency.

'Wow. Until last year, I might have fallen for this bait. Back then, I still believed in the importance of going for the exchange programme or becoming a prefect. It was about getting validation from you and the headmaster and the other teachers. Getting "selected" and being "chosen" had some weight behind it. But now that I know what kind of people you all are, I really don't care for your false positions and fake admiration.'

'Tiana, wait. Think about it. Being a prefect could benefit you in the long run,' said her father.

'I don't think so. Besides, like I said, Pia and Zoravar deserve this.'

'Tiana, what have we always taught you? To rise above the nonsense that other people do to you. You should strive to be better. Tit for tat is never the right way and you shouldn't stoop to the level of negative people,' said her father.

'You're right. I have tried my best to not stoop to the level of negative, hurtful people. I had a great opportunity to throw my friends and this school under the bus but I stopped myself. I stopped because I love my school. I stopped because my friends feel horrible about what they did. They had been trying to make up for it. They were even going to confess on their own. If I had turned them in, it wouldn't have been fair on my part,' said Tiana.

'Then why did you give this Pia girl's photo to Ina?' asked her mom.

'Ever since the term began, Pia, who is Zoravar's girlfriend, has been spreading rumours about me, and Zoravar has been forcing boys to bully me. They took a bad situation and made it worse. His dad came to school and started yelling at me. Luckily, Ina recorded the entire fight and you'll all see that I did nothing wrong. They tried to label me a liar but it backfired on them. I tricked Zoravar and Pia into admitting their guilt on camera. So the photos are redundant. There is a video now.'

'You know about this video?' Tiana's father asked Mrs Banerjee.

'Yes, but Pia feels horrible.'

'So what? Why are you making Tiana feel bad about the photo? You're making it sound like she broke her word,' said Tiana's mom.

'She did!'

'No, she just outsmarted you. If Zoravar admitted his guilt, then it's all on him. After that, if the photo becomes public, it only corroborates his own admission. Don't put this on my daughter and don't you dare falsely accuse her of anything else in the future or else you will be facing a lawsuit,' said Tiana's father angrily.

'And you will make her a prefect next year,' said Tiana's mom.

'Mom, no.'

'I can't do that,' said Mrs Banerjee haughtily.

'Yes, you will, otherwise this conversation we just had, I will make it public too. I will tell everyone how you play favourites with your students and trust me, after the release of the documentary, everyone will believe us too. They will know what a liar you really are,' said Tiana's mom.

'I'm sorry, but Tiana doesn't fulfil the criterion to become a prefect. I was going to put in extra efforts to make her one but if she won't help Pia, then I can't help Tiana. Besides, girls who have boyfriends aren't considered serious and we don't like to give them prefectorial posts. I would have asked Tiana to break up with her boyfriend first, only then she would be considered.'

'Umm...I'm not dating anyone.'

'Don't lie, Tiana,' said Mrs Banerjee.

'First, I believe my daughter. Second, Pia is head girl and yet she has a boyfriend. How is that okay then?' asked Tiana's father pointedly.

'Well, when she became head girl, she wasn't dating anyone,' said the senior mistress.

'That was convenient, wasn't it?'

'If Tiana is serious about her future, she should break up with Ronit,' said the senior mistress, changing the subject.

'I'm not dating Ronit.'

'Yet I see you with him all the time. You both are always lurking near each other. So many times, I have seen the two of you together, without any of your other friends around you.'

'That doesn't mean anything. Tiana and Ronit are childhood friends,' said Tiana's mom.

Tiana wanted to laugh out at how wrongly Banerjee had read the situation between her and Ronit. Now that they were hanging out *more,* they were even further *away* from dating.

'I'm telling you what I see. Tiana should focus on her studies and extracurricular activities. Then she has a chance to be selected a prefect. Now if you'll excuse me, I have other meetings.'

Tiana left the office with her parents.

'Wow. That woman is really something,' said her mother, stroking Tiana's hair softly.

'Yeah.'

'So tell me honestly, T, are you really dating Ronit?' asked her mom.

Great, back to talking about Ronit. A mere mention of his name was starting to become like prolonged torture for her. Either he was in front of her or someone was talking about him. There was no escape.

'No.'

'Good,' sighed her mom.

'Why good? What if I was?' asked Tiana timidly to see what her parents felt about her having a boyfriend.

'It's good because it means you are focusing on yourself. After the year you've had, you can't afford any more distractions,' said her father.

'We've known Ronit since he was a kid and he is a great boy but right now he will be a distraction, Tiana,' added her mom. Tiana felt like her mother could understand her unsaid feelings.

'Well, don't worry. I'm not dating him. There is no chance of that happening at all,' said Tiana, giving her parents a faint smile.

Until last week, all she had wanted was to clear her name and nothing else could have felt like a bigger problem to her but now suddenly this Ronit situation seemed like a much worse conundrum to have got stuck in. She couldn't confide to anyone, not her parents or her friends and least of all Ronit.

Ronit didn't want to date her. Her parents didn't want her to date Ronit. Everyone wanted Tiana to move on, even Banerjee. It should have been simple.

But it was far from simple.

Thirty-Nine

*'Great blunders are often made,
like large ropes, of a multitude of fibres.'*

—Victor Hugo

She hadn't realized that her friends weren't going to make it easy for her to move on. At all. Misguided as it was, they thought they were helping her but that didn't mean that they hadn't created a mess. A mess which spilled right before the dance performance. Everyone was dressed and ready, in costumes which were ridiculously ugly, made of silver and gold polyester with frills and big sleeves. It was an outdoor night performance, so they were waiting on the corner edge of the athletic field waiting for the gymnastics performance to finish.

'Why do school costumes always have to be so disgusting? They could have picked better colours at least... Silver and gold together? Why are they torturing us?' exclaimed Bella.

Even though the costumes were ugly, Tiana still wished she could have worn it and been a part of this dance with her friends. She was missing out on creating this fun memory with them. Soon everyone began taking pictures and of course they included her in those because that's what friends do. While everyone was laughing and rehashing their steps, Ronit came to Tiana with a very serious look on his face.

'Is there something you want to tell me?' asked Ronit hesitantly.

If only he knew, thought Tiana but she said, 'Umm...no.'

'Are you sure?' asked Ronit.

'Okay, what's going on?' asked Tiana.

'I think you need to talk to Leila, Savera and Bella,' said Ronit.

'About what?'

Ronit looked uncomfortable so Tiana took charge of the situation and called her friends to come where they were standing.

'Okay, Ronit. Here they are. What's up?' asked Tiana.

Ronit looked at Leila and said, 'Do you want to tell her?'

'Ronit, chill,' said Bella.

'Yeah, it's not such a big deal,' added Savera.

'What the hell is happening?' asked Tiana, irritated at being left out of this big secret.

'They made Ria cry today for talking to me,' said Ronit flatly.

Tiana looked around at her friends. Leila and Savera stared back blankly and Bella just looked bored.

'Which Ria?' asked Tiana.

'Ria Virk,' replied Ronit.

'You guys made a *junior* girl cry?' asked Tiana, addressing her friends.

'It was nothing, T. We were just talking to her,' said Leila.

'She started crying for no reason,' said Bella.

'Why were you talking to her at all!' exclaimed Tiana.

'Ria is my friend. I met her in my extra class last term and we became friends. That's it. We hang out occasionally but that doesn't mean anything,' said Ronit, looking at Tiana.

'Ronit, you don't have to explain yourself to me,' said Tiana, embarrassed about what her friends had done.

'No, I do.'

'Really, you don't.'

'To you, I do,' said Ronit, staring into her eyes and she felt butterflies in her stomach.

'But there is no need to attack her like that. Just for hanging out with me,' said Ronit to Leila.

'Dude, Ria likes you. I hope you know that,' said Leila.

'No, she doesn't,' said Ronit.

'Wow, you're really oblivious, man. I have observed Ria around you and she *likes* you a lot! That's why we told her to stay away,' said Bella.

'You guys are out of control! Ronit can hang out with anyone he wants to, don't interfere in his life!' exclaimed Tiana.

'Fine! We were just looking out for you but now you deal with this yourself. Don't cry and mope around when he moves on and you are still stuck on him,' said Bella.

'What?' asked Ronit, his eyebrows raised as far up as they could go.

Tiana had covered her face with her palm in mortification. Bella pouted and nodded her head.

'You know what, Ronit, now I believe that you didn't realize Ria likes you. Not knowing when a girl likes you is kind of your specialty,' said Leila, walking away with all her friends.

'Tiana?' asked Ronit softly.

Tiana uncovered her face and looked at him, 'I had no idea that this happened. I promise you, I didn't ask them to go to Ria, much less make her cry.'

'I know that. Of course, I know that. I came to you because I knew that your friends wouldn't have behaved like this unless they knew something. Which is why I asked you if you wanted to tell me something,' said Ronit.

'Seriously? You tell me first. Did you really think my feelings would disappear in a week? You'll say let's move on and I'll just flip the switch? That's not how feelings work,' said Tiana.

'Don't you think I know that? I'm going through the *same* feelings here. I thought we are doing this together, so we don't end up hating each other. If we avoid each other that would suck and if we start dating that would also suck because we still haven't resolved our issues. Just moving on from those feelings and staying friends is the only way forward. It's the only way we don't end up losing each other completely!' cried out Ronit.

'Arghhh! Why is this so hard?' yelled Tiana.

'I don't know!' yelled back Ronit.

'Well I don't know either!' exclaimed Tiana.

'If I asked you out today, what would you say?' asked Ronit suddenly.

Tiana was caught off guard. Just a few hours ago her parents had asked her to not date anyone. She didn't know if she would have said yes instantly if that conversation hadn't taken place between her and her parents but now that it had, she had to hold back and be sensible. She was trying to formulate a response when she realized that their entire batch was standing on the sidelines listening to them and waiting to hear Tiana's response.

'How is it that all of you are wearing these *ridiculous* costumes, yet I'm the one who has become the spectacle?' asked Tiana, looking at Ronit but then she gave a stink eye to her friends who had caused this scene in front of everyone.

Ronit then grabbed her hand, which caused more butterflies, and pulled her to a corner, away from everyone. Before he could ask her again, she decided to respond.

'I would say no,' said Tiana softly.

'Why? T, I don't understand you at all. Clearly, you've been upset about us. Upset enough that even your friends noticed and went and made a girl *cry* because they thought she was coming too close to me,' said Ronit, not letting go of her hand. Tiana tried to pull away, but he didn't let her, and instead stepped right inside her personal space. He was so close that his proximity took her breath away.

'Why can't you just let go of the past?' pleaded Ronit.

'Ronit, even if I did, I still don't think I could date you,' responded Tiana, looking into his eyes.

Staying logical was becoming increasingly difficult for her and suddenly all she could think about was kissing him.

She remembered the last time she had kissed him; it had been her very first kiss. Tiana remembered the kiss had been prefect. No matter what, Tiana and Ronit kept coming back to each other without actually being with each other. Till that moment, all they had been trying to do was fix the breach of trust that had followed their first and only kiss.

Now when she was dreaming about kissing him again, it seemed she was capable of letting go of the past but it was her present that was the problem. Her parents and their concern for her. She had put them through a lot this year and keeping her word to them was important to her. She had always marvelled at how easy it was for a lot of her friends to lie to their parents or to do things against their wishes. She sometimes wished she could be like that but it was truly something she couldn't do. Maybe it was because of how they had raised her. They had never stopped her from doing something without first having a discussion about why they were stopping her. They made their reasons clear and Tiana had never found her parents to be unreasonable and that was why she had always agreed with them.

For the most part, they had let her do whatever she had wanted. Sleepovers, trips with friends, going out for parties, and even staying out late occasionally. Even when she had been dating Karam, they had never made an issue out of it. Having open and honest conversations had been the most important aspect of her upbringing. Even when she messed up, they trusted her to tell them the truth so they could fix everything as a family. Her parents had always trusted her and she didn't have it in her to break that faith.

So, if they didn't want her to date anyone for some time, then that's exactly what she planned on doing. Her feelings for Ronit were strong but they weren't stronger than her love for her parents. Using that strength, she managed to push Ronit away from herself.

'Are you really so stubborn, Tiana? You can't leave the past in the past?' asked Ronit, perplexed at Tiana's behaviour.

She couldn't really tell him that her parents didn't want her to date. He wouldn't understand. Neither would her friends. They would just make fun of her for being a 'good little girl'. They would all think that it was a weak excuse and she didn't want to spend the rest of the term defending herself. So telling everyone the truth was out of the question.

'We need to go back to what we had discussed earlier. Let's move on,' said Tiana in what she hoped sounded like a determined voice.

Ronit was quiet for a few seconds. Then they heard the dance choreographer yelling at everyone to get into their starting formations.

'Fine. Will you make sure your friends understand as well?' said Ronit flatly.

'Yeah. I'll talk to them. They won't go after Ria or any other girl you hang out with in the future. Move on or date whomsoever you want,' said Tiana quickly.

'I didn't realize I needed your permission but thanks, I guess,' smirked Ronit.

'That's not what I meant and why are you sounding mad?' asked Tiana.

'You know what, let's go back to how we were originally. Let's just stay away from each other because I don't think I have the energy to pretend that we are just *friends*. I'm not good at acting like you,' said Ronit sarcastically.

'Okay, that's way too harsh. Also we can't ignore each other. My parents just told me that you will be staying with us for the Founder's holidays because your parents are travelling and you can't go to Bombay. So let's not turn this into a fight,' said Tiana.

'Oh no no,' laughed Ronit.

'What?'

'I'll find somewhere else to stay, thank you very much. There is no way I'm going to spend any time near you now that I know how stubborn and irritating you can really be, Tiana,' said Ronit.

'How did we go from almost kissing to this?' exclaimed Tiana.

'Ask yourself!' cried out Ronit.

'Ronit! Do you need a special invitation to come and stand in your position?' yelled the choreographer.

'Sorry, sir, coming,' said Ronit, walking away. He didn't look at Tiana at all as he walked away.

'Great!' she thought to herself.

Forty

'What is found in the effect was already in the cause.'

—Henri Bergson

By evening, the students of Hill View were all released from school for a week-long holiday. When Tiana reached home, she was surprised to see her brother Sid waiting for her.

'I can't wait to see this documentary! Honestly, it's all anybody talks about, from Leila and Karam to Ronit,' laughed Sid.

'Yeah. It caused a lot of excitement for a while in school,' smiled Tiana.

'And my baby sister was the star,' said Sid as he air quoted the word 'star'.

'You bet I was! No one else has managed to bring in as much drama into school as I have. Drama follows the star,' laughed Tiana as she air quoted around her head.

'Hey, I'm just glad that you and Leila have made up for good. My sister hating my girlfriend was too awkward for me,' said Sid.

'Oh, you mean just like my brother dating my best friend had been awkward for me three years ago?' said Tiana sarcastically.

Sid just made a face in response.

Leila and Karam came over to their house later. They brought Ronit with them. Tiana was surprised to find out that of all people, Ronit was staying with Karam. Until the fight, the two of them couldn't stand to be near each other and now they had suddenly become such good friends that Ronit felt comfortable enough to stay with him. Ronit ignored Tiana. He greeted her parents and then went to play video games with Sid and Karam in the family room.

'Did he really just ignore you?' asked Leila.

'Yeah. I don't blame him,' shrugged Tiana.

They were sitting on a couch far away from the boys but it seemed as if Sid heard Leila because suddenly from across the room he yelled at her, 'Tiana, how does it feel that two of your ex-boyfriends would rather hang out together to avoid you?'

'Sid! Don't be an ass,' yelled Leila.

'It's okay. At this point I'm immune to what Sid says.'

However, Ronit and Karam didn't take it as coolly as Tiana. Ronit threw a cushion at Sid's face and Karam trapped him in a chokehold.

'Okay! Geez... So touchy! Tiana didn't even blink and look at you both,' said Sid, giving up and straightening himself after Karam released him.

Leila rolled her eyes at him. At that moment, Tiana's cell phone began to buzz. It was a FaceTime from Bella.

'Hey, what's up?' asked Tiana.

'You won't believe what happened!' Bella's voice rang out so loudly from Tiana's phone speakers that everyone stopped what they were doing and turned to look at Tiana.

'What?'

'So Krish just told me. Apparently Ina was going to tell you tomorrow but Krish let it slip by mistake. The documentary... our episode... It's out already! It's on YouTube!' said Bella excitedly.

Tiana inhaled sharply, her hands suddenly felt clammy. She hadn't expected it to release so soon! Panic was starting to set in. Who knew exactly what Ina had sent out into the world? For a while, she had been nervous about the release of the documentary, but she had consciously kept blocking it out. She had kept telling herself that what was done was done. She would have to deal with it whenever the film released. Now, without any warning, that day was here and all the worries that she had blocked were flooding her mind.

'Oh God, I'm so nervous!' exclaimed Leila.

'Let me grab my laptop,' said Sid, rushing to his room.

Tiana looked at Ronit and saw that he was staring at her too. He looked just as nervous. The documentary had exposed him just as much as it had her. But the moment between them passed quickly and they averted their gaze at the same time. Sid returned with the laptop.

'Wait wait! I can't watch it! I can't. What if it's horrible? Or I seem like an idiot?' said Tiana, pacing across the room. Her stomach felt queasy, and she felt she was going to get sick at any moment.

'You won't,' said her father.

Tiana turned around and saw her parents entering the family room.

'Sid told us,' smiled her mom.

'Oh God, Oh God. I can't. I can't watch it!' said Tiana, holding her stomach with both her hands and bending over.

'Stop being so dramatic,' said Sid. Their father gave him a playful smack on the head.

'Tiana, chill! I'm on YouTube right now and guess what? It was released this morning and by evening the video has got 500,000 views!' said Bella.

In her panic, Tiana had forgotten that Bella was still on FaceTime.

'Have you seen it?'

'Halfway through! It's awesome!' said Bella.

'Really?' asked Tiana in disbelief.

'Watch it! I'll come over tomorrow to discuss. Bye!'

Sid was about to play the video but Tiana left the room.

'Where are you going, T?' asked her mom.

'I need to watch it alone. I'm sorry. I can't watch it with you all,' said Tiana, rushing to her room. She locked her door and grabbed her laptop.

Forty-One

*'Challenges are what make life interesting.
Overcoming them is what makes life meaningful.'*

—Joshua J. Marine

The film was funny, sarcastic and thoughtful. Everything was balanced. Serious scenes were followed by hilarious ones. At 40 minutes, it wasn't too long and didn't feel stretched. The love triangle scene in the classroom was fun to watch. Ronit and Bella's interview was emotional and sweet. The scene where she was left with no dance partner made her look relatable. Her interview had turned out well too. Tiana was glad that she had been able to say everything that was on her mind that day. The fight scene with all the boys showed how she had been calm while talking to Mr Singh and how she had tried to stop the fight. The fight itself looked equal parts serious and funny. The scene that Sara had shot secretly worked very well and revealed Zoravar and Pia's reality.

Tiana now understood why Ina had focused so much on her personal life and on all the love angles. Those parts of her life definitely made her story more watchable. Most of the things she had said in the film were either in self-defence or were anti-establishment. She could have come across as unlikeable and aggressive, if not for the quirks and silly things that were going on in her life. Ina had layered funny scenes with the serious ones and the result had been very entertaining. Tiana had been presented as a determined person with a messy life and that inherently made her a watchable character.

Bella and Ronit had had a similar effect. They had both messed up, but they had been brutally honest about their mistakes. They sounded genuine when they said that they were sorry and were trying to be better than before. This redeemed them as characters.

The school looked beautiful in the film and luckily its reputation didn't suffer much either. Ina somehow managed to get an interview with the headmaster and she showed how strict the school was with the students but that sometimes things could go wrong.

As soon as she was done watching, she called Ina.

'I was waiting for your call,' said Ina.

'How did you manage that?' asked Tiana incredulously.

'It required some manoeuvring but I guess I'm just good at this,' laughed Ina.

'Why didn't you tell me you were releasing it today?' asked Tiana.

'I thought it would be better for you to find out organically. I didn't want you to freak out. I thought once you saw that it's doing so well and is getting so many views, you'll feel more confident about it,' said Ina.

'I won't lie. I did freak out,' said Tiana.

'Also, my producers wanted to release it today because they knew that all the students from the school would be out for the holidays. They would have their laptops and phones and will watch it because the film is about their school and they saw it being shot in front of them. We were counting on the students and their families to make the video viral and it worked. Now it has a life of its own. But don't worry, we will keep promoting it.'

'Wow,' said Tiana.

'Don't worry, so far the response has been positive. People are loving you and your friends. People your age can relate easily, and adults are getting reminded of their own school days, so that's good. Even the comments are mostly positive as of now.'

'You said, don't read the comments,' reminded Tiana.

'Well, if they are good, then you should read them for sure!' laughed Ina.

'How did you manage to get the headmaster's and other teachers' interviews?' asked Tiana.

'I showed them the footage of Zoravar confessing and of how he and his dad were the ones who caused the fight in school. Once the headmaster and some of the other teachers saw that those two had implicated themselves on their own and that I also had photos of him drinking on campus they decided to speak up against him too. Your headmaster is a smart man. He knew the story was going to leak out either way, so he thought it would be better for his image if he was on the side of the truth. He spoke against Zoravar's father's interference in the school and how, going forward, no parent would be allowed so much influence in school, no matter what their background. The teachers had been dying to speak up against Zoravar but they had been scared for their jobs. Once they saw that even the headmaster was speaking up, they agreed to give their interviews too,' explained Ina.

'You *really* are good at this,' admitted Tiana.

'I know. It was great working with you, Tiana, and if you ever need a job in Bombay, I would love to have you join my team,' said Ina.

'Thank you so much, Ina. For everything,' replied Tiana sincerely.

'Oh and be prepared, if the views keep going up at this rate, then some reporters might want to interview you in the coming days,' said Ina.

Tiana returned to the family room and she was instantly engulfed in hugs and kisses from her family and Leila. Once they left her, Karam came to give her a hug and to tell her how great it had turned out.

'Great job,' said Ronit, maintaining his distance.

'Thanks,' replied Tiana.

'I'm super impressed! Everything you said made so much sense,' said Sid.

'Yeah, that's what everyone is writing in the comments. People who are still in school are going through the same stuff and they can relate so well with you and your friends' life,' said her father.

'Even grown-ups can relate. I remember teachers being vicious for no reason at all when I was in school. Someone needed to voice it and you did it so well,' said her mom.

'You read the comments?' asked Tiana.

'Yeah, mostly they are positive. Don't worry about the negative comments. It's good that the film is starting a discussion. As long as people talk about it, they will watch it too. That's the point,' said Sid.

'Yeah. I guess,' smiled Tiana.

Later when Leila was leaving, she pulled Tiana aside, 'I hope it's okay that Ronit is staying with us.'

'Of course, yeah.'

'I don't know how but ever since the fight, Karam and Ronit have become friends. I guess, now that both of them have given up the idea of being with you, they have no reason for hostility.'

'I wish my presence or absence had nothing to do with it and they had become friends a long time ago,' said Tiana.

'Oh, you should know that the comments are also filled with people wanting to know who you ended up with... Karam or Ronit,' laughed Leila.

'What?'

'Yeah, everyone noticed the love diagram in the film. And the fight with Zoravar shows both of them coming to your rescue and in their interviews both of them have said how amazing you are and blah blah. So by the end of the film, people thought they would see who will end up with you but that doesn't happen,' said Leila.

'So, that's what they are discussing in the comments?' asked Tiana mortified.

'Ina told you that people like drama,' said Leila.

As if on cue, Karam came over too. Leila left them alone, sensing that he wanted to say something personal.

'I wanted to tell you that I broke up with your cousin.'

'Oh, I'm sorry,' said Tiana.

'No, she had been lying to me. Not just about what she did to you but about lots of other irritating things as well. I'm telling you personally because I wanted you to know it had nothing to do with you. I know, Leila must have mentioned what people are saying in the comments. I didn't want you to think that I broke up with her because I think I have a chance with you,' said Karam awkwardly.

'Oh of course, I get it. Don't worry, I won't be getting any ideas about us,' laughed Tiana.

Karam relaxed a bit, 'Yeah, I think we work best as friends and we'll always be that. So if you ever need a friend, don't hesitate to reach out, okay?'

'Okay and that goes for you too,' smiled Tiana.

'Also, now that I've spent some time with him, I think Ronit is a really cool guy.'

Tiana nodded.

'I can see why you like him,' said Karam casually.

Tiana raised her eyebrows.

'It's not a secret, you know. You've liked him for years now. Why can't you guys just figure it out?' said Karam.

'Good night, Karam!' smiled Tiana.

As soon as her guests left, she rushed to read the comments.

'I hope she chose Ronit!'

'Who did she end up with?'

'Why didn't they end the story by telling us who Tiana ended up with?'

'Ronit is sooo cute!'

'Karam is adorable!!!'

It went on and on and on. Tiana was surprised that random strangers on the internet were so invested in her love life. But then, she had consciously decided to put her entire life out there for people to see. Now she couldn't force them to only focus on the parts she wanted. People were free to focus on whatever they wanted and they wanted boy drama.

~

In a couple of days, almost two million people had seen her story. It was insane. She had never thought that there would be such an instant reaction. She had expected the views to increase gradually but she hadn't considered Ina's influence. She knew that Ina's previous film had reached 10 million views but she hadn't thought that her own story could be interesting enough for so many people to watch. People were sharing and reposting it so quickly that Tiana didn't know what to think of it.

She felt exposed but she also felt a slight sense of pride. This film was the first thing she had created in her life and it was now being watched by millions of people. It was an exhilarating feeling because even though Ina had done all the hard work, Tiana had not missed out on this opportunity. She had sensed a chance to do something different, the decision to be featured in the film had been taken by her alone and it had paid off. Now its success was giving her immense confidence. For that, she was grateful.

Forty-Two

'The mind is its own place,
and in itself can make a heaven of hell, a hell of heaven.'

—John Milton

A couple of days later, the students were back in school and everybody told Tiana how much they liked the film. Everyone could relate so well with the things she had said. The teachers were a little less forthcoming because Tiana had criticized their methods rather boldly in the film. Still, some told her that she had spoken well and had done a good job.

Bella constantly kept going to the computer lab to keep checking and updating everyone on the number of views the film had garnered. In the seven days since its release, it had reached 3.5 million views.

'It's crazy that so many people know who I am,' said Bella incredulously.

'Okay relax, Bella. They don't *know* you,' said Savera.

'Excuse me, but my Instagram is out of control. Since the film came out, almost 60,000 people have started following me!' said Bella.

'What! Why are people following you?' asked Sara.

'I guess they just love me!' shrugged Bella happily.

'Tiana, what about you? Did your followers increase too?' asked Leila.

'I didn't check,' admitted Tiana.

'Omg! We need to check. Computer lab, now!' exclaimed Bella, pulling Tiana with her.

'We'll check later,' said Tiana.

'Now!'

So they went all the way to the computer lab and when Tiana finally logged in, she was shocked to find that her followers had increased from 90 people to 200,000.

'What the hell!' exclaimed Tiana.

'Like I said *crazy*! Now let's check Ronit's followers,' said Bella excitedly.

Ronit had 90,000 followers now.

'Wow,' said Tiana.

'So you know that people are dying to know if you are dating Ronit now?' asked Bella.

'Yeah, and they can keep guessing,' said Tiana, rolling her eyes.

'Come on! Tell me at least!' pleaded Bella.

'Am I dating him? No.'

'That's not what I meant. Tell me when you will date him.'

'I don't think I will.'

'Come on!'

'I'm serious, Bella. Nothing is going to happen.'

'But—'

Tiana shook her head and Bella just gave up.

After watching the film, Jasmine finally decided to speak to Tiana as well. One afternoon, once classes were over, she went to speak to Tiana. Although she didn't like how she was portrayed in the love triangle scene, she still acknowledged that she had behaved unreasonably with Tiana.

'You know, after watching the entire film I realized it was silly of me to think that you and Aditya might have anything going on. You're clearly into Ronit,' smiled Jasmine apologetically.

'Jasmine, that's not the point. Aditya and I are friends. You have to respect that and not make it dirty. It's not fair. Aditya might have more friends who happen to be girls and if you don't respect his friendships, he will end up breaking up with you.'

'Did he say that?' asked Jasmine, looking worried.

'No, he would never say such things, but he has looked unhappy ever since you made him change his place at the dining table. Distancing him from his friends is not the healthy way forward for your relationship.'

'I'm sorry okay, but with you, I never know. All these boys behave like such idiots around you. I mean, Aditya even got into that fight for you. I find this very confusing,' cried out Jasmine.

'In that case, judge me by my actions, not the actions of people around me. Have I ever given you a reason to think that I like Aditya? Have I behaved inappropriately?' asked Tiana, raising her eyebrows.

'No.'

'If you saw the film you must have seen that the fight was between Karam, Ronit and Zoravar. Aditya and Aryan jumped in to defend their friends. It was instinctive and nothing else. So please, let's just end all this negativity,' said Tiana.

'Yeah. Let's.'

The last person to come and talk to her was Tea. Tiana had been sitting at her study table reading and when she looked up, she saw Tea looming over her.

'What do you want?' asked Tiana, returning her gaze to her textbook.

'Can you forgive me for what I did? I miss having you in my life, Tiana. We used to get along so well before all these boys messed things up.'

'Tea, your transparency is laughable,' said Tiana.

'What?'

'Karam told me you both broke up. Now that you are alone, you want to come close to me? No, thank you.'

'Tiana, please, I'm so sorry.'

'Tea, I have forgiven everything and everyone but I'm not

going to lie to you, we can't go back to being the way we used to be, I just don't get good vibes from you. I can't help it. So, we're cool and everything is good but that's it,' said Tiana and when she watched Tea walk away she felt nothing.

༄

After Founder's Day, all the fun and games were over. For the next two months, the focus was to be kept on final exams. As the term went on, the days became shorter and colder and the study load kept increasing. It was dreary with both the weather and the prep work for finals bringing them down. Tiana's misery kept mounting because in addition to these, she was still dealing with her heartbreak.

Every time she saw Ronit, she had to work extra hard to not show any signs of feelings that went beyond basic friendship because she knew her friends were observing her behaviour. However, such instances were rare because the only time Tiana and Ronit were near each other was when their entire group was chilling together on Sundays. For the rest of the week, Ronit stayed away from her. He had changed his place at the dining table again and returned to his original seat at Leila's table. He no longer sat behind her during assembly. Even during their common classes, he made sure to sit on the opposite end of the room. Tiana didn't know if this distance was helping her move on from him or if it was making her more miserable than ever. She couldn't wait for the term to get over. She needed space, an escape from seeing him every single day and acting like he meant nothing to her and even worse, from knowing that she no longer meant anything to him either.

Two months went on like this and finally a week before final exams, the headmaster called her to his office after breakfast.

'Tiana, how are you?'

'I'm good, sir,' replied Tiana.

'I hear your film has reached 15 million views as of today.'

'Oh! I didn't know. We've been so busy with studies that we forgot to check,' said Tiana.

'I'm glad to hear that you are so focused on your studies. A few of your teachers and I have been very impressed with you, Tiana. We have noticed your go-getter spirit, ability to follow the rules and your focus on school work. I also remember in your friends' drunk driving accident, you had impressed us all by being the only one present there who had *not* gotten involved with drinking. You helped save your friends' lives that night and when the media covered that incident you had been the only saving grace for the school.'

Tiana smiled awkwardly in response because she was not used to so much praise from a teacher.

'That is why I am going to make you a house prefect next year.'

Tiana was stunned.

'I think you suffered a lot because of the school's mistake and you didn't deserve it, Tiana. Consider this a reward from us,' smiled the headmaster.

'Thank you, sir, but if you feel there is someone more deserving than me then please give the position to them. I already got my reward with the documentary,' said Tiana honestly.

'Yes, that documentary has done wonders for you but as I see it that was a reward you gave yourself. This is something I feel I must do. You were the only one who suffered amongst the 25 students and I do believe that you weren't drinking that night. I know you to be an honest person, Tiana. Barring Zoravar and Pia, none of the other 25 have faced any real consequences. They got away with it and that's their reward, but this is yours.'

'Thank you, sir,' smiled Tiana.

'Besides, the documentary has been good for us. The country

had forgotten about our school but now they have been reminded. The feedback that I have got is that parents are happy with how the school has been portrayed in the film. We come across as a disciplinary school where students can't get away with wrongdoing easily and that we are not afraid to suspend and expel such students from the school. Also, that when we are wrong, we accept it instead of covering it up. People appreciate our transparency and parents love our strictness with the students. I know you spoke against the strictness but remember that Indian parents love strict teachers and that's why teachers are the way they are. If teachers weren't strict, then not only the students but even the parents won't respect them,' said the headmaster pensively.

'Can I say something?' asked Tiana.

'Go ahead,' smiled the headmaster.

'I understand why teachers need to be strict, but there is no need for them to be downright mean and sometimes even demeaning. Many teachers, I feel, cross that line and when they are reminded of it, they turn even more vicious because they feel students shouldn't be allowed to express their opinions. Speaking up is often considered disrespectful by the teachers and that's not fair,' said Tiana.

'How about, next year, when you are a prefect, we can start a committee of students and teachers to facilitate better interaction? You can lead it and help out other students who are struggling. Sounds good?' asked the headmaster.

'Thank you again, sir. Sounds good,' said Tiana, getting up to leave.

'Good, now go and do well in your finals and don't be like the rest of your friends. Focus on yourself and not on boys.'

Tiana's smile faltered and her heart, which had temporarily lifted, sank again as she walked out of the office. Becoming a prefect meant that there was one more hindrance on her path to Ronit.

On top of everything else, as she walked towards her classroom, she saw *him* in the corridor which was currently secluded because assembly was going on. Ronit was standing under one of the stone arches talking softly to someone. At first, she couldn't see who it was because they were partially covered under the arch, but as she reached closer, she saw him talking to a junior girl, it wasn't Ria. This was some new girl. Tiana had seen her around, she was two years younger than them but she couldn't remember her name. It didn't matter. They were holding hands. She inhaled sharply and turned around instantly and walked away.

'Tiana!' said Ronit.

Oh God. He had seen her too.

She gave him a thumbs up sign without turning back to indicate it was all good and that there was no need to talk about it. But Ronit ran after her.

'Listen,' said Ronit.

'It's okay. I don't care,' said Tiana, turning to look at him for barely a second before turning back and continuing to walk away.

Her parents, the senior mistress, the headmaster, all the grown-ups in her life were right. She needed to focus on herself and her senior year. Feelings would come and go. Feelings were all over the place. Maybe Ronit still had feelings for her or maybe he didn't, but she had asked him to move on and he seemed to be doing just that. That was the healthy thing to do after all. He wasn't going to mope around forever, and neither would she. To see him move on gave her the strength to do the same and she was going to put in all her efforts to do so and presently, there couldn't be a bigger distraction than finals.

Forty-Three

'Hearts will never be practical until they are made unbreakable.'

—The Wizard of Oz

It was done! The final exams were over. It was the last day of the term and the new prefects for the next year would be announced during the last special assembly which took place in the evening. Tiana was officially made the Austen House Prefect. She had already told her friends and whether they were jealous at the time, Tiana didn't know, but they had been happy for her. Now, it didn't matter because Savera became the new head girl and Leila became the Austen House Captain. Sara became the deputy head girl and Bella didn't care about being a prefect because she was too happy to have influence outside the school. Her Instagram followers had reached 400,000 at this point. Tiana still didn't check her own account but Bella told her that she currently had 700,000 followers. Amongst the boys, Aryan became the new head boy and surprisingly Ronit became the Austen House Prefect, the same post as Tiana, which meant in the future they would have to collaborate for House activities.

After a lot of cheering and hugging, Bella yelled out, 'Time to get ready for Break Ups!'

'That is the most ridiculous name for a farewell party,' said Ronit.

'I think the *most* ridiculous name is "farewell party", where's the creativity in that?' scoffed Bella.

'Yeah, you're new that's why you think it's funny but since

we were 10 years old, we have referred to our farewell party as Break Ups. It's school tradition,' said Leila.

The last night of the term was time to send off seniors into the real world. It was the most bittersweet party of the entire school year. After living together for eight years, leaving the comfortable bubble of the school and of childhood friends was difficult. More time had been spent in school and with friends than with parents at home in this time period. Tiana was sure that students in day schools felt sad when the school year ended or when they left school for good but in boarding school the attachment was much stronger. At the end of every year, even though they knew they were coming back, they always got emotional. And next year was going to be their last year. Just one more year and it would be their time to break up with the school, with constant friendships and even with school-time relationships. The farewell party was very aptly named Break Ups.

The party was taking place in the school gym. The entire school was already inside, waiting for the seniors. The tradition was for seniors to enter in pairs. It was also tradition that before the seniors, the new prefects enter in pairs according to their rank. So Savera and Aryan as new head girl and head boy were going to lead followed by deputies Sara and Ravi and then the house captains of all four houses. So Leila was paired with Austen House Boys Captain Jai. Finally, the house prefects of all the four houses, which meant Tiana was paired with Ronit.

'Guys, take your positions fast! Find your partner and hurry. We are running late!' yelled Savera, already taking on her head girl role seriously.

'Can't I skip this?' asked Tiana, looking at Leila.

'Just get it over with. You only have to enter with him. After that, you can avoid Ronit as much as you want. But just so you know, we are all going to be running Austen House together next year. And we'll have *many* prefect meetings and dinners and trips.

It would be better if you guys get along without awkwardness,' smiled Leila.

Tiana rolled her eyes. Leila was already behaving like the house captain. She wondered what she was supposed to do as house prefect. She ranked second in Austen House after Leila now. Next year was going to be interesting for sure.

People were already starting to fall into a line and through the commotion she saw Ronit. He waved at her. She smiled and waved back, and went and stood next to him in the line.

'Congrats,' said Tiana.

'Thanks, and to you too. I didn't expect to become a prefect, considering I joined the school just this year,' said Ronit.

'Oh, that's not a factor. You're good at both academics and sports and that's what matters to them. In my case, headmaster was impressed by how I handled the documentary,' said Tiana.

'You did well with the film for sure. Speaking of the film, I have like 150,000 followers on social media now,' smiled Ronit.

'Let me guess. Bella told you?' asked Tiana.

Ronit nodded.

'That girl is obsessed!'

The new prefects entered one by one and were cheered by all the students. After entering together Tiana had left Ronit's side. She could sense that Ronit wanted to say something more but the polite conversation they had shared before entering was as much as she could handle.

Soon, the seniors made their entrance and there was more hooting and cheering. Eventually, Karam and Pia gave a farewell speech on behalf of the seniors. After that there was a lot of sentimentality as everyone said goodbye to each other.

Almost before midnight, when their feet were hurting from dancing and the gym began to feel hot and sweaty, Tiana and Bella stepped out to catch their breath. They were sitting on the porch steps that lead to the gym.

'Can you believe that we are *seniors* now? asked Bella.

'I can't believe I'm a *prefect* now,' replied Tiana.

'Please be a cool prefect. Let Leila be the mean one. Whatever Leila asks everyone to do, you should come in and be like "guys, don't do it", that way everyone will love you,' laughed Bella.

'Cool. Except that will make Leila hate me,' said Tiana, raising her eyebrows.

'That's nothing new. You've handled that problem before,' laughed Bella.

'Tiana, can I talk to you alone?'

Tiana and Bella turned and saw Ronit standing behind them.

'Okay, I'm going to go now,' said Bella, getting up quickly.

'Bella, just stay please,' said Tiana.

'Oh, no way. My days of being your third wheel are over. It's about time you guys talked anyway,' said Bella knowingly.

'What does that mean?' asked Tiana.

'It means that you both are miserable all the time. The rest of us have noticed and even discussed intervening but the finals were coming, so we let it go,' replied Bella.

'I'm not miserable,' said Tiana uncomfortably.

'Oh please, you're both constantly grumpy, moody and distant. You're not fooling anyone, T. Well maybe you both are fooling each other but the rest of us see right through your silliness,' said Bella, walking back into the gym.

Tiana was shocked to find that all her efforts had been in vain. She avoided looking at Ronit because the situation had become very awkward.

'I know,' said Ronit, without offering any additional information.

'What?'

'That day when the documentary came out and I had come to your house with Leila and Karam, your mom pulled me aside and told me that she and your dad were the ones who asked you not to date me,' said Ronit.

Tiana was stunned to learn that her secret had never been a secret. She had been holding on to all her feelings, not discussing them with anyone for nothing. She had held on to it to save face in front of Ronit but apparently her mom had robbed her of that dignity without even informing her.

'Why would she tell you that?' asked Tiana.

'I guess because she is perceptive. She saw that we were barely looking at each other and that things weren't normal between us. I guess senior mistress also told your parents something about me. They were worried about you and didn't want any teacher to cause any more problems for you,' said Ronit uncomfortably.

'I can't believe she told you! Why would she do that? Why didn't you tell me you knew?' asked Tiana, upset at this turn of events.

'Look, she told me because she didn't want me to blame you for it. She actually said that. I guess from her side she was trying to save our friendship,' said Ronit.

'That's not what happened,' smirked Tiana.

'I told you, Tiana, it was difficult for me to just be your friend when I didn't know what you were thinking or if you had forgiven me. But once your mom told me the truth, I understood that you wanted to keep your word to them and that's something I love about you, the way you respect your parents and you never break their trust. I wish I had that ability, but I don't. I have caused so much pain to my parents in the past but since I've come here, I've changed. They see it too and it makes them so happy, which made me feel proud of myself for once. So I understand the sense of fulfilment that you get from seeing your parents happy.'

'So that's why you were keeping a distance?' asked Tiana.

'Yeah. If there was no chance of us being together, I thought maybe it would be best if we stayed away and tried to move on. I thought it would make things easier,' said Ronit.

Tiana nodded.

'Though going by what Bella just said, apparently we've been miserable and they could all see it,' said Ronit, smiling at her.

His stupid smile. It got to her every single time.

'At least you've been more successful in moving on,' smirked Tiana.

'That was nothing okay. I was just hanging out with Tanya and yes, I was flirting with her because I was trying to keep my mind off of you, but it was useless. It didn't work. Nothing ever works when it comes to moving on from you,' said Ronit softly.

'Ronit, please. You know there's no point in talking about this.'

'Yes, there is,' replied Ronit, taking a step closer to her and taking her hand in his own.

'What's the point?' asked Tiana.

'Tell me if it hadn't been for your parents, when I asked you out on Founder's Day, would you have said yes?'

This time it was Tiana who took a step closer to him and without taking a beat to think, she said, 'Yes.'

The way Ronit smiled took her back to their summer in Bombay, three years ago. She hadn't seen that smile in a while. He slipped his hand around her waist and pulled her closer, 'So that means you've forgiven everything that happened last term as well?'

'Yes,' smiled back Tiana.

'And you've forgiven me for ruining your first kiss?' murmured Ronit in her ear.

'That one I will always hold to your head whenever you piss me off,' replied Tiana.

'But when I'm not pissing you off?'

'When you're not pissing me off, which will be rare, yes, I'll forgive that too,' smiled Tiana, looking into his eyes.

When their lips met, the butterflies she felt were even

stronger than the first time she had kissed him. The happiness that she felt from his closeness was so dynamic that the aching piece of her heart healed itself. It wasn't until they heard clapping and hooting that they abruptly stopped kissing. It was of course their friends.

'Finally!' said Sara, smiling at them.

'I know!' exclaimed Bella.

'About time, guys,' said Aliya, rolling her eyes.

'Also, stop kissing now. We're still in school and if a teacher caught you then you would get in trouble all over again,' said Leila.

'Yeah guys, don't get so handsy,' teased Aryan.

'Okay, thanks for your commentary. Bye now,' said Ronit, laughingly waving off their friends.

As their friends walked away, they did pull apart though. Not just because they were in school but because Tiana remembered her promise to stay away from Ronit. That was not working out so well.

'Ronit, listen—'

'I know we still can't date. But it doesn't matter to me,' said Ronit.

'What do you mean?'

'It means that I don't care about labels. I don't have to be called your "boyfriend" to feel like your boyfriend.'

'I thought you were sick of being stuck in a limbo,' said Tiana.

'I said that when I didn't know how you felt. It felt like you were still making up your mind about me and I guess you kind of were but I hated being left out. I didn't know if you were going to forgive the past, I didn't know if you wanted to go out with me. Everything was confusing and I didn't like being stuck in that situation.'

'But now you know.'

'Yes. I know you feel the same way about me, so I don't care if we don't declare that we are dating. Somehow, we've managed to be honest for once. I don't care about anything else,' said Ronit.

'How would that even work?'

'What is dating in this school anyway? It's just talking! Everyone is constantly being watched. Teachers have a problem if a boy and a girl talk to each other and hang out away from others on their own. So we won't do that. I'll come back to your table, I'll sit behind you in assembly, I'll sit near you during classes, and on holidays and Sundays we'll hang out together with all our friends, the way we always have. As long as we can hang out and talk, I don't care about anything else,' said Ronit earnestly.

'We're not going to fool anyone like this,' said Tiana rationally.

'As long as we're fooling ourselves,' said Ronit, smiling contagiously.

Romantic feelings can make a person rationalize anything. The optimism that romance generates can't be controlled by anyone, least of all the ones affected by it. So even though Tiana knew that this plan wouldn't work in the long run, she said, 'Okay, let's try your silly plan.'

'We'll make it work as long as we can and who knows, maybe in a few months, your parents will relax once they see you doing well in school. They were okay with you dating before so maybe they will be again,' said Ronit hopefully.

'So in other words, the fate of our relationship depends on me getting better marks in the future?' teased Tiana.

'Hell yes! Now you focus on studying and I'm going to make sure you take extra classes if you need to. There's no escape now.'

'You know, on second thoughts, I don't think I like you *that* much. So maybe this was a mistake...'

Ronit interrupted her by kissing her again but he had to let go quickly because they really couldn't allow themselves to get caught.

Forty-Four

'Swim against the current:
Even a dead fish can go with the flow.'

—Jim Hightower

'So, Tiana, your film has reached 15 million views. Personal details of your life were captured and put out there for entertainment. Strangers discuss you and have opinions about you. How does it make you feel?' asked the news reporter.

'Indifferent. The film was about telling my truth and that's what I did. I knew that people may or may not believe me and I knew they would discuss me. I feel lucky I got to clear my name and that would have never happened if I hadn't been a part of Ina's film. It's because of her that I got an opportunity to express myself. Now whether people agree or disagree with me is irrelevant,' replied Tiana.

The winter holidays were going on and Ina had set up some interviews for her because the documentary was still trending, and people were curious to know more about Tiana. A lot of reporters had been interviewing her for the past one week. But those had been written interviews or phone calls. This was her first media interview on camera and Tiana was happy that she wasn't nervous to face the camera at all. Ina had made her so comfortable with talking in front of the camera that now it felt like second nature to her. She even understood all the camera, light and sound equipment lingo being used by the crew. Fleetingly, she thought that she should intern with Ina next summer because working in the media seemed interesting to her.

'You have been lucky that a lot of the reactions have been positive. Why do you think that is?'

'I'm guessing that may be the raw honesty that touched people, especially with teenagers who are my age and still in school. They get it. They understand that we are in this awful age together,' replied Tiana.

'Is it really that awful? Or is that hyperbole?'

'It is awful. I'm not trying to be dramatic for effect. I, in particular, had zero control over what happened to me. Some teachers from my school made a wrong decision and if I hadn't taken control of the situation, I would have felt like a victim forever,' said Tiana.

'Teen years are a time to learn about patience, yet you seem to be in a rush to bypass a period of learning in order to do things yourself. Do you think that will help you in the long run, not learning important lessons in your teens?'

This reporter was clearly old-fashioned and didn't approve of Tiana's teen power but Tiana wasn't going to back down.

'Grown-ups can choose to surround themselves with like-minded people and then they can talk about people they dislike without actually having to face them. They have the freedom to cut people out of their lives. Maybe that's why they can be civil during short social interactions with the people that normally they won't be able to tolerate over a longer period. This privilege is not afforded to teens in high school. You are forced to face the people you hate all the time. They cross you in the corridors, they sit behind you in class, they eat at the same table, they play sports with you and if you are in a boarding school, their bed might be next to yours and you might have to sleep next to them. When you wake up in the morning, the first thing you see is their face. Adults think that teens are impatient but in reality, they have just forgotten what it was like when they were young themselves. If anything, teens can teach adults a thing or two about patience because their patience is tested every single day. So no, I'm not bypassing any essential learning because of lack of patience,' replied Tiana.

'You have spoken up against the teaching methods of some of your teachers. Is that fair?'

'Yes. Teachers go unchecked in our country. They say cruel and horrible things and no one bats an eyelid. They deserve respect but they should give it too. Just because we are much younger than them, it doesn't mean we have no dignity or feelings. The things our teachers say to us can impact us for a long time. Negativity can be detrimental to our growth. I had a math teacher who called me an idiot every single day in front of my entire class in the eighth grade and it crushed me. I became worse than I was at math because I really started believing that I was an idiot. So yes, I think it's about time someone questioned the teaching methods in our country,' said Tiana.

'You have gained a lot of social media followers after this film. How does that make you feel?'

'That's the biggest sign of approval for the film. Those numbers are a visible proof of how much people connected to the story.'

'What will you do with this social media power now?'

'These things are temporary, but while I have people listening to me, I will continue to express myself realistically and maybe reach out and help other teens who are going through similar issues or are unable to speak up for themselves.'

'What happened to Zoravar and Pia after the film?'

'Since it was their last term in school, they weren't suspended but they lost all their power as seniors which can be a humiliating experience on its own. Nobody listened to them for the rest of the term and whenever they tried to mess with me, I had the support of my teachers and friends. So they ceased to exist for me. Mr Singh tried to get the film banned but he wasn't successful.'

'Because of the fight scene?' asked the reporter.

Tiana nodded, 'Yes, it shows him yelling at me, a minor, when he didn't even have permission to speak to me without a teacher present.'

'On a lighter note, a lot of the viewers were disappointed because at the end of the film they didn't find out if you ended up with Karam or Ronit. Would you like to share any news on that front?'

'Regardless of which boy I date today or in the future, the one person that I will always end up with is myself. This film was an attempt to stand up for myself and I'm so proud that I did just that. Self-respect and self-love were the real themes of this film and going by that theme, I guess I ended up at the right place. Compared to this, which boy I ended up with is such a trivial issue,' smiled Tiana.

'So, you won't tell us?'

Tiana just smiled sweetly but there was a sparkle in her eyes.